On the floor, set into the stone, is the Seal of the Agency, complete with warlike bird and "CENTRAL INTELLIGENCE AGENCY" lettered around its circumference. On the interior side of the rotunda is the main Security Clearance checkpoint.

As the five men passed through the heavy doors, it was to this checkpoint that Bishop was leading Colter when the voice went off in Colter's ear.

Too many men in the rotunda.

He remembered instantly — no one ever stopped to chat here; it was an overdone entrance hall. On top of that, its acoustics made it possible for anyone to hear what you were saying. Yet now there were four distinct groups of men off to the sides of the hall. And no women. The complex was lousy with female secretaries, yet not one was in sight.

But because he had deemed his earlier alarm unnecessary, he did something that it was not his custom to do. He hesitated.

DAWN'S EARLY LIGHT

STEPHEN JOHNSON

Tudor Publishing Company
New York and Los Angeles

Tudor Publishing Company

Copyright © 1989 by Stephen Johnson

ISBN: 0-944276-36-9

Printed in the United States of America

First Tudor printing — January, 1989

For Sharon

PART ONE

THE INVITATION

CHAPTER ONE

BLOOD POUNDING IN HIS EARS.

No matter how many times he did it, the swim from the beach to the reef excited him. There was a bittersweet tang of fear involved, easily attributable to the unseen creatures in the water all around, or to the sheer depth of the water, as he passed over the volcanic trenches so deep no one had ever discovered the bottom. Actually, the basis of the tingling sensation that started in his groin and spread over his body in waves had more to do with the sheer mystery and grandeur of this undersea environment. In terms of natural habitat, he didn't belong here, and he knew it.

The black rubber fins pushed him steadily along, and the mask and snorkel allowed him to gaze at the coral formations dotting the bright sand bottom some forty feet below him. The water was that impossibly bright ultramarine combination of blues and greens that can only be found near deep water islands. On another day he might have lingered for a while, diving on the coral formations and playing tag with the Moorish Idols and the French Angels like a tourist. But that would wait for another time. He had a distance to cover, and he was on an errand.

The reef was closer now, and he could hear the surf

breaking over it. He stopped momentarily, treading water easily, removing the mask in order to have a look around. His grey-green eyes swept the surface, checking for nearby fishing canoes, swimmers, anything. Satisfied, he replaced the mask and resumed his strong, surely pace.

The average tourist would have been spent by now or, if not, his back would have been so sunburnt that blisters would already be appearing. The sunshine was seductive but horribly intense in French Polynesia. Many a visitor had returned to his home country with little to remember of the islands save for the unguents, swelling, and incredible discomfort of a real South Pacific sunburn.

But Mitchell Colter had no such worry. Since his arrival on Bora Bora some years ago, he had acquired the kind of tan that never really goes away. After a long day in the sun, it would be a shade or two darker, with perhaps a suggestion of red in it. After one of the infrequent rainy periods, or a couple of weeks away from the islands, it might be a shade or two lighter, but that was it.

Colter was at the reef now. He planted his flippered feet on a massive head of brain coral below the surface and stood, breathing easily, waist-deep in the restless lagoon. He raised the mask again and, looking around, spotted the launch from the airport slowly making its way toward the town pier. It was along way away, but he was not squinting. He was frowning.

The Bora Bora airport had been built by the U.S. Army Corps of Engineers during World War II, to be used as a refuelling and resupply stop for military aircraft and personnel in the Pacific theater of operations. The island itself presented no site for an airfield, but the reef did. Except for tidal breaks, the reef completely encircled the island, at widths measuring from a few yards to almost a quarter mile. The army had bulldozed part of it flat, then laid down a temporary chain-link airstrip. With grudging improvements over the years, it still served. Passengers traveled back and forth between the reef airport and the island proper via a shuttle launch.

Colter turned to his task. Replacing mask and snorkel, he took several deep breaths in preparation, then dove into the water. To the side of the coral head on which he had stood, the bottom of the lagoon fell away dramatically. At the bottom of the rocky cavern was another, very distinctive coral formation. It was long and cylindrical, of a much more regular shape than the surrounding growths. It was in fact a U.S. Navy Mark III torpedo, long forgotten and covered in living coral. Colter had come across it two years ago while chasing after a particularly elusive octopus. He had found it by accident, which was the only way it could be found. Because of the angle of slope and force of tide, a small side-cavern had been formed into which very little light ever penetrated. From the surface, even Colter had trouble pinpointing the spot.

But now, in close proximity, Colter's movements were swift and sure. He picked up a broken piece of corroded propeller blade and scraped away the sediment and new coral which had appeared in the painstakingly excavated grooves of the access hatch. He lifted the hatch door away, placing it carefully aside on the sandy shelf under the scrutiny of a passing grouper. Now, needing to return to the surface for air, Colter reached inside the huge old exploding cigar and withdrew a metal container slightly larger than a family-sized thermos bottle. Checking it for leaks, he slowly returned to the surface. He swam over to the reef. There was an area of raised, relatively smooth and flat volcanic rock about twenty meters away, and pulling himself easily up onto it, he once again looked around to make sure that he was alone. There was no one in sight.

The container's watertight seal was intact, and surrendered with a soft pop as he opened it. The contents were in small polyethelene bags, durable and reusable. He laid them out next to him.

Passports. One American, one French, one Canadian, and one Swiss. The Swiss had been the hardest to get. Colter removed a waterproof pouch from the pocket of his swim shorts and took out a fifth passport, this one the shabby-looking gray-and-maroon document of the German Democratic Republic, East Germany. He replaced it with the others, and turned to the other items.

Paper money. Two rolls of U.S. fifties, a roll each of English five-pound notes and Swiss hundred-franc notes.

Diamonds. Gem-quality cut stones, varying in size from less than a carat to one that was the size of a jellybean, a large jellybean. There were around a hundred stones, in two of the clear plastic bags.

Pistol. A .22-caliber Beretta automatic.

Ignoring the rest of the cache, Colter opened one of the bags and took out a diamond. It was approximately the size of a pencil eraser, and Colter held it up to examine it more closely. A faint blue-white light seemed to burn at its center. Satisfied, he jammed it into the pocket of his swim trunks and closed the protective velcro flap. He resealed the packet and replaced all the glassine bags in the waterproof cylinder, making sure as he closed it that the seal was tight. Then, replacing mask and snorkel, he dove again to the torpedo.

After two more dives, he was satisfied that even if some nosy tourists found the torpedo, they would find no evidence of his work. He turned his six-foot, two-inch frame around and pointed it toward the island, allowing the briefest of smiles to play across his features. He had been to the bank, and made a withdrawal.

As his body settled into the task of returning to the beach, Colter allowed his mind to return once again to that other, colder land, so far away, from which he had so recently returned.

* * *

"Shuffle."

The pit supervisor nodded to the dealer, barely glancing at Colter. He made a note on a small pad of paper, and sauntered away in the direction of a gaggle of middle-aged ladies just sitting down at the roulette wheel. The crowd was still very light, just the regulars who always came in as soon as the doors opened at five in the afternoon and the odd tourist or two drawn to the elegant old casino rather like pilgrims toward Mecca.

Colter sat comfortably at the table, smiling at the dealer as the thin Spaniard ruffled through the cards with practiced ease.

"Beautiful old building, more beautiful than the Palace, don't you think?"

The dealer almost let the cards slip, but covered the momentary awkwardness smoothly. It was the exact phrasing he'd been told to expect, but it still took him by surprise. He had already summed up the man sitting at the table as a European engineer with the dam project, and having classified him, had moved on.

"It depends on the kind of gambling you want to do," he replied.

"High stakes. What's the limit, Benito?"

The dealer, whose name was Benito Delgado, let his eyes flicker over the man briefly, reassessing. Something about the eyes. . . yes, he hadn't noticed at first glance. The man had the rugged look of the engineers from the dam, he dressed the same way, and yet there was something more. . . He abruptly decided that he knew enough, and got on with the business at hand.

"Five thousand per hand," the dealer intoned.

"Let's play." Colter put five one-thousand peseta plaques on the betting square.

Per routine procedure, Benito glanced over towards the supervisor and called softly and casually, "Maximum bet plays," then began to deal. On hearing this, the supervisor strolled back toward the table Colter had chosen, looking over the action. As he neared, he pasted an oily smile on his features and showed it to Colter.

"Good evening, senor," he began.

"Generalissimo," countered Colter.

The supervisor's expression slipped just a bit, and he gave the dealer a quick, involuntary glance. The dealer just nodded. The supervisor scanned the casino furtively for casual onlookers, then pretended to relax, leaning against the adjacent table, effectively masking the play from the rest of the casino. Colter read his cards and slid them under the corner of his wager, indicating that he didn't want another card. The dealer's hand showed a five, and he turned over his hole card, revealing a nine. Fourteen total, and he drew another card. A queen. Dealer busted, Colter won.

Colter let the money ride, stacking the plaques in front of him. The dealer dealt the next hand. Colter had twenty, and stayed. Dealer turned over an eight to go beside the ten that showed. Colter won again. He let the money ride.

Next hand. Dealer seventeen, Colter nineteen.

Next hand. Colter got blackjack, ace of hearts and jack of clubs.

Next hand. Colter had seventeen, dealer had to hit a fourteen, got a nine, and busted.

Next hand. Colter had an ace and a three, and asked for a card. He got a seven. Dealer busted.

The stack of plaques was now almost unmanageable, but Colter knew he didn't have to keep track. They would let him know when he had reached the point.

Next hand. Dealer showed a six, and Colter stayed on a hard thirteen. Dealer had another six in the hole, and hit it with the king of diamonds. Busted.

And right then, the supervisor leaned over to Colter. In a voice that was just a little bit shaky, he asked, "Would the senor care to play a little Baccarat?"

Colter smiled. "Maybe later. I think I'll just have a drink right now. Could you have someone help me with all this?" He gestured at the enormous pile of counters on the table, and the supervisor nodded quickly.

Colter looked at the dealer, and picked up a ten-thousand-peseta plaque from the array. He handed it to Benito, and said, "Thank you, senor. Most memorable." Colter headed for the hallway to the bar, not even waiting for the money. He knew that it would reach him before his drink order could be filled.

It had all been neatly and quickly handled, he thought. Not at all like the last time he had been in Chile. But that had been Santiago, two-hours' drive inland from here and several years in the past. Here in Vina Del Mar, the summer playground of the moneyed elite, all that seemed a very long time ago.

Normally Colter received payment for services rendered in a more orthodox manner, but in this instance he was being paid by a very nervous regime. They had arranged this method to be proof against any later claims that Colter had worked for them. On closest inspection, Colter had gotten lucky at the tables.

There would be witnesses, and if necessary the films taken by the casino's "eye in the sky" cameras could be produced. No one paid Colter for anything. It just happened that Colter had gotten lucky only hours before he left the country, after a visit of almost three weeks.

During the last three weeks, Colter had done what he was hired to do with a speed and a ruthlessness that had astonished even the people who had hired him. The teetering moderate faction in the ruling Junta had been threatened by a small cell of fanatical right-wing terrorists called the Twenty-fourth of May Movement. The moderates had begged the CIA for help to no avail, but the local station chief had "leaked" the name of Mitchell Colter to the moderates' leader, one Pietro Vargas. Vargas had cabled Colter, and he had come.

Vargas had pointed Colter in the right direction, but then Colter had disappeared. After a few days, Vargas was worried. After a week, he began to think that Colter had been killed. But at the end of the second week, reports began to come to him that a mysterious series of incidents had been occurring in the seedy waterfront quarter of Valparaiso. Bodies were discovered, and identifications made. The Twenty-fourth of May Movement was suffering a loss of membership.

It had all come to a head two days ago, when an emergency action session had apparently been called by the leadership of the Twenty-fourth of May terrorists. The conjecture at the headquarters of the Guardia Nacional was that one of the terrorists' homemade had gone went off by accident, but Vargas knew very well that he was watching the hand of a less random influence at work. Colter had taken out every one of the terrorists, yet windows just across the alley from the terrorists' apartment were not even broken. It was an expert job, and frightening enough to a man like Vargas that he never even considered the option of refusing to pay Colter and denying any complicity. He put the machinery for the payoff into immediate operation.

Now, Colter had the money and a few hours' leisure before his return to Bora Bora. He sat happily in the elegant bar of the casino, regarding the check which the casino man had just delivered to him. He rolled it into a tight tube and placed it inside the ball-point pen he carried inside his jacket, tossing the ink cartridge and spring into a nearby trash can.

As the waiter brought over his Tanqueray and tonic, he glanced around, automatically registering the only familiar face in the room. He didn't react to seeing Geoff Forbes at the bar, because he never knew when a CIA man was operating under cover, but he made a mental readjustment regarding his own status, deciding that Forbes probably meant him no harm. The decision was confirmed moments later when Forbes picked up his drink and made his way over to Colter's table.

"Hi, Mitch. Mind?"

Colter nodded toward the other chair, and Forbes sat down. Geoff Forbes was older than Colter, and had been slightly senior to Colter during the years of Colter's CIA employment. He was slight-looking, just under five-ten and wire thin, with sleepy-looking eyes and a sallow complexion. He was also one of the best field men in the Agency, and not a man to be taken lightly. Colter and Forbes had worked together some years before, on a very successful op in the Pyrenees. Forbes had dark shadows under his eyes, and he sipped at a Pernod with only a vague pretense of enjoying it.

"Good to see you, Geoff. How's Jillian?"

"Oh, Jillian. . . Well, she's fine, last I heard. She's running a travel agency in Sausalito."

"Sorry to hear that."

"You know how it is."

"Funny bumping into each other like this."

9

"Yeah, *amazing* coincidence, huh?" The two men looked at each other, and abruptly smiled. There was not one chance in a million that Forbes was here by accident. "So I guess you're about ready to go back to Bora Bora, right? All finished on my patch? Paid up? Plane warming up at the airport?"

"Your patch?"

"That's right, Mitch. My patch." Forbes leaned in, and lowered his voice. "I don't say I disapprove of you taking out the Twenty-fourth of May. You did a damn good job of it. But you might have talked to me first. Hell, I was the one who gave your name to Vargas."

"I know that. Thanks."

"Thanks, he says. So now Vargas and the whole moderate faction stabilizes, and I'm out in the cold. I'm busting my hump here, Mitch. Couldn't you have told me the when and how, so I could put my guys in position to take some of the downrange political gravy?"

Colter sat back. This was the game as he remembered it. This was part of the reason he'd arranged to retire from the Agency. It wasn't important who got killed, who got power or who lost power; it was only important in terms of how it was perceived. Forbes didn't care that a cell of terrorists had been eliminated. He didn't care that the moderates now had at least an even chance of living through the summer. What he cared about was that because Colter had done it so efficiently and quietly, he didn't have time to set it up so that the CIA could take credit for having stage-managed it. He was upset with Colter because Colter hadn't taken him into his confidence on a step-by-step basis.

"Maybe next time."

"Next time, your ass, Colter. You better come back to earth, my friend. You're not operating in a vacuum. Not here, not anywhere."

"Cheer up. I didn't set you up for the op, but I

didn't set anybody else up either. I never do."

"Big favor."

"You want the credit, do the work." Even if it had been Forbes who had told Vargas about Colter, it had been necessary for Colter to do it. Forbes had not been willing or able to commit Agency personnel to the task. Colter was getting irked.

Abruptly, Forbes sat back in his chair. "What the hell," he muttered. "That's what I told them you'd say. On top of which, you're right."

And then it became clear to Colter exactly why Forbes was here. "Somebody on the fifth floor is cranky, is that it?"

Forbes smiled. The "fifth floor" is the euphemism for the offices of the Director of the CIA and his section chiefs. And, of course, Colter was exactly right.

"The way it was put to me was, 'We can't hold the bastard, but give his chain a good hard yank before you let him go.'"

"Sounds familiar."

"Be a little easier if the Agency had a chain on you to yank, of course . . ."

"If anybody asks, I'll say you scared the hell out of me."

"I'd appreciate it, Mitch." Forbes put down the half-full glass of Pernod and got to his feet. "Anything you need? When are you leaving?"

"No, I'm fine, thanks," Colter replied, casually ignoring the second half of Forbes's question. He never told anyone his exact travel plans.

Forbes squinted off in the direction of the grand entrance as a group of Japanese businessmen was escorted inside by a tour guide. He nodded, thinking, and then turned a genuine smile on like a lamp. "Take care of yourself, Mitch. It's a wicked, wicked world out there."

"See you around, Geoff. Get some rest."

"That'll be the day." Forbes took a pair of aviator's sunglasses out of his pocket and put them on, making his way out of the bar and into the grand corridor. Colter watched him go, and then finished his drink. Rather than wait for the waiter to come around, he fished in a pocket and threw a crumpled bank note on the cocktail table, making his own way out.

The last sight Colter had had of the CIA man was just as he'd gotten to the entrance of the casino. It was just at twilight, and the plaza was flooded with coppery, humid light. Forbes was getting into a taxi, and the two men caught sight of each other at the same moment. They didn't wave. Forbes got inside the cab and it drove off into the gathering night.

An hour later, Forbes was dead.

And now, a man had come from Virginia.

CHAPTER TWO

The man from Virginia was sweating. He was also hungry, thirsty, and tired, but the main discomfort he faced at the moment was the sweat. It ran down his face, his back, his legs, and his arms. It ran into his eyes. It got on everything he touched. His brand new LaCoste shirt was sopped, and his designer jeans were becoming more uncomfortable by the minute.

He had been traveling for a long time. First the 747 from Dulles to Los Angeles; then the UTA L-1011 to Papeete, Tahiti; then the inter-island DC-3 to Bora Bora. The man from Virginia was not only tired, he was edgy.

His luggage had arrived at the same time he had, by virtue of the fact that he had carried it with him for the entire trip; he now stood smugly aloof from the gaggle of frantic tourists whose swimsuits, leisure wear, and blow dryers were now well on their way to Australia. The baggage handlers at Papeete International Airport were much the same as any other organized group of Tahitian workers; they always showed up for work, unless they decided to go fishing instead.

It had been a half an hour since the group had disembarked from the antique airport launch, and they were waiting for the arrival of the island's only form of public transportation, fondly known as *le truck*. It was literally a truck, usually a flatbed relic, gaily painted and equipped with benches for the tourists to cling to as *le truck* creaked around the uneven circle described by the island's only road.

The few passengers who could afford to stay at the Hotel Bora Bora had already been picked up by that hotel's maxi-van, and the rest of the group had been properly resentful. The man from Virginia could have stayed there, but he preferred Michelle's. It was clean, and the food was good, and it was inconspicuous. And, of course, there was Michelle.

Michelle D'Alene was one of the good ones. She made you feel alive and comfortable, both at the same time. Fiercely loyal, and vulnerable as a kitten. She had come out to the islands when her brother, Jean-Louis, had died of a stroke, intending merely to close up the inn and sell out. She had fallen in love with the islands, the inn, and the way of life almost instantly, and had never returned to Europe. The man from Virginia had met her on his last trip out here, and she had fed him, mothered him, teased him, and finally slept with him.

Thinking back to that time, the man became dreamy with remembered pleasures, and he felt the stirring of an oncoming erection. It jolted him out of his reverie like an alarm bell going off, and he instinctively checked his surroundings for any changes, chiding himself for the lapse. *It's these damned islands*, he thought.

And the heat. *Le truck* was never going to come. He picked up his grip, mentally preparing himself to walk to Michelle's. He wanted nothing more than a shower and a few hours' sleep, but he knew that it would have to wait. He was on an assignment. With a short sigh, he set off walking down the dusty, midday road.

* * *

Michelle D'Alene knew he was coming. Ordinarily, she would have tried to start up her ancient, beloved Citroen *deux-cheveaux* and gone to meet him at the launch. But today, for the first time in months, the delivery truck had shown up on time. She was needed to supervise the unloading of the supplies she had ordered two months ago from Osterman-Petersen in Denmark. Cheeses, wines, cases of Tuborg beer, canned foodstuffs. . . all had to be checked off against the list as it went into the *godown*, or else she would become hopelessly disorganized. This had been the case last year, and she had gone three full weeks with little to offer her guests except variations of mahi-mahi, the local mainstay fish, which did not lend itself to haute cuisine.

She was not especially tall, but she carried herself with a grace and a purpose which gave her stature. Her light brown hair had been gradually turned blonde by her time in the islands, and she wore it casually tied at the nape of her neck with a small scarf from Hermes, a legacy from her prior life. At forty, she had the French disdain for numerical age, and thought of herself merely as a grown woman, in the lush, full-bodied flower of her life. Her facial features were regular, with a wide mouth giving the lie to her aquiline nose. Her eyes were such a deep, warm brown that they were all but hypnotizing. Her breast were full and round, with just a hint of wanton sag beginning, and her belly and thighs were firm and brown.

As she checked off the last item on her list and closed the pantry doors, her thoughts were on the American. She would be glad to see him, of course. But he always brought some trouble with him, and this was not the right place for trouble. It didn't seem real,

15

not here. Trouble was for the crowded, busy mainland nations. . . not Bora Bora. She sighed, leading the workmen from the truck into the courtyard of the inn to give them a cool beer. The American would want to see Colter, of course. Right away. Everything had to be right away, with Americans. But no, that wasn't true. Colter was an American, or had been, and he wasn't like that. Colter was. . . more like a cat. A big, dangerous, unpredictable cat. She smiled. Eh bien, but he had fine manners when he wanted to. He knew a lot about women, that one. Even Frenchwomen. *Dieu!*

Giving the beers to the driver and his friend, she squinted down the road, toward the little village where he would be coming from. *Le truck* was overdue, of course. Perhaps he would walk. Always in a hurry. He would rush off to find Colter, and they would talk about their secret things, and then, this evening perhaps, they would come back here for dinner. Her mind began reassessing her new stock, automatically preparing a menu for the evening. Her frown deepened. Then Colter would go away. Perhaps soon, perhaps for a long time. Perhaps. . . forever. She did not know what Colter did, but when he came back from these trips he was exhausted and tense at the same time. Sometimes he was scarred. Whatever he did, it was very dangerous, she was sure of that. Yes, one day he would be gone, and he just wouldn't return. *Stupide*. Why leave, when you lived in a place like this?

* * *

Colter came out of the shop, satisfied. The China-man appeared behind him, coming out as far as the porch. He had stopped moaning about how badly he was being cheated, because the deal was concluded. It was more of a ritual than a negotiation, anyway. The fair-market value of diamonds didn't change that much; it was more a matter of establishing the true weight and quality, then settling on a price.

Colter had enough cash to last him for months, and the Chinaman would make a decent profit on his own sale of the gem.

They looked at each other, then bowed slightly. The old Chinaman retreated into the shadows of the shop.

Colter began walking, his mind turning to less pleasant things. Bishop was here, he was sure of that. Even if he hadn't known to expect him today, he would have felt his presence on the island. He couldn't explain how that happened, but Colter had always had some kind of extra sensitivity, and it had saved his life on more than one occasion.

His mind flickered over the time in Munich, when he had suddenly awakened from his sleep, sure that something was wrong. Another man might have dismissed it as a dream or a random sound outside and rolled over to return to sleep, but Mitch Colter had learned to trust this sense. He reacted instantly, grabbing slacks and sweater on his way out the window, putting them on only when he had reached a safe distance from the house. He had waited and watched, and, just when he was beginning to think he had been foolishly paranoid, the men had come to kill him. They had been KGB professionals, swift and silent. The first thing they had done was to close off any possible route of escape. If Colter had been in there, he would never have gotten out alive.

And there had been other times. Once they tried to bomb his car. In Tunisia, that was. He had gotten into the driver's seat, and he had frozen, terribly alert. There had been nothing out of place, nothing visibly

17

wrong. No smudge marks in the dust on the hood, no extra wires extending from underneath the dash, nothing. Yet his alarm bells had gone off, so he carefully got out again and walked away. As it turned out, the pressure of his weight on the driver's seat had triggered a sixty-second timer and, just as Colter rounded the corner, walking away in search of a telephone, the bomb had exploded, leaving one passerby dead and another seriously injured.

There were some people at Langley who were actually upset by this trait of his. It didn't fit into their concept of reality, so they became suspicious and even fearful. Colter smiled. It was fine with him if he didn't belong in their reality, because they sure as hell didn't belong in his.

Colter was a CIA "dropout." As Colter himself looked at it, he had retired early. Officially, of course, this situation never occurs. You don't simply walk away from the CIA. Not after they had selected you, trained you at the Farm for "field work," and then entrusted you with all the dark, dirty secrets of the supposedly nonexistent Nightshade Section of the Covert Operations Division. Nightshade handled the "wet work" and was one of the Agency's most closely held cards. You couldn't just step away, not after you had become one of the best field agents they had. And certainly not when you had become one of the most highly skilled assassins in the world.

Except for Mitchell Colter. He had become fed up with the bureaucratic bullshit early on but continued for some years in spite of that, propelled by a genuine, natural patriotism. But the CIA had made a mistake. They had lied to Colter. They had lied, and a friend of Colter's had been killed. They explained the whole thing to him very clearly afterwards, and Colter had nodded and told them he understood. These things happen.

Seven months after that, the Agency controller who had lied to Colter lost his life when his car skidded out of control on the icy George Washington Parkway and sailed over a guard rail, dropping seven hundred feet to the rocky banks of the Potomac River.

The whole unfortunate affair caused Colter to take a long, careful look around the Company. And what he saw did not please him. Oh, he knew the need for an intelligence apparatus, and had nothing against a lot of what he saw, except that he found he could envision with frightening clarity just what his life would be like if he continued with the Agency.

As he progressed, he would be given more and more responsibility. He would direct whole operations, and the gut-wrenching, nail-biting, chain-smoking burdens of decision and result would be his. He foresaw an endless parade of gray little rooms full of gray little men, living in the grey little areas of life. As he aged, he would come in from the field . . . if he lived. The Nightshade Section had a sickeningly high mortality rate. But if he survived, he would get his own office at Langley, and maybe he would be able to afford a house in Arlington or McLean, if he was lucky and played the political game well.

So he quit.

He knew, of course, that he couldn't just hand in his resignation. *You didn't just quit.* So he took his precautions first. He set it up, just as he would have done had it been another of the field operations. Over a period of months, he assembled the various elements of a plan: papers, travel, false leads, escape routes, back door, timing, and money. And then he disappeared.

One day, he just hadn't been there. The Agency was naturally upset, suspecting he had been snatched by the Other Side and was being squeezed dry in some remote safe house. They put their formidable machinery to the task of locating him. By the time they found out where he was, his resignation was more or less a *fait accompli*. He had holed up on Bora Bora, and wasn't coming to work anymore. He was out of the Agency, that was for sure. The only question was, what to do about him? They couldn't just *leave* him out there. . .

So, as Colter had known they would, the CIA decided to "terminate with extreme prejudice." That is, murder him. They sent an assassin named Van Dyke to Bora Bora. They gave him an immaculate cover as a member of a package tour of the islands. Van Dyke actually spent several days just relaxing on Moorea and Huahine before arriving in Bora Bora. Then, his first night at the Hotel Bora Bora, he had awakened to find Colter sitting on his bed, a silenced automatic in his hand.

Colter sent Van Dyke back to Langley with a message: *I am not available for execution.* And then he added the terms on which he might continue to do business with the CIA, among them the specific instruction that any further contact must come to him by way of Stephen Bishop, who was the only CIA operative he knew that he could trust. They never sent another killer, but Bishop appeared about a month later.

Since then there had been several jobs; always difficult, but always highly paid. Colter took payment in the form of diamonds, and the Agency paid promptly and according to his instructions. With only a few exceptions, Colter was always paid in diamonds. Not that he had any particular obsession with the jewels; it was simply that their value was constant, they were easily transported, and they crossed borders with minimum bulk and no language barrier.

And so Colter had retired. He had his secret cache

out near the reef, in his torpedo. He had enough money to live well here in the islands for a long, long time. It was one of the most beautiful places on earth, the people were friendly, and nobody tried to kill him anymore.

Except when he went away on a job. Colter frowned, remembering Bishop's presence on the island. His natural curiosity made him want to know what it would be this time, but he didn't think he'd take it, no matter what it was. He didn't need the money, and he wasn't bored, so he'd probably turn it down. Bishop wouldn't like it, but that was his problem.

He'd listen to the pitch, though, just out of good manners.

CHAPTER THREE

Colter walked up the pathway which led to his house. It looked like many of the houses on the island, rustic and weather-beaten. In fact, Colter had been lucky to get it; it was fairly new, large enough to be comfortable for one person with room to spare, and— best of all — very difficult to approach without being seen. He had bought it from an Italian trader who had moved out the month after Colter had arrived in the islands, and Colter had made a few modifications right away, including an assortment of unpleasant surprises for unwanted visitors. Nothing lethal, but it definitely helped to be an invited guest.

So Colter didn't need his sixth sense to tell him that he had a visitor. One look at the old weathervane attached to the roof of the house told him that. It was a tremendously simple device, really; most of the more effective ones were. When the house was entered by anyone who didn't know its tricks, a switch was automatically triggered which turned the vane to face the rocky hills behind the house, the one direction from which the wind never came. Just like the flag on a mailbox. One look, and you knew whether the house was empty or not.

The house was not empty. Colter suspected that it

was Bishop, but the weight of his training and experience prevented him from *assuming* so. He left the path and entered the jungle like foliage at the edge of the property. Making his way silently and quickly to the rise of volcanic rock at the back of the house, he watched for traces of activity in the house. Satisfied, he moved up close to the large window next to the verandah. This particular window was another of his "improvements." Appearing to be a normal, sash type window, it opened soundlessly, like a door, at a push from inside. Colter peered inside and smiled.

Bishop was asleep on the battered old couch. A bottle of Hinano beer stood half finished on the coffee table, but the dauntless agent had allowed the trip to catch up with him. Soundlessly, Colter swung the window wide enough to enter, lifted himself over the sill, and secured the window behind him. Colter cat-footed over to the easy chair next to Bishop's head and sat down, comfortably sprawling into a position that made it seem as though he had been there for hours. As though picking up the thread in the middle of a conversation, he began to talk.

"There *are* hotels on the island, but I can see why you prefer it here. Michelle was expecting you, but . . ."

Bishop woke with a start, instinctively moving away from the source of sound. His memory and consciousness came back at the same instant, and he found himself at the other side of the room, leaning against the wall in what he imagined was a casual manner, furiously pretending that he hadn't dozed off.

"Yes, well, no, I'm staying at Michelle's . . ." he began, but sensed he could never keep it up. He sagged. "Jesus, Mitch. Don't do that, okay?"

"This beer you poached," grinned Colter, "has gone warm. You want a cool one?"

Bishop stared at him, and then nodded. As Colter

moved to the kitchen, Bishop shivered. "I must be getting too old for this shit. You should never have been able to get that close to me." He rubbed his eyes. "What if you'd been an Indian?"

"You'd be dead. Have a beer."

Between themselves, they had always referred to the two "sides" in any given confrontation as either Cowboys or Indians. It amused them, and seemed to lend a certain clarity to messy situations. But at the moment, Bishop had plenty of clarity. More than enough. Colter had just scared the hell out of him; it was perfectly true that no one should have been able to do what Colter had just done. Of course, he comforted himself, probably no one but Colter could have done it. But Colter had also done him a favor. He had reminded him, once more, that the price of lowering one's guard, of relaxing anywhere in the field, even for a moment, could be very high. The Indians wouldn't give you a break because you were tired from the traveling. You just wouldn't wake up.

Colter came in from the kitchen with two bottles of Hinano beer and gave one to Bishop. As they raised the bottles to each other in an unspoken toast, Colter eyed his visitor. The gray-green eyes swept him like a metal detector.

Bishop, uncomfortable under the scrutiny, spoke first. "Iaorana, Mitch." The all-purpose Tahitian greeting. Aloha. Hello. Goodbye. Have a nice day.

Colter nodded at him. "You look like hell. They've got you in an office, haven't they?"

"Not today, they haven't."

"Next year you'll be the color of library paste, and you'll weigh another twenty pounds."

"Good to see you, too," Bishop replied from the corner of his mouth.

"You ought to stay here for at least six months. A

year is better."

Bishop made a face. "Nah, I'd just end up like you. Overgrown beach boy with a flat brain-wave."

Colter went back to the easy chair and sat down. They never engaged in the hand-shaking, good-to-see-you, how-have-you-been routines. Never had.

Bishop asked, "You knew I was coming?" Colter nodded, slowly. "Bullshit," Bishop continued "I used a different name and travel profile this time."

"The coconut telegraph doesn't care much about names," drawled Colter.

"Coconut telegraph, my ass, you've probably been banging one of the UTA airline stews that was on my flight."

"Actually," Colter began, neither confirming nor denying this suggestion, "the coconut telegraph does exist and function, but you have to live here a while to be able to read it. Tahitians are very careful about people from outside, until they decide whether you're a Cowboy or an Indian."

Bishop shrugged. "It doesn't much matter. I wasn't trying to keep my arrival a secret from you."

"Good."

Bishop winced. Colter's response was the same as saying, *I'm glad you weren't trying, because if you were, you failed.*

Bishop decided to get on with it. Colter would never ask what brought him here; he had already become too Tahitian for that. Organizing his thoughts, he went over and sat on the couch.

"I'm here on business, Mitch."

"Imagine my surprise."

"Come on. Can I lay it out for you? Now?"

"Just a minute."

Colter got up, languidly, and disappeared into the next room. He reappeared a moment later, having activated a small device which he now carried in his hand. The tiny battery-operated transmitter would make gibberish out of their conversation, should anyone be eavesdropping electronically. He placed it on the coffee table.

"You never know," he said. "Okay. Now. Who stole the secret papers?"

Ignoring this, Bishop fixed his eyes on Colter's. "The Director wants you to come to Langley, Mitch. The Agency's being hit, and we need your help."

* * *

It had all started a couple of months before, but no one at the CIA had become aware of it until recently. It had taken the new computer, affectionately code-named Einstein, to point the way.

Neil Carlton, a thirty-five-year-old field agent from Waycross, Georgia, had died of a stroke while on a routine surveillance in West Berlin. Because he had been on an assignment at the time, an autopsy was ordered but revealed no sign of foul play. A stroke can take you out anytime. Regrettable, even tragic, but these things happen.

Two weeks later another field agent, Jerry Aldrich, had died in a traffic accident. He had been visiting his parents in Bradenton, Florida, at the time, and there was absolutely no reason for anyone to suspect that a homicide had been committed. Another traffic fatality. Awful, but it happens all the time.

But the subsequent weeks went by, and six more seemingly unrelated accidents occurred. Always the man who was dead turned out to be a field agent. They were from different sections, under different controllers, so no one pushed the panic button, but Personnel began circulating a bad joke about transitioning steno pool personnel into Field Ops.

When an agent dies, his contacts, sources, and actual operations in progress simply disappear. Some of the agents are controllers for other agents, and, when a controller is removed without notice, so is his link with Langley. Incoming information had started to dry up. "Einstein" routinely ran efficiency summaries, gain versus loss ratios, and probability surveys. When Geoff Forbes's body was found in a dry dock in Valparaiso, ostensibly the victim of a slip and fall, Einstein set off the bells and the lights at the print out terminus and started to scream. The probability was now 946,000-to-1 that the sudden loss of field men was *not* accidental. Somebody was killing CIA agents.

Paxton Fairbanks, Director of the CIA, felt a chill at the base of his spine as he was briefed by the computer experts. He knew Einstein was right, but it didn't make *sense*. In the world of professional intelligence-gathering organizations, this kind of thing just did not happen. Oh, sure, you lost a man from time to time, that was in the scheme of things. It happened, usually because the man had gotten careless, or sloppy. It happened if he didn't follow orders, or didn't use his head. That was to be expected.

But when, say, the KGB killed one of our men, there were ramifications. Sometimes we killed one of theirs. Sometimes trades were made, prisoners exchanged, even formal protests channeled through the embassies. But the original killing always had a *reason*. It could be understood, looked at in terms of cause and effect.

Nobody just killed American agents because they were American agents. First of all, very few people knew who they were. Sure, the Director, his deputies, the Langley staff . . . these people were *visible*. But trained field agents had much lower profiles.

They were not invisible. Probably all the intelligence services of the major nations had lists of definite or probable CIA operatives. Kept closely guarded, of course. No one wanted you to know that they knew, even if you already knew they knew.

But *who*? The KGB didn't operate like this; Fairbanks knew that from years of experience with them. Couldn't be. . . not even that lunatic Krasnevin, the new chief of the Committee for State Security, KGB, could get away with anything like this. His masters would carve him into little tiny pieces.

MI-5? MI-6? Nonsense. They depended on our apparatus almost as much as we.

Mossad? The Israelis were not stupid.

China? Absurd. To what purpose?

Mentally Fairbanks checked them off, one by one: every major intelligence service in the world, allies right alongside enemies. Dead end.

His mind then shifted its focus to the *how*. Who in the world could pull it off? Who had the means? But, realizing his own limitations, he addressed this question to Einstein. Although Fairbanks himself held to an old-fashioned dislike for mechanical logic, he knew very well what a valuable tool the computer could be when it came to legwork on a global scale.

Thirty hours later, Fairbanks summoned Stephen Bishop to his office and sent him to Bora Bora, to call Mitch Colter back to Langley.

* * *

Colter had listened carefully as Bishop laid out the

request. It was not an assignment, as such, the way Bishop put it. It was a call for help. Bishop said the computer gave Colter's name as the one to summon for help. But it was not a summons, it was a plea.

The shadows outside the house had grown longer during Bishop's recital, and the island was becoming even more beautiful in the softer light. Colter stood up, stretching, and walked out the front door.

Bishop, surprised, followed closely to find the big man leaning against the porchrail, staring out at the light green lagoon and the dark blue ocean beyond it. He seemed to be miles away.

Bishop followed his gaze, and almost immediately felt his fatigue returning. The pure, placid serenity of the island filled and whispered to him. The other world, full of deceit and treachery, darkness and death, seemed to be a memory; a shadow which had passed, not real. *Stay*, the island whispered.

Bishop's mind drifted in the fantasy. He could learn to sail, a skill which had always awed him, but never had time to learn. He could dive in the coral lagoon, he could lose his office pallor and eat coconuts and swim and fish and. . . *relax*. That would be the best of all. He could stop living with the fear, the constant fear of almost everything. Here the act of relaxing was natural, not a dangerous mistake.

By an act of will, Bishop shook off the fantasy and returned his mind to the present. He was still on duty, and Colter had given him no indication of his reaction to the message from the Director. He turned his eyes away from the hypnotic beauty of the lagoon, and found Colter watching him. Colter nodded to him, slowly, almost sadly. Damn the man, thought Bishop, am I so transparent?

Colter perched on the porchrail and regarded Bishop speculatively. "What does the Director want me to do, exactly?"

"That's outside my brief," Bishop replied, shaking his head. "Ask him."

"What's your feeling, Steve?"

The piercing eyes made Bishop feel as though he were wired to a lie detector. "It feels like he wants to use you as a consultant. It's standard procedure. You're top expert in the field. I guess you're supposed to help them find out who's doing it."

"And then?"

"And then," Bishop repeated, "make them stop."

Colter grunted. That meant a termination. A contract killing. An assassination for money. Colter, too, was under the spell of the islands, but much more deeply than Bishop. This was already Colter's home, and the longer he lived here, the less inclined he was to leave.

Bishop felt reluctance coming off Colter in waves, so he quickly qualified his last statement. "Of course, I'm just guessing. I don't know. That would be your decision to make later. The only thing I'm supposed to do is to talk you into a plane ride. The rest is up to the Director."

Colter nodded absently at this. Then he stood up, vanished into the house for a moment, and reappeared in a clean pale blue shirt which he was tucking into his cut-off Levis. "Come on," he said, "I'll walk you back to Michelle's."

Bishop was impatient. "So, what do you think?"

"I think I'm hungry. Let's go."

* * *

They ate dinner in the courtyard at Michelle's Inn,

beginning with bottles of cold Tuborg beer and an appetizer course of deep-fried *pauah*, an abalone-type delicacy from the lagoon. One of Michelle's friends had caught a *roroa*, and she made delicate fillets of it and served it with her own sauce Veronique and a bottle of crisp white Bordeaux. Then they had small green salads, and, as they began to nibble at the plateful of fresh pear slices, Michelle came over to join them, bringing a bottle of her best cognac and three large snifters.

"There will be no charges for the cognac," she said as she was seated, "and for the rest," she gave a particularly Gallic shrug, "Americans are all rich."

There had been no mention of business since they had left the house, and now, Bishop realized, there would be none. Colter would talk to him when he was ready and not before. Bishop abandoned himself to the easy warmth of the evening and the companionship.

Michelle trapped Bishop with her enormous eyes. "It is very good to see you again, Stephen. I am glad you have come back."

"It's only for a day or two, I'm afraid."

"Ridiculous." She turned to Colter. "You hear this, *cherie*? *Alors*, he is your friend, you must make him stay."

"Him?" Colter looked at Bishop with mock skepticism. "Look at the color of him. I think he's sick."

"Of course he's sick," she replied, "that's why he must stay."

"No." Colter was firm. "If he stays, he will become healthy, and strong, and not as terrible to look at as he is now. He would become attractive to simple-minded Frenchwomen."

Michelle was delighted. Laughing, she openly confided in Bishop "He pretends to be jealous, this one," she said, pointing a thumb at Colter, "while every *wahine* on the beach and most of the tourist women from the hotels are crawling up the path to his house."

Bishop smiled. "I wondered why he seemed so relaxed . . ."

Colter put on a long face. "Michelle has gone insane from too much mahi-mahi. It happens, sometimes. The fact is, I am a poor old man who lives the lonely life of a recluse, hiding from the worldly pleasures of the flesh."

"*Oui*, I think your hiding place has been discovered, though."

"We must be patient with him, Michelle," Bishop put in, "he is becoming senile in his old age. He forgets things easily. For example, he seems to have forgotten that Danish Pan Am stewardess. And the German tourist-lady. And those sisters at the Club Med . . ."

"And that damned Italian movie actress," Michelle contributed.

"I taught her to play chess," Colter retorted. "It helped to pass the time, while you were preoccupied here, entertaining the director of the film."

Michelle shrugged a small smile at Bishop. "Jealous, you see?" She thrust her chin at Colter. "Always pretending to be jealous."

The casual banter was fun, and done in good spirits, but there was an underlying current of truth behind the joking. When Colter had first arrived on Bora Bora, he and Michelle had been instantly attracted to each other. It had been hot and heavy for a time, and Colter had actually lived with her at the inn while he was looking for a house to buy. But they were both fiercely independent people, and had the emotional scars to prove it. They knew they could not sustain an exclusive relationship, and as soon as Colter's house became available, he wasted no time moving out, nor did Michelle try to stop him. They were still strongly attracted to each other, and slept together when they felt like it. There was no active jealousy, but each was well aware of the other's sometime love affairs.

Besides, the Polynesian attitude toward lovemaking had little to do with that of the modern, civilized nations. Here, couples went to bed without thinking much about what it meant; they merely wanted to make love with each other. No one wore much clothing; the "facts of life" were not classified information, as they are in many of the so-called "civilized" societies. In fact, some of the European old-timers in the islands referred to the sex act as a "Polynesian handshake." Sex was not casual, or meaningless; it was just not dirty, or secret. Rape was unheard of in the islands, and the concept of being a bastard could not be understood as a bad thing. The closest Tahitian translation meant "having many families."

When Michelle had take Stephen Bishop to her bed, Colter who had seen it coming for days, viewed it almost with relief. The next morning, Bishop had been painfully uncomfortable around both Colter and Michelle at breakfast, and finally, unable to deal with his conscience, he had taken Colter aside and confessed, manfully, that he had slept with Michelle the night before.

Colter had growled like a wounded lion, grabbed Bishop by the scruff of the neck, and paraded him into the kitchen of the inn to confront Michelle.

"Is this true? You actually took this poor innocent puppy into your bed?" Colter roared at her.

"Yes, and he's twice the man you are!" she roared back, trying not to laugh.

"He is?" Colter gawked at the crimson-faced Bishop. "Well. That's okay then."

Whereupon the tension was released. Everyone in the kitchen had burst out laughing, and all three of them had sat down to coffee in the courtyard. Bishop had been absolutely radiant, once he realized that he had nothing to feel shame over except his tendency to feel shame, and the trio's relationship had been easy and friendly ever since.

Now, sitting in that same courtyard, the talk drifted to gossip; Henri Chagrin, a grizzled old ex-Legionnaire who ran a cafe/bar in Faanui Bay, had become so drunk that he had taken his ancient .45-caliber revolver and announced that he was going to kill DeGaulle. His friends became upset and sent for the local *gendarme*. A small, worried crowd had arrived at the ramshackle pier at the sound of shots being fired, to find the pot-bellied old soldier sending bullet after bullet into his own *pirogue*, a battered old outrigger canoe christened *DeGaulle* on the bow of which Henri had painted an enormous nose. Extremely relieved, the crowd gathered around, gendarmes included, to shout their applause and offer advice. Henri damaged the boat, but it would not sink.

Bishop smiled and listened for as long as he could. Earlier, he had had hopes of getting Michelle to himself, but he had been counting on his ability to stay awake. That ability had deserted him. He sent all his energy to the task of keeping his eyes open for one more minute, but failed. The next thing he knew, he was being helped to his room. At the door, he surfaced long enough to kiss Michelle and to extract Colter's promise to meet him in the morning. That done, he stumbled out of his clothes, collapsed on the clean sheets, and was asleep.

Colter returned with Michelle to the front of the inn and helped her close things up and put things away. There wasn't much to do, and when they had finished, Colter turned to her.

"Shall I stay?" he asked softly.

"I would like that, Mitch."

They went back to her cottage, behind the main buildings. He held the door for her as they entered, and, just for a moment, they stood in the front room holding hands, facing each other. Then, slowly, she unbuttoned his shirt, and reached inside to touch his skin. It was very warm, and she could tell the heat came from underneath the brown skin. The shirt slid to the floor easily, and she quivered as he undid the knot of her pareu, the one-piece dress of native cloth which was all that she wore. She leaned toward him as the light cloth fell away from her body, but he held her back for a moment, almost at arm's length, admiring the rich femaleness of her. She moaned softly, reaching to unfasten his shorts, which he tugged off himself, half turning with the cat-like grace she knew so well. As he turned to her again, she whispered to him, "Can you have grown even bigger in the past few days?"

"No," he rasped, "I have grown bigger in the past few seconds."

Their mouths met, hungry, searching. Her full breasts pressed against his smoothly muscled chest, and their hands explored the curves of back, shoulder, and hip. Her mouth was on fire, and her head was reeling. No one had this effect on her. Her hands searched for his hardness, cupping him, stroking him, teasing him. She felt an incredible heat building at her center, and the familiar hot wetness between her legs. Her knees were all watery, and she had trouble breathing. His hands were on her breasts, her buttocks, all over her.

"Now," she moaned, "Please, now. Hurry."

He lifted her smoothly and quickly carried her through the house to the familiar bed, joining her on top of the coverlet, stretching out to their full lengths. As he slid himself into her, she felt the pressure of him all the way up to her lungs. There was ecstatic relief for both of them in the act of joining their bodies, and they breathed easier for a moment, chuckling to each other, but then the overpowering need became white-hot again as their hands became busy, searching, grasping, their mouths hot and wet on each other, and the rocking, rocking motions became more urgent. Colter reached behind her and lifted her slightly at the small of her back, quickening their pace. Suddenly, Michelle cried out his name, almost in surprise. Her excitement fed his, and they called out once to each other as they were swept overboard into the blinding seas of ecstasy, locked utterly together.

* * *

"Mitch."
"Yes."
"Will you be going away with Stephen?"
"What?"

Colter looked up from her breasts, which he had been teasing. She met his gaze with those huge brown eyes, full of directness and vulnerability.

"I'm not blind, Mitch. Stephen comes. You talk to him. Sometimes you go away. You do something dangerous, I think, and then you come back, angry, with scars, tired."

"Michelle . . ."
"Are you going?"

There was a silence in the dim light. Colter looked out the window, then back at this extraordinary woman.

"Yes. For a little while."
"Mitch?"
"Yes?"
"Please. . . be careful."

CHAPTER FOUR

The Pan Am 747 lowered itself into the glide slope to Dulles International just as Colter rose out of his light sleep into full consciousness. He had learned a long time ago of the dangers long flights posed to stamina, especially eastbound flights. You flew against the sun, against the time zones, and your only defense against the draining fatigue universally known as "jet lag" was the simple mechanism of sleep. Eat the large, main meals, but ignore the drinks, the movies, the snacks, and the other passengers.

Colter had followed this plan, and woke up feeling relaxed and refreshed. He unbuckled the belt he had kept over him and stood up. The three seats in that row had been empty, and with the armrests removed, it hadn't been too bad. Less lumpy than his own couch at home, even. He returned to first class quickly, and stepped into one of the lavatories. After relieving his bladder, he took the electric shaver provided and removed the beard stubble which had accumulated since leaving Bora Bora. Quickly running the razor over his face, his thoughts touched briefly on the last hectic twenty-four hours.

Once he had decided to accompany Bishop back to Langley, he had seen no reason for delay. At dawn he had returned to his own house, quickly packing a carry-on bag. He dressed in a clean white shirt, faded blue jeans and his relatively new Bata running shoes. He picked up his wad of new money, which he had received yesterday in exchange for the diamond, and decided to take all of it. For a passport, he saw no need to get fancy or go back out to the reef for a fake, so he took the one he kept on hand, a worn but up-to-date American passport which he kept taped to the bottom of a drawer in the kitchen. He grabbed his navy blue satin warmup jacket, the kind pro ball players wore, and put it with his bag.

He took five minutes to close the house, carefully setting the various switches which maintained its security. Without looking back, he picked up his gear and walked back to the inn.

He woke Bishop and told him to start, moving and Bishop, to his credit, hadn't wasted any time with questions. The Air Polynesie launch took them across the lagoon to the airstrip, and Bishop started making furious arrangements for quick-connecting flights. They had touched the ground at Faaa International in Tahiti long enough to have coffee and pastry, and at LAX, Los Angeles, not quite that long.

Now, the flashing sign in the lavatory of the big jet told him to return to his seat, and he did. He looked clean and fresh as he walked past the bedraggled tourists and businessmen who, because the liquor had been free, had decided that it was more important to have fun on the flight than it was to arrive in good operating condition. One look was enough to judge the merits of that decision.

As Colter sat down and buckled himself to the seat, Bishop regarded him enviously. He had tried to sleep but couldn't. At least, not enough to refresh himself. His eyes were red and grainy, and he needed a shower.

He had not tried to keep Colter entertained with conversation during the time they took meals or, for whatever reason, found themselves awake at the same time. He knew that Colter was preparing himself. It was no small matter to go from that enviable life on the island to the adrenalin pump that is CIA Langley.

As the pilot magically placed the landing gear of the hundred-ton aircraft on the eleven-thousand foot runway at Dulles, there was a general release of tension among the passengers. Air travel was taken for granted, yes, but most people held onto the armrests, along with a deep-seated fear of a flaming, spinning death, until the landing was actually completed. Conversation and laughter broke out like a virus among the travelers, and the inevitable eager ones began gathering their possessions together, already beginning their push to be first off the airplane. It didn't bother them that their next stop, the baggage carousel, didn't care who got off when. They just wanted to be first.

As they approached the ramp, the war broke out between the stewardesses and those who were already standing in the aisles jockeying for position. It was won decisively by the flight attendants.

Colter and Bishop had already cleared Customs and Immigration in Los Angeles, so they went directly to the taxi ranks outside, having no checked baggage to wait for. They were being met, Bishop said, by an agent Bishop knew. There was a pervasive stink of Jet-A fuel and automobile exhaust in the air around the terminal, but the green, wooded countryside around them beckoned with the promise of better breathing.

Colter spotted a dark blue Ford LTD approaching them, maneuvering to get in next to the curb. "This looks like Agency motor pool," he said signaling to Bishop. "What's the guy's name?"

"Beckett. I don't think you know him, he's relatively

new."

The LTD found a break in the flow and pulled up in front of them. Colter leaned down to peer past the dark-tinted window glass. There were two more men in the back seat. "Yup, that's Beckett driving," Bishop chirped.

The rear door opened and a man stepped out, smiling and offering to hold the door open for Colter to climb into the back with him and his buddy. Colter ignored him and circled the back of the car, opening the other rear door himself and sliding in, causing the third man to scoot into the center position in the back seat. Nobody objected, there had been no time to object, but Colter had been meant to sit between the two men in the back seat, and he had reacted instinctively. He never liked to get hemmed in.

The LTD pulled out of the arrivals area and followed the green-and-white signs for the Parkway to D.C. The driver, Beckett, was asking Bishop how Bora Bora was, how come he didn't have a tan, and so on, but the chatter was a bit empty. Colter took the time to examine the two men in the back seat with him. They were big, healthy-looking young guys, one with jet black hair and an eyebrow deeply scarred at the end, the other with reddish hair and very pale blue eyes. Colter's mind classified them instantly and automatically sent them to his memory bank tagged *muscle*. They were here to make sure he arrived undamaged, Colter mused. Interesting. Somebody must think there's a danger of getting hurt.

Reflexively, Colter positioned himself deep in the seat so that A) he became a poor target, and B) he could keep an eye on the traffic behind them in the rear and side-view mirrors. The chatter died away naturally, each man's mind returning to his reason for being there. Colter opened his window a bit to enjoy the fresher air of the rolling Virginia countryside. His mind focused briefly on his upcoming encounter with Paxton Fairbanks.

The two men had met only once before, and there had been immediate friction between their personalities. At that time Fairbanks had been a deputy director, and as ruthless as they come, a bureaucratic shark. He wanted the number-one job in the Agency and was out to get it. And he got it: partly because no one tried to stand in his way, but partly because he was a natural for it. He curried political favor but had variable politics himself, standing foursquare behind whichever administration was in power. At the same time, he was no fool. He made decisions quickly and based upon the best advice available, the hallmark of any good administrator. He backed up his men when they were right, and was deaf to excuses when they were wrong. He also hated Mitchell Colter.

Colter offended Fairbanks' sense of order, of control. That a weapon of Colter's caliber should be allowed to "retire" on his own terms was unacceptable to Fairbanks. Colter knew too much and had been trained too well. The one time the two men had met, the chemistry between them had proved volatile.

It had been at a routine debriefing of Colter following a highly successful penetration mission inside the Soviet Union. Colter had been introduced to Fairbanks, and the two men had sized each other up.

"So. You're Colter."

Colter did not reply.

"I hear you're the new Agency hotshot. A real super-spy."

"And you're Fairbanks. You're shorter than I thought you'd be."

Fairbanks winced. "Yes, I hear you're a real killer type. A legend in your own mind." He smiled smugly at

41

what he imagined was a joke.

"And I hear you think you're going to be the DCI when you grow up."

"That possibility worry you?"

"Some."

"Don't worry. I doubt you'll be around. Hotshots don't last long in this Agency."

"I won't worry. If you make Director, I definitely won't be working here."

The two men had stared at each other for a moment. It was a suspended piece of time. The next moment might have contained laughter, or bloodshed. As it turned out, Fairbanks called on his reserves of self-control and merely turned on his heel and walked away. But both men had marked the other down in the mental category of "Dangerous; Use Caution."

The same color kept appearing in Colter's field of vision, and he snapped his attention back to the present. After a moment, he realized that he was seeing the same metallic-gray Datsun over and over as his glance swept from front to side, to sidemirror to rear-view, and back to front. He tapped the driver on the shoulder.

"Beckett, is it?"

"Yes, sir?"

Colter winced internally at the guy calling him "sir." but left it alone. "You supposed to be alone?"

There was a split-second's hesitation before Beckett answered, "The gray Datsun?"

"Uh-huh."

"One of ours, sir. Just extra insurance."

"Okay."

Bishop turned in his seat to see the Datsun, and grinned at Colter. "Jumpy, jumpy. I guess Fairbanks just wants to make damn sure you arrive in one piece."

Colter decided to return the smile. "You know me. Surprises make me nervous."

"Sorry, I should have mentioned them," put in Beckett "You know how it is. If they're doing it right, you forget they're there."

They settled back to watching the beautiful green countryside give way by degrees to the advance of civilization, as they approached the parkway exit marked simply but plainly "CIA." Colter was becoming uneasy. It was one hell of a lot of "extra insurance," in his book, to order a tail car for an airport pickup. Unless the rule-book had been changed, they were laying on a whole lot more manpower than was necessary, and that was not the usual procedure.

The LTD glided up the exit ramp and followed the tree-lined roadway toward the guardpost. A short way beyond lay the huge parking lots and the enormous office-buildings complex. Colter experienced a quickening of pulse, a tightening of his stomach muscles. This had never been home, exactly, only Headquarters; but he had spent too many years with the Agency for him to remain unmoved by the sight.

Beckett presented his ID to the guard, and the car moved forward. Suddenly, Colter's alarm bells began to chime, faintly but firmly. He became terribly alert, using all his senses to search for the cause.

"Stop the car."

Bishop reacted first, looking back at Colter. Beckett's eyes flashed to the mirror, seeking Colter's.

"Now."

They were in the middle of the parking areas, and for the driver of the vehicle it was sort of a pain-in-the-ass place to go stopping. . . but something in Colter's tone of voice gave the distinct impression that there was an emergency situation developing, and all the occupants of the car knew better than to delay a response by asking questions. The LTD came to an immediate, abrupt stop. Colter was out of the car instantly, before any of the others could ask questions or interfere. He walked away from the car, towards a battered old Cadillac. Only when the Cadillac was between him and the LTD did he come to rest, almost sensing the air, like an animal.

Bishop came up, at a lope. "What's the matter?"

"Not sure yet. Something's not right."

"Well, what?"

Colter looked at him. "Why didn't the guard at the gate ask for my ID?"

"What?"

"The only ID he saw was Beckett's. There were five of us in the car."

"Hell, I don't know," Bishop groaned, "why don't you ask him? He recognized everybody, I guess."

"He didn't recognize me."

"You were with us. In an Agency car. Besides, the parking lot isn't exactly what you'd call a high-security area." Bishop stared for a moment, then grinned. "You know what I think? I think you just felt left out. We'll all be thoroughly screened once we get inside, don't worry."

The gray Datsun which had followed them was pulling up to the gate. After a perfunctory look at the driver's ID, the guard passed it through, and it pulled up at the empty LTD, where Beckett went over to talk to the driver.

Colter made a face. "Maybe you're right. Maybe it's just been a long time since a gate closed behind me."

"You're on edge. That's good. But come on, Mitch. This is the Ranch - where the Cowboys live. Remember?"

Colter began to nod, slowly. Bishop was right. They had gone to some extra trouble to get him here safely, and here he was, safe. "Yeah. Sorry. You're right."

"Can we go in now?"

"Sure. Let's go."

Colter and Bishop walked back to the LTD Bishop gave the Datsun driver a "thumbs-up" signal and a wave, and the Datsun pulled away. The five men got back into the car and proceeded along to the main entrance. Beckett and the two escorts were careful not to comment on the incident, or even raise their eyebrows at Colter, and Colter found this unaccountably annoying. He would be glad to get inside, he decided.

The main entrance to CIA Headquarters, Langley, is an imposing edifice in the Federal style, much like many other government buildings. Inside the brass-and-glass doors is a large rotunda, a circular foyer with a vaulted ceiling. On the floor, set into the stone, is the Seal of the Agency, complete with warlike bird and "CENTRAL INTELLIGENCE AGENCY" lettered around its circumference. On the interior side of the rotunda is the main Security Clearance checkpoint.

As the five men passed through the heavy doors, it was to this checkpoint that Bishop was leading Colter when the voice went off in Colter's ear.

Too many men in the rotunda.

He remembered instantly — no one ever stopped to chat here; it was an overdone entrance hall. On top of that, its acoustics made it possible for anyone to hear what you were saying. Yet now there were four distinct groups of men off to the sides of the hall. And no women. The complex was lousy with female secretaries, yet not one was in sight.

But because he had deemed his earlier alarm unnecessary, he did something that it was not his custom to do. He hesitated.

At the instant he broke his stride to look around him, all the men in the rotunda went into action as if a starter's pistol had gone off. The red-haired escort grabbed Colter's right wrist and elbow in an incredibly powerful grip, and the dark one with the eyebrow notch did the same with his left. Beckett seized Bishop and ran for the interior of the room. The four groups had formed a circle around Colter, isolating him completely. One man came up behind Colter, grabbed the cuffs of his blue jeans, and pulled his legs out from under him. Instantly, Colter was on his stomach on the cold hard stone of the Seal. Each man had an assigned task, and the sound of metal against metal rang through the rotunda as Colter felt himself handcuffed at the wrists and above the elbows, then shackled at the ankles. Powerful hands searched him for weapons and emptied his pockets. Two more men grabbed him under the shoulders and returned him to his feet. It was all very professional. The entire process had taken just under twenty seconds.

Colter had offered no resistance, of course. That was a good way to get hurt. This kind of treatment was reserved for someone who is considered very dangerous indeed, and he endured it in stoic, pliant silence. He knew he would be punished for showing any resistance whatsoever, and the agents in the hall had held all the cards, from the moment Colter had stepped through the doors.

He was confused, however, and very angry. Angry at Bishop for setting him up, angry at Fairbanks, whose orders these men must be following, and most of all, angry at himself. He had ignored his own disquiet. He had *known* something was wrong, but he had gone on anyway.

It wasn't an escort that had been provided, it was an armed guard. That's why those two muscle-types had offered him the middle seat in the back of the LTD. Containment, not protection. The extra tail car. The gate guard had recognized him, all right. Prisoner in custody, do not interfere. He must've given them a bad moment in the parking lot, Colter mused grimly. Bishop had been very good. Very good indeed.

But what in the hell was the problem?

Just then, Paxton Fairbanks stepped into Colter's line of sight. "Well, well. Colter. The renegade returns."

"Hello, Fairbanks. Don't bother with a handshake."

"Still the smart ass?" Fairbank's eyebrows went up. "That's all right, we'll take care of that." He turned to three uniformed guards. "Take him down to Detention One."

"What are you doing, Fairbanks? Do you know?" Colter seemed genuinely curious.

"Shut up, Colter. You're a dead man."

CHAPTER FIVE

Palma de Mallorca fled in the June heat, the crowded streets filled with the first wave of package-tour visitors from the Continent. Each summer, the small Mediterranean island was inundated with tourists from Denmark, Sweden, England, Germany, and anywhere else in the world where the weather never really got hot. All types of people came to stay for as long as they could afford to, from secretaries to royalty. Whole areas of the island were block-booked by travel agents according to nationality. Although the island itself came under the rule and government of Spain, you could spend entire weeks in Mallorca without once hearing Spanish spoken. In Cala Santa Ponsa, for example, the Germans landed with what amounted to an occupation force. In Cala Ratjada, at the southeastern end of the island, there were Frenchmen in droves. And women. Many, many women.

Mallorca is one of the playgrounds of Europe. By day, in season, the beaches are filled with semi-nude holiday-makers, and by night the disco beat from the boites can be heard throughout Palma, the only large city on the island and its major port.

There is an elegant casino called the Sporting Club de Mallorca located some forty-five minutes west of the city of Palma, along the Paseo Maritimo, past beautiful old windmills and down a newly cut road. The Sporting Club grounds encompassed a sprawling apartment complex, tennis courts, swimming pools, one of the most elegant dining rooms on the island, and direct access to the sea. Gambling had been outlawed in Spain for forty years under Franco, but after his death permission had been obtained for the Sporting Club's casino, and the resort was quickly becoming a very magnetic attraction. It was staffed with experienced young dealers and croupiers from England, and the management had wisely kept the betting limits and playing rules in line with those of their successful predecessors.

If a swanky casino on a pleasure island filled with nubile Danish secretaries in bikinis under cobalt skies seemed an odd place to find the CIA Operations HQ, Eastern Europe, the effect was intended. Following the example set by the KGB, most Western intelligence *apparats* were now run from removed physical locations. Mallorca held the additional advantage of being a plausible location for almost anyone to visit; that was what you *did* with Mallorca - you visited it.

James Minton had been Head of Station for a year and a half. He was forty-one years old, in nearly perfect physical shape, and one of the best agents the CIA had ever put in the field. He had been recruited out of the Special Forces in Vietnam.

On the morning of the last day of his life, he had awakened feeling easy and relaxed, unusual for a man in his position. He maintained a spacious suite of rooms in the main building, under the cover of being one of the casino owners.

It was a particularly good cover, as covers go, in that Minton had been with the resort casino almost from its start; he had not been "brought in" after the operation was under way. He did actually do useful work for the

Sporting Club, was fluent in Spanish, and was socially graceful enough to be accepted into the higher circles of island society. So successful was he that he had been granted a membership in the prestigious Club Nautico, a high honor indeed for a foreigner. This famous yachting club was the center of high society during the summer season — *the* place to see and be seen.

Additionally, there is a wariness on the part of the international public when it comes to the activities of a casino manager. The taint of the underworld clings to the most honest of them, thanks largely to their notorious brethren in Las Vegas and their antecedents in Sicily. This feeling of dangerous undertones in the air is fostered carefully by the managers, as it adds a certain spice of romance to the atmospheres of their clubs.

Therefore, James Minton was never questioned about his activities. He could make trips to Berlin, Vienna, Tunis, or simply disappear for a few days; no one asked why. He could send and receive cables in what was obviously some sort of code, and nobody would raise an eyebrow. And if the maid had come across his .357 Colt Python while she was cleaning his suite, she would have made sure she had forgotten all about it by the time she had closed the door behind her.

As James Minton ate breakfast on the last day of his life, he mulled over his schedule of activities for the day at hand. It was fairly light. Before the casino opened at 6:00 p.m., he had to meet Aguilar in the Plaza Heroes des Baleares, but that wasn't until quarter past noon. The operation in East Berlin wouldn't need his attention for at least two more days, but he would still need to check his dead-drops as he always did, to make sure no emergency was brewing. And the death of the agent in Vienna had effectively halted any reporting from that area.

Minton had heard just last night that Mitch Colter

was being held at Langley, and now, as he thought it over again, his frown deepened into a scowl. Mitch Colter? Minton and Colter had worked together. They had gone through some parts of their training together. The idea that Langley could think that Colter was working against them was barely possible, but systematically assassinating field men? It was inconceivable.

Still, the signal had been clear enough.

> RE CARLTON SIG 12 NOW
> TRIPHAMMER OFF CENTRAL
> STOP MEMOIRS COMMENCE
> STOP WILL ADVISE CS 1612.

"Triphammer" had been Colter's working codename during his life as a CIA field agent. It had achieved a measure of fame in intelligence circles, and in some cases had become legendary. As for the "memoirs" reference, that clearly meant that Colter was being or was about to be chemically debriefed, the current Agency euphemism for "squeezed dry." "Carlton" was the computer-assigned designation for the recent catastrophic series of deaths among field agents.

Minton found himself amazed for several reasons. First, that Colter had allowed himself to be taken alive for interrogation at Langley. All by itself, that would argue persuasively for Colter's innocence. If he had been in any way guilty, they never could have managed it.

Second, he was amazed that any suspicion had attached itself to Colter in the first place. Unless he had gone completely crazy, it was not something Colter would become involved in. He was — well, he was *Colter*.

Still, Headquarters had sources of information that he didn't. Not his job to reason why, as the saying went; he didn't have the equipment for it.

James Minton, dressed in his favorite linen suit and stepped out into the warm sea breeze of the patio overlooking the unbelievably blue Mediterranean. He savored the beauty and comfort to which luck and hard work had consigned him. He would meet with Aguilar, then pop round to the *Club Nautico* for a drink. Perhaps he might run into the commodore's niece again.

The barest hint of a smile was beginning to flirt with the corners of his mouth when someone hit him in the chest. Off balance suddenly, he stepped back a couple of steps and sat down, hard, on the patio flagstones. He looked around in a flash, but there was no one there.

WHAT THE HELL . . .?

Minton rubbed the heel of his palm against the spot he had felt punched, and felt the warm slippery wetness there. He was confused. Looking down, he was annoyed that he had begun to bleed - blood would be impossible to get out of the fine linen. He rubbed at it. Trying to stand up, he found that his knees and feet had gone all funny, making the simple act of getting up quite difficult.

OH, MY GOD, NO. . .

It was at that exact moment that he realized he had been shot. A burst of adrenalin coursed through his veins, fighting the hollow chill which threatened to paralyze him, and he stood up.

WHY? FOR GOD'S SAKE, WHY?

He thought he saw light reflect off what might have been a rifle barrel, on top of the next group of buildings down the hill some hundred meters away, but he couldn't be sure, because it was getting dark outside. He decided to go indoors and turn on some lights. There sure was a lot of this blood getting on his suit. He'd have to change clothes.

Then somebody hit him again, in the neck. Now

that *was* surprising. He wanted to call out to whoever it was that was shooting him to stop, please stop. But he was choking on the blood now.

Besides, he was tired. It would be okay. He'd make the man stop shooting him, but first he'd have a little nap. It was getting dark anyway, it was time for sleeping. But he'd better go inside, where he wouldn't get shot anymore. Except he was on the ground again, and the doorway was way over there. How did it get that far away?

James Minton died in comparatively little pain, with an expression of complete surprise on his face.

* * *

The man who was called the Doctor watched Minton die through the telescopic sight on the rifle. There hadn't been much noise. The Czech-made silencer had reduced the rifle shots to a muttered *phutt*. His concealment was good, and he had no fear of discovery. He just watched. When he was absolutely certain that Minton was dead, he methodically dismantled the 30.06 Enfield and put it into its carrying case, which was a lead-shielded, black leather doctor's bag.

* * *

The death of James Minton put a very big chunk of fat in the middle of an already very hot fire. The repercussions were channeled through embassies, intelligence services, Langley, and Dzerzhinsky Square. In Mallorca, the information was leaked that it had been a gangland-style execution. This seemed to satisfy most of the curiosity which had been aroused by the spectacular killing. Most, but not all.

Mallorca made a good listening post for the American intelligence organization; it had also become an important station for British MI-6, their counterintelligence section, and for the Mossad, the Israeli Secret Service. In the comparatively short time since its inception, the Mossad had become one of the foremost intelligence *apparats* in the world. This was due in part to keen support from its own government, which wisely realized the value of clandestine information and the uses to which it could be put; but in a larger measure, it was also due to Mossad's own recruited personnel. Mossad picked the *creme de la creme* from the army, the universities, even the Knesset staffers. They were relentless, they were ruthless, and they got things done.

When James Minton was killed, the CIA sent a man named George Jassey to Mallorca to confer with the local police, Interpol, and Minton's own staff and stingers, and to generally clean up the mess. He was also charged with meeting the men from MI-6 and Mossad, and to enlist their help and opinions, as allies, with the aim of finding out who had killed Minton and why.

He was to meet with an Englishman named Peter Loring, from the British side, and Mark Entmann, the Mossad's Chief in Mallorca. The three men met, by mutual agreement, late in the afternoon on the day following Minton's killing, at the Plaza del Toros on the Calle Archduke Luis Salvador. It was midweek, and the bullring was abandoned at this hour, awaiting the throngs of the following Sunday. It was one of the few places where they could meet and be hidden from sight while still in the open, thus preventing anyone from getting close enough to either hear them or shoot at them.

The stadium was eerily quiet as the three men walked slowly through the seats, in the deep shade of the western side of the arena. The Englishman was speaking.

"Dunno what you want from us, old son. Not really our show, do you see?"

"I appreciate that," said Jassey, "but I have to know if there is any indication of a reason, or any particular personal enemy of Minton's, you might be aware of. It's a small island. You knew Minton."

"I knew the man, yes," replied Loring, "but not the details of his ops. Look here, it must be that he was onto some operation or other that set off a ruckus with the other side. But you would be the ones to know about that. Just for the sake of argument, what *was* he working on?"

"That's the frustrating part," Jassey grumbled, "there's nothing like that to go on. In fact, it's been very damned quiet."

After a few seconds, the Mossad agent spoke. "There has been not much activity, but some. The obvious place to look is the KGB, of course, but we have no information of Russians coming into the island who would be candidates for an assignment like this. It was very professional."

Jassey encouraged Entmann with a raised eyebrow. "I went to the casino myself, yesterday," continued Entmann, "and found the spot the shot came from. No traces, no unusual comings or goings, nothing interesting in the guest registers."

Jassey was silently impressed. Entmann had moved quickly and had been very thorough. To get access to the guest lists was not a simple task. God only knew how the Israeli had managed that one.

"Nevertheless, it's got to be the KGB." Loring

seemed sanguine about it, almost to the point of seeming bored.

"Why?" Jassey fought a growing irritation with the Englishman.

"Well, who else?" Loring seemed surprised at the question.

"Bullshit. Even the KGB doesn't kill agents for no reason," Jassey said.

They had reached the presidente's box, and they stopped to rest and survey their surroundings. The sand floor of the bullring was clean and raked. On Sunday, it would be bloodied with the killing of six bulls in ninety minutes. It was a traditional entertainment.

"Is Mitchell Colter still at Langley?" Entmann asked.

Jassey was startled, even shocked, to find that this particular fact was known to Entmann. He himself had only been told because of this mission. As he looked at Entmann, he failed to conceal his surprise. Loring picked up on this immediately, belying his sleepy demeanor.

"What's this? Colter's back at Langley?"

"Wait a minute, you guys," Jassey put in, "wait a damn minute. First of all, the Colter thing is supposed to be on a need-to-know even for our own top guys. . ."

"Come on, Jassey," Entmann barked, "don't start up with that kind of crap now. We're either together on this one or we're not, all right?"

Jassey was silent for a moment. Then he said to both of them, "All right. Colter is being held at Langley."

"*Held*?" Loring was openly astonished.

"The Director ordered it," Jassey continued. "That's all I know." To Entmann he said, "And what the hell has that got to do with Minton?"

Entmann was impatient. "I'll tell you what it's got

to do with Minton. The CIA has been losing agents all over the world. Your ops are down by more than forty percent. My God, you think the other services haven't *noticed*? These are top-level, class-A assassinations. You take Colter into custody, who just happens to be maybe the top man in the world for that kind of work. And now Minton is hit. Colter sure as hell didn't do it."

The three men looked at each other, and silence fell over them for just a moment as they looked out over the empty killing ground. Then Entmann gave his quiet voice to the thought that was in their minds.

"So the question is, who the hell did?"

* * *

In Moscow, James Minton was not mourned, but his death was noted without pleasure.

The Premier of the Soviet Union could feel the focus of international suspicion on the Kremlin. Publicly, of course, there was not even a ripple of disturbance. But as the vigorous, balding man strode into his office, he was feeling the heat. Every damned intelligence service in the world was wondering what was going on, and they all felt that the Russians were *somehow* responsible. Even his own people! As if the Soviet Union would undertake this kind of madness - especially now.

The Premier was right on the crest of the new wave of Soviet-engendered internationalism called *glasnost* by the Western press, celebrated as the dawning of the new day of thinking. It was his brainchild, his life's work, and his responsibility. If it came crashing down because of some damn-fool KGB-CIA residual enmity, it would be the end of him and all he had given his life to further.

The Premier was not stupid. He knew that the clandestine relationship between the KGB and the CIA had reached a form of stasis. There was tension, certainly, but they operated according to a set of unwritten laws. Very tough laws, with swift and final punishment for their infractions, but *laws* all the same.

And now the whole damned structure of the sweeping new agreements he had spearheaded at the Summits for the easing of tensions, the de-escalation of the nuclear arms madness, the beginnings of movement toward a sound economy for the Soviet Union at last -- all of it was threatened by some new form of terrorism he could not identify, let alone understand.

For terrorism it was, even though it made no headlines. The Premier was aware of this. In fact, his first thought, when he realized the scope and nature of this outbreak of CIA murders, had been to seek out the culprit from among the known organizations of terrorism, especially that madman in Libya. This was just the sort of thing that would appeal to the shortsighted baboon.

Krasnevin, his head of the KGB, had sent agents to Libya, Palestine, Germany, and Iran. They had put their most sophisticated computers to work on the problem. They had run down every possible combination of motive, opportunity, and means, just like a Western detective boardgame. The stickingpoint, of course, was always the same; whoever was doing it had a list in his possession. A list of CIA agents, their covers, their locations, and, it was beginning to appear, their actual job functions. Until recently, the Premier had felt secure in the belief that the Soviet Union was the only possessor of such a list in anything like complete form outside of Langley, Virginia.

The Premier lifted his telephone and gave instructions for Krasnevin to be admitted the moment he appeared and for all calls and appointments to wait until he had finished speaking to the KGB chief. He replaced the instrument, and stared unseeing out the great window behind his desk, recalling the momentary euphoria - was it only days ago? - as Krasnevin had given him the information about the agent Colter being taken into custody at CIA headquarters. Everything had suddenly made sense. Of course! A renegade agent in their own ranks, a trained professional killer whose mind had snapped - who had turned on his own. Some injury in the past, real or imagined, had amplified itself in the mind of the man living in so-called "retirement" on that island.

The Premier gave a snort. Retirement, indeed. The CIA showed a certain callow innocence, letting that one live. Things aren't done in such a slipshod way in the USSR.

At any rate, it had been a perfect solution. It made sense. The man Colter had obviously become obsessed, insane, and gone on his own campaign of retributive destruction. Reading Colter's KGB dossier, the Premier had believed in the success such a man might have. Frightening. But at last it had been over. A closed file. For a few days.

The killings had continued now, and the whole theory concerning Michell Colter was out the window. He would have to send Krasnevin back to the hunt.

Krasnevin appeared a few moments later, resplendent in his full-dress uniform. The Premier's aide ushered him into the office and withdrew. Krasnevin politely declined the offer of coffee or vodka, and seated himself near the Premier's desk. The Premier studied him for a moment.

Krasnevin looked younger than his fifty-six years, due to an almost fanatical dedication to physical health and culture. Indeed, there were times when the light of the true fanatic shone in his dark eyes. The Premier mentally shrugged that off; after all, one must be something of a fanatic, these days. Krasnevin had risen to his extremely powerful position at a very early age, considering. Krasnevin had taken to wearing the uniform more frequently lately, the Premier noticed. No matter. When you're the head of the KGB, you can wear whatever you want to, he supposed.

As the two men bent to the task of renewing the search for the mysterious killer of CIA agents, Krasnevin showed no sign that he was other than a loyal Party member and servant of the Soviet Union.

* * *

Krasnevin was, however, quite insane. Some time ago, he had reached the level of being a certifiable sociopathic psychotic, a schizophrenic with an uncontrollable homicidal rage directed and focused with maniacal intensity at the Central Intelligence Agency of the United States.

He found it surprisingly easy to get along, in spite of the Voices which drove him ever harder, due to the nature of his job and the position in which it placed him, which was very high in the "pecking order." People were so easy to deceive - it was childishly simple.

The Voices had started to come to him when he had been little more than a child. He had been raised by his aunt Katya, a feeble, whining woman who complained constantly and from whom Krasnevin had isolated himself as much as possible. His father had been a serving officer in the GRU Military Intelligence who was killed "in the line of duty" in 1936.

Actually, the man had become hopelessly drunk while carrying out a menial surveillance assignment and had fallen asleep in the snow, where he froze to death.

These details, however, never reached the boy, who extrapolated a hero's death for his father from the single phrase "in the line of duty." In his isolation, he imagined his handsome Hero of the Soviet Union father being ruthlessly tortured and then gunned down in cold blood by *Agents of the West*, while fighting bravely to his last breath.

In school, he applied himself vigorously to political studies, history of the class conflict, and the unending struggle to overcome the West. During World War II, his concept of Agents of the West became embodied in the Office of Strategic Services (OSS), which then became the CIA.

He formed no friendships, but appeared friendly; he developed no cravings for sex of any kind, but he appeared normal to those around him. It was at the age when most young men become preoccupied with their developing sexuality that the Voices began to come to him in earnest; periodically he was compelled to cause the death of some living thing. At first he satisfied the Voices with animals - cats, dogs, or a sickly farm animal which he figured no one would miss very much. He would trap them, take them to a secluded spot, and kill them, quickly at first, to satisfy the Voices. Later, he experimented with drawing out the process, curious to see the mechanism of death at work. In his fantasies, many of the animals became Agents of the West.

Then came the announcement of a program whereby he could, with his aunt's permission, enlist in a special army school for training and possible higher education and advancement. When Krasnevin took the permission forms to his aunt for her signature, the old woman whined that he could not go away and leave her alone, and she wouldn't sign the paper.

Krasnevin felt no emotion. She was merely a problem which had to be solved. He strangled her the next morning after breakfast, leaving her body in her own bed. Before leaving for school, he started a fire in the old woman's kitchen, and when he was certain that it could not be stopped from consuming the entire house, Krasnevin hurried cheerfully to his classes. When they came to give him the bad news at noon, he was convincingly confused, then shocked, then grieved; everyone was very sympathetic.

A week later, as a ward of the state applying on his own behalf, he was accepted into the army program. He had committed his first homicide, and it had been a huge success.

He gravitated naturally into intelligence work, and won his commission early. Officers of much higher rank began to take note of him as one who produces outstanding results. So open and friendly was Krasnevin's outward demeanor that no one considered him dangerous until it was much too late. He learned quickly, and used his knowledge ruthlessly, and the Voices were pleased.

But as time passed and Krasnevin escalated up the ladder into positions of higher trust and higher authority, a vague unease slipped into the tone of the Voices. The Cold War, VietNam, and other operations of the KGB increased his status as each was completed. He even salvaged a personal enhancement by distancing himself from the fiasco in Afghanistan. But it did not bring him peace. The Voices became hungry again.

Then, one night in January, as Krasnevin sat in his Zil limousine on the way to the Bolshoi, the solution just came to him, brilliant in its blinding simplicity.

CIA agents were not dying fast enough.

Here he was, having worked all these years to get

himself to this penultimate position, the head of the KGB, where he finally had the means to do *anything* he wished. The Voices screamed their approval. He would launch a campaign to kill CIA agents. Not a KGB operation, of course; that would be considered insane. But an operation nonetheless, to be directed by him personally, aimed at every single CIA agent known to the KGB. It only remained to select the instrument with which he would operate.

Two hours later, he had surreptitiously obtained the file of the man he had known all along would have a destiny like this. The thick, Most Secret file of the perfect man for the job. Opening the file, he gazed thoughtfully at the photo of the man. Glancing down, he read the printing underneath.

Operational Code Name: DOCTOR.

CHAPTER SIX

Paxton Fairbanks had a headache.

He knew that he should take two aspirins, lie down for ten minutes, and then get back to work, but he didn't want to. He wanted to run away from Langley, get in his car and drive out into the open spaces and never think about intelligence work anymore. He had these little spasms of irresponsibility once in a while. They didn't last.

He had just returned to his office from the regular biweekly meeting with all of his section chiefs. The situation was growing worse - there were, literally, too many chiefs and not enough braves. Operations all over the world were virtually at a standstill, paralyzed with confusion.

Early that morning, Fairbanks had been called to the White House for a "special conference." The president, just like the Soviet leader, had been informed that Mitchell Colter was in custody and that no more killings were expected. The "renegade CIA agent" theory had made sense to him, too, and he was annoyed that it didn't hold water. He had instructed Fairbanks to "stop playing tiddlywinks" and go find the assassin.

When Fairbanks returned to Langley, he was five minutes late for the Sections meeting, a situation he deplored. The content of the meeting didn't help. Morale seemed to have dropped across the board, and the status of worldwide operations hadn't exactly lifted it.

Now, back in his office, Fairbanks forced his mind to look at the situation. Colter was still down in Detention One, the new super-secure holding tank which had been installed primarily for the holding of captured enemy agents, moles, or defectors who couldn't be trusted not to get away.

It had looked so good, when the link had been confirmed between Colter and Geoff Forbes at that casino in Vina Del Mar. It was the last time Forbes had been seen, and Colter had been there. Fairbanks had always believed there was something a little too special about Colter, and so was predisposed to believe that he might have "gone sour".

They had not, thank God, begun the process of chemically debriefing Colter as yet. That involved a whole protocol of drugs which, once begun - well, at least they hadn't made that mistake. The news of James Minton's killing had come in and arrested the process. The damnable part was that whoever it was out there wasn't even attempting to disguise the killings as accidents anymore; the use of the 30.06 Enfield demonstrated a knowledge that no one would believe it was an accident, in any case.

He had to release Colter. That was certain now, and he saw it in the eyes of all who knew of "Triphammer's" incarceration. The section chiefs, his deputies, his number-two man Harold Miles, even the president. It was not an attractive idea, for Colter would be justifiably angry, and the thought of the enmity he had incurred with one of the most dangerous men in the world was, to say the least, daunting.

Harold Miles, the deputy director, knocked softly

and opened the door far enough to poke his head in.

"Got a minute?"

"Unless you've brought bad news," Fairbanks replied, waving him in.

"Just got the new run from Einstein, negative."

"Fucking computer."

"Yeah. We've got to cut Colter loose, Pax."

"Yes, all right. I'll take care of it."

"Only I was thinking . . ."

"Yes?"

Miles went to the Director's desk and sat in the chair next to Fairbanks. Instinctively, he spoke in a low tone.

"Remember the legend we gave Bishop?" The background information, whether true or false, upon which a field agent operates in any compartmentalized operation is called the "legend." In this case, Miles was gently reminding Fairbanks that they had lied to Bishop, and that it had come back on them.

"You mean that we wanted to hire Colter as a consultant?"

"Right. I was thinking. . . This whole thing keeps coming back to the fact that somebody out there has a listing of our people. Somebody knows who our guys are and where they are, and it's current information."

"Yes?"

"Colter isn't current. I didn't even think about that before, because when you're dealing with Colter a lot of ordinary things don't really count. But what about this? Suppose we stayed with the legend we gave Bishop?"

"Go on."

"We appeal to Colter. See if we can enlist Colter to give us his help. You've got to admit that A) he's an expert in the field, and B) we're not having much luck so far, and he couldn't hurt our efforts. So why not ask him if he'd be willing?"

"Are you fucking nuts?"

"What?" Miles blinked, twice.

"It's a little late for that, isn't it?"

"Wait a minute. Judge the idea first. Don't assume, just for a minute, that he'd rather kill us both."

"Harold. You don't ask a gut-shot rhino how it feels about gun control . . ."

"Just assume for a moment. Make it hypothetical."

Fairbanks took a deep breath, squinting at his desk in the effort to envision the situation. Finally, he nodded. "Yes, I see. Too bad we didn't start out with it. He might have been of great value, I agree. *So*?"

"So I think we ought to see if we can't arrange it."

"You realize that when he gets out of here we'll be lucky if he doesn't bomb our cars just for openers? For *fun*?"

"Wait. You're thinking of it as if he were already out. But he's not. Of course he'd turn us down if we took him to the airport and then asked him. Of course. You would, too. But remember, he's a prisoner. And one of the things we know best about prisoners is that they are always willing to play "Let's Make A Deal.""

Fairbanks sat back in his chair. Miles was correct to the extent that he had, in fact, been thinking of Colter as already released. And correct, too, in that there is a distinct psychological advantage in being the one who holds the keys to a person's freedom, an advantage that he had been forgetting. That was a slip on his part, but it was also Miles's job to bring it to his attention. And in this situation, the Agency needed every single advantage it could lay its hands on.

He had to release Colter unharmed, of course. He had already given his word. Any vague fantasies he might have entertained about Colter having "an accident," or just simply vanishing off the face of the earth, were no good.

67

Pity, really. Fairbanks had always felt that Colter should have been terminated with extreme prejudice. Colter had been in operations that were now dangerous skeletons in the closet. He had led others. It was really horribly sloppy to have him running around loose.

What Miles suggested was very nice, though. It was conceptually pleasing. Faced with the choice of assisting his captors in exchange for his freedom, balanced against what he must naturally assume would be further discomfort or possibly death, it might be plausible that Colter could be talked into making a deal. If in addition it were made clear that he would also be proving his loyalty all over again, by helping the old school. . .

"It's a good idea, Harold. It might work. And God knows Colter would be the perfect man for the job. How do we go about it? You want to tell him a tale?"

Fairbanks used the tradecraft expression for what translates into English as "tell him an enormous lie." It originally came from professional con artists who set up their victims with plausible accounts of, for example, just how it was that they happened to come to *own* the Brooklyn Bridge in the first place, so that when it came to explaining the need to sell it at such a loss, the details were quite believable. You isolate the mark and tell him the tale.

Miles, however, shook his head at the idea. "I don't think so, Pax. This guy is a little too sharp, and we've crossed him once, from his point of view. I think we ought to lay the whole thing out in front of him, holding nothing back, and see what he says. I know he's an outsider now, but that's what I'd recommend."

Fairbanks didn't like it. Any suggestion of opening up any operation all the way to anyone, let alone Mitch Colter, wasn't likely to excite his approval. But in this case there were operational reasons and a definite urgency factor. It would be worth it if it worked.

"I suppose so. Yes, all right. I'll want you with me."

"Of course," Miles replied.

Fairbanks paused. In a few moments he would be explaining his own actions and decisions to that fucking hotshot downstairs. He hated the idea. He began to cast about in his own mind for ways he might frame his proposal and his, shall we say, explanations. . .

He'd blame it on the computer.

Not in so many words, of course, but the truth was that Einstein had singled Colter out for attention. Colter was one of the few men known to the computer's memory banks who was actually capable of an operation of this nature, scope, and magnitude. And he was the only one whose location was compatible with the criteria given for the memory-search, in that it could not be demonstrated that Colter couldn't have been present at each killing. In the other cases, there was firmer data. Therefore, the computer reasoned, it had to be Colter.

It was a simple matter, really. Surely Colter could be made to understand. Had their positions been reversed, Colter would certainly have taken the same action. In the bureaucracy, it was an action one could not afford not to take. After all, you had to cover your ass. If anyone ever found out that the computer had given him Colter's name and he had failed to act upon it, he would be finished as the Director of the CIA. That was certain. Never mind those nagging personal doubts that whispered that it just couldn't be Colter, he wasn't the kind of man who would do something like this. The computer had printed out Colter's name, and that had been that. Colter would be able to see that, surely. After all, the man was many things, but he wasn't stupid.

"All right," Fairbanks sighed. "Have him brought up

here - no, wait. Might as well press the advantage of the situation. We'll go down to Detention One. As you pointed out, he's not released yet . . ."

"Very good," smiled the deputy director.

Fairbanks and Miles walked through the sterile corridors of the Langley complex, coming at length to the elevator marked Director. They entered and descended into the labyrinthine bowels of the building, impatiently showing their ID cards to the guard who sat at the control point. There was a bank of television monitors next to the guard's desk, and Fairbanks' eyes were drawn irresistably to the one marked Detention One. It showed Colter's sleeping form, face down under the covers.

"He's still asleep, for Chrissake?" Fairbanks growled.

The guard peered at the monitor. "Going in to see the prisoner, sir?"

Fairbanks restrained himself from an angry retort, limiting himself to a mild, "Nice guess."

"Sir, S.O.P. is that you'll have to be accompanied by an armed guard."

Fairbanks was not about to make anyone else privy to his plea for help to the likes of Mitchell Colter, so he nodded in the direction of Miles and said, "He's a black belt. Instructor. My personal insurance policy."

The guard glanced over the thin-shouldered, thick-waisted, bespectacled form of Harold Miles and inwardly shrugged. He nodded. It satisfied the regulations. He reached under the counter and pressed a release buzzer.

As they headed for the door, Fairbanks muttered, "This will be to our advantage. Hit him with it while he's still a little disoriented from sleeping."

Fairbanks and Miles walked briskly down the corridor to the cell and heard the buzzer sound change as they got closer and the door electronically unlocked. Miles opened the door and held it for Fairbanks, who entered and was moving purposefully toward the form on the bed when he suddenly stopped cold, frozen in midstride.

"No," said the Director.

Miles hurried to see what the matter was. He could detect nothing wrong, except that Colter was still asleep.

"Get on your feet, Mr. Colter, you've got . . ." And then he took a second, longer look at Colter.

It was a very good improvised replica of a sleeping human form. Miles guessed that the substitute for the hair had been worked from mattress stuffing, probably pigmented with coffee. The shape under the bedclothes was just right. From the television monitor, it certainly appeared to have been the sleeping form of Mitchell Colter.

But it wasn't. It was a very sophisticated, well-executed dummy, but it was a dummy.

Miles' first instinct was to whirl and look behind him, even though he knew Colter couldn't be there. The walls were solid plexiglass, they were being monitored, and there was simply no place he could be hiding.

Fairbanks, white-lipped, had bent down and picked up the covers and was examining the workmanship of the sculpture Colter had undoubtedly learned at the Farm, the CIA's own academy of dirty tricks. When the guard at the video monitors saw this, he hissed, "Jesus!" and pushed the Security Alarm button, then dashed down the corridor to the door of Colter's cell. Before he could really think it out, he groaned to the Director of the CIA, "Where the hell *is* he?"

Fairbanks whispered, "He left."

* * *

Two days later, Mitch Colter was having breakfast back on Bora Bora. He was on the patio of the Hotel Bora Bora, chatting quietly with Arthur White, one of the owners of the famous old hotel.

It had been a busy two days. The most difficult part of the escape had been getting out of the Detention One area itself. He had spent better than a day working it out, after he had overcome the anger he had felt and the confusion over being imprisoned. They had lied to him. Again. And he had come walking placidly in under his own power, that was the thing that really burned him. The reason was anybody's guess - he would deal with that another time. For the present, he found himself inside a classic example of the CIA's version of the "escape-proof" cell. It was formidable, all right. Plexiglass walls, remote-operated electromagnetic door with magnetic locks, TV monitored around the clock, all in a secure underground area of a highsecurity installation.

It was laughable.

The CIA had spent uncounted thousands of dollars training Colter how to get out of any situation, including the so-called "box," the escape-proof cell. Now they turned around and put him in one, and then blithely assumed that he couldn't get out of it.

This is the government way.

Plan A had been simple but unnecessary. No drugs. He had anticipated that they might come after him with needles full of the latest hybrids of scopolamine, pentothols, and hallucinogens. If he allowed them to start this process, there would be no end, no escape. His senses would be unreliable in any escape attempt.

He would have to prevent it with personal combat and try to force his way to the door quickly and with the maximum of injuries inflicted on the way.

If he could. Inspecting the seal between the walls and the floor, he could see tiny openings at about two-foot intervals. Those would be gas jets. Colter had smiled grimly. That was good news, and also bad news. The bad news was that they could flood the cell with nerve gas or its equivalent at the touch of a button if he became troublesome or if they wanted to disable him in order to do something to him. The good news was that this was, then, the kind of advanced toy jail which tends to make the jailer too dependent on the pure gadgetry of the place, forgetting that the most difficult single factor to overcome in a prison environment is direct, armed supervision. An alert twenty-four-hour guard, placed five feet on the other side of the glass wall to personally watch him, would make all the other escape-proofing virtually unnecessary. Colter was delighted to note that there was no such guard.

There were several other flaws, too, which Colter saw right away. The bed had an innerspring mattress; a textbook mistake. There was, unbelievably, a electrical outlet. The hatch through which the meal trays were pushed looked flimsy enough to be forced; Colter could examine that later if necessary.

Mentally, Colter turned his escape efforts into a training exercise of the same kind he had undergone at the Farm. Piece by piece, he assessed the strong points and the weak points of his environment. He appeared docile, depressed, and resigned to being a prisoner. After the passage of a couple of days, he realized that his old employers did not intend to use chemicals right away at least, so he put Plan A on the back burner and turned up the heat under Plan B. He listed all the weak spots he had been able to discover, and looked for a way to use them all at once. Once he decided on a course of action, he was still not finished. He had to make several more plans, for once he was out of the Detention One area, he still had to get out of the building; once free in the Langley grounds, he had to get transport through the fence; once outside, he must return to Bora Bora. And, at each step, he had to design a backup plan in case something went wrong. This was where many good escape attempts turned into disaster - the failure to provide for the unexpected. Something could always go wrong.

The timing had been just plain lucky. Colter had made his attempt a bare eleven hours before the Director had come down to deal with him.

The guard at the TV monitors had been reading a copy of *Sports Illustrated* when there had been a brief electrical failure accompanied by a soft popping sound. His eyes flashed immediately to the TV monitor, which was still operating, but the screen was dark because the cell lights had failed. Later he would find the bent section of bedspring, doubled into the cell's outlet, which had been the cause, but at the moment, he hesitated. His own area was unaffected by the blackout, and the prisoner was asleep anyway. The lights would probably come back on in a second.

And they did, just as he was beginning to feel that he should do something. He checked on Colter, who was still there and didn't appear to have even moved. There he was, sleeping away, just as he had been before. He turned his attention back to the article on Magic Johnson and the leadership that had enabled the Lakers to repeat as champions.

Colter had been right in his assumption that the door would fail along with the lights. When his stand-in (or lie-in) was in bed, perfectly arranged, he had placed both palms on the door and pressed in and to the side.

The magnetic locks were disengaged, and he had simply stepped out and closed the door behind him. He was relieved he hadn't had to use the backup plan on squeezing out through the meal-tray hatch; it would have been a tight fit and would have consumed precious extra minutes.

Now, he placed himself at an angle from which he could observe the guard without stepping out into plain view. He had made no noise, and the guard was reading a magazine. So far, so good.

Ideally, Colter would make his escape without alerting this man to any sign of trouble; he was prepared, of course, to knock him out and hide him somewhere, but that was definitely a last resort. Colter might get lucky - the man might leave his post for a few minutes, to go to the bathroom or get a cup of coffee - or he might get unlucky. He had no way of knowing when the guard shifts changed. It might be an hour, or it might be six hours. He waited, silent, watching.

Colter saw the door he wanted, thanks to the CIA's high expectations of its "escape-proof" toy. It was clearly marked EXIT STAIRS, with a smaller sign reading USE IN CASE OF FIRE ONLY: ALARM WILL SOUND just above the old-fashioned Bushman push-bar alarm latch. That wouldn't present much of a problem, if Colter could manage to reach it unseen. Colter wondered when the guards' shift changed.

If it happened soon, Colter had the option of taking out both guards and then leaving by the elevator, armed with the off-duty man's uniform, ID, and pistol. This would be a little better than his last resort, but not much. In the other man's uniform, he would run an unacceptably high risk of being recognized, at least as being an imposter. The chances were better than even that the alarm would be sounded, and Colter wanted to be well away before that happened.

Why didn't the guy just go to the bathroom? He was drinking coffee, didn't that go right through your system? Hell, Colter himself had to take a pee. His eyes roved over the checkpoint area, absently resting on the door down the hall marked MEN.

Colter blinked. His pale eyes flickered back and forth between the guard and the sign marked MEN as he figured angles of vision and the percentages. It was good. It was worth a try.

Colter eased himself away from the wall. The restroom was about thirty feet away, at the entrance to another hallway. It was on the guard's blind side as he sat hunched over his magazine, more or less facing the elevator side of the open space. Colter moved silently and very, very slowly, his soft-soled shoes making no sound on the stone floor. The guard was not looking, but any time you move through air you're not supposed to be in, you were mindful not to upset it. He assumed the guard was normally sensitive, and it was amazing how many times air currents were responsible for giving people that "feeling" of not being alone.

Colter reached the door to the bathroom, and fought back the impulse to open it normally. He very slowly cracked the edge of it enough to get the fingers of his right hand behind it, and very, very slowly opened it to a distance of about eight inches. Doors cause air disturbance, too. He slipped himself behind it and took the same kind of caution closing it, slowly, slowly, and with no noise whatsoever. He silently praised the maintenance division which had kept the hinges adequately oiled.

Colter looked around. Perfect.

It was just like most of the other restroom facilities at Langley, and that was what Colter had been hoping. He now faced another door, identical to the outer one, between himself and the bathroom proper. Right beside him was a third door, clearly marked Maintenance Supply. Colter quietly opened it, making sure it met his needs, then closed it and proceeded through the inner door to the bathroom.

Three urinals, two stools, two sinks, two mirrors, and there it was, the object he had been looking for, in all its metallic glory, the hot-air hand-dryer. In 1958, these forced-air blowers were installed throughout the complex, replacing the nasty old unsanitary cloth-towel rollers which had been the original equipment. No muss, no fuss. Punch the dollar-pancake-sized chrome button, and sixty seconds of heated air pumped out the nozzle, in which stream one dried one's freshly washed hands.

Colter did actually have to urinate, so he went in the sink next to the dryer. Relieved and zipped, he took a moment to mentally prepare for his next moves. Then, taking a step toward the door, he extended his arm back to the dryer and gently pressed the large shiny button.

As the noise of the little blower started, which sounded like a battalion of industrial vacuum cleaners in the enclosed, tiled space, Colter made his way quickly past the inner door and stepped into the supply closet, allowing the doors to close normally.

Outside, at the guard desk, the sound of the hand dryer was having the desired effect. The guard ignored it for a moment before realizing that it was out of place. At this hour, no one else was around to be using the john. Besides, he had heard no slushing sound, no water running. He made a face in the direction of the men's room.

He sighed. Might as well check it out.

The guard put down his magazine, marking his place with a government-issue pen, and strolled over to the restroom door. He opened the outer door, stepped through and opened the inner door, and marched into the noisy bathroom.

As Colter heard the second door close behind the guard, he slipped quickly out of the closet, still being quiet about it, but aware that he was covered by the noise of the dryer for a few more seconds he slipped past the outer door, now in a hurry.

The guard looked at the blower machine, scowling. He checked out the stalls, looked at the ceiling, then back at the dryer, which promptly stopped running. His ears still rang with the noise of the thing, but all was quiet again. Mentally, he shrugged. Probably something electrical. A sort of hiccup from the wiring, like that lighting off-and-on business a while back. Damn government buildings. Everything goes to the lowest bidder.

Colter was working on the fire door as he heard the dryer quit. *When you're in a hurry, slow down.* The old maxim whispered itself in his ear, and he listened.

The guard paused briefly, considering whether to go to the bathroom or not. Better not. Better get back to the desk, the relief will be here in less than an hour, he thought. Besides, he was supposed to keep a "Constant Vigil" on the joker named Colter. Big deal. He wondered whether to make a log entry about the hand dryer, and decided against it. He'd just mention it to a maintenance guy when he saw one. No sense getting anybody in trouble by writing them up in the log.

After checking his appearance briefly in the mirror, he returned to his post. Glancing around the desk area, he saw that all was as it should be, and his eyes swept over to the monitor for Detention One. Yup. Guy hadn't moved a muscle.

Big deal, this "Constant Vigil" number. Special instructions from the Watch Commander in person, special ammo for his sidearm, all that. Just like to see the guy try to get out of this place.

Colter, meanwhile, was climbing the stairs. Remembering what he knew about the Langley complex, he figured that he shouldn't encounter any insurmountable difficulties in getting out. The whole place's security design was intended to keep outsiders out, not to prevent someone who was already inside from leaving.

Still, he couldn't just march out the main gate. Mentally, he reviewed his prior planning. Avoid contact, remain invisible. Only as a last resort should he have any contact with anything or anyone on the premises. Don't steal a car here, don't crash the gate, don't pull any fancy ID switches, just stay invisible and disappear.

At the ground-level landing, Colter found what he needed: the exterior fire door. Of course. He was standing in the emergency stairs, having penetrated one emergency fire door. In case of an actual fire, there had to be a way outside, and here it was. Having already practiced his lock-slipping skills on the door downstairs, Colter had no trouble convincing this one to open up without sounding any alarms.

Outside, Colter simply vanished into the shadows. It was work he had been trained for, work at which he was experienced, and he did it well. And, of course, he wasn't supposed to be there, so no one was watching for him. Within twenty minutes he was at the high wire fence which surrounded the complex. Here again the design was intended to keep would-be intruders out. The top portion of the fence slanted, heavy with barbed wire, toward the *outside*. Colter was over it in seconds.

Now he faced a new set of problems, including how to get to the airport, how to buy a ticket with no money, and how to get some kind of a passport so he could get back to Bora Bora. All his money, ID, and luggage was somewhere in the bowels of CIA Headquarters.

First things first. He started jogging at a sedate but steady pace until he came to the access road, where he increased his pace, knowing it would be just over a mile to a point from which he could hitch a ride up the parkway. He found a spot near the parkway entrance and stuck out his thumb.

He tried to look embarrassed. He grinned slightly, almost shrugging as he showed the thumb at the last minute. His whole attitude said to the passing motorist, "You won't believe how dumb I was. Wait till you hear."

Fifteen minutes later, a Dodge pickup truck driven by a fat, foul-smelling middle-aged man pulled over next to him and stopped. Colter leaned down, shaking his head, and grinned in at the driver.

A short time after that, Colter was driving toward Dulles International in the pickup, leaving the fat man, whose name was Jody Selkirk, tied to a tree in the middle of a stand of fragrant Virginia pines, naked, with his own smelly socks wadded into his mouth, firmly held in place with a rawhide bootlace. He would be rescued eleven hours later by a pair of homosexual furniture salesmen from Georgetown on an outing to Manassas, who heard his screams while stopped on the roadside to pour capuccino from a thermos bottle. Jody Selkirk would never pick up another hitchhiker in his life.

Dulles International produced an Air West flight to Los Angeles departing at 2:45 a.m.. Colter purchased his ticket using Jody's American Express Gold Card. He went first class.

Colter elected not to wander around Los Angeles International aimlessly looking for his next necessity, so he walked over to the theme restaurant at the center of the sprawling complex and took the elevator to the top-floor restaurant-bar to have a quiet look around.

In just under an hour, he found what he was

looking for. A man, clearly a successful executive type, stood up from a table of men who wished him a safe journey. He was a tall man, well built, and his coloring was close enough to Colter's that they could pass for brothers. Colter rode down in the elevator with him.

As the elevator reached the bottom floor, there was the predictable crush to get out of the car, met by the press of eager travellers to get on, and Colter was pressed against the businessman, seemingly quite by accident. Colter muttered "Excuse me" as he stepped away. It was a very neat one-handed lift, and yielded nine hundred dollars in cash, as well as the passport and another thousand in Bank of America traveller's checks. Colter vaguely hoped the poor bastard would notice before he boarded his flight.

Colter took the first flight he could find that was headed west, which turned out to be a United Airlines 747 to Oahu. His passport now proclaimed him to be Richard W. Sinclair, 42, of Beverly Hills, California.

Reluctantly declining the free drinks, Colter settled into his seat and closed his eyes. After a few moments of methodical mental exercise, he entered a semihypnotic state of "alpha," and turned his mind to an analysis of his progress so far, as if he were going to give a critique of the exercise.

It was almost 9 a.m. in Los Angeles, so it would be almost noon at Langley. By now, the Agency would certainly know he was gone. The question was, how would they respond?

Colter smiled as he envisioned Fairbanks' reaction to the news.

Probably they would put out some kind of discreet alert, calling for locals to assist them in detaining anyone of his description for "questioning." Colter was not worried about a possible reception in Honolulu; he knew that he had been moving much too fast for them to be thinking of covering airports other than Dulles, yet.

There was not much chance that the CIA would go to the FBI with this problem, asking for help. The friendly cooperation between those two agencies was just a newspaper story, promoted by the Public Information Office of whichever organization. The simplest thing for the CIA to do, if they wanted to catch him and bring him back, would be to keep a very close watch on Faaa International Airport in Tahiti. They would know, of course, that he would be headed for home.

Under other circumstances, Colter would head for the south of France for just that reason. He had other arrangements he could make there on short notice, but in this case he felt safe simply because of the timing. Colter didn't think they would get to the stage of watching Faaa for another day or two, and by that time all that would be there for them to find would be a record of Richard W. Sinclair passing through customs.

Meantime, Fairbanks would most likely be throwing the CIA version of a dragnet over the surrounding countryside, tracing stolen vehicles, questioning suspected accomplices, and asking his precious computer what he should do next. By the time they found out about Jody Selkirk and traced his American Express purchase of a ticket to Los Angeles, Colter would be back on Bora Bora.

Not bad.

Then, for the first time, Colter allowed himself a taste of the anger he had been suppressing since his capture. Most of it was directed at himself, for being such a greenhorn as to allow it to happen, and it was quite fierce. But there was an enormous confusion, too. *Why*?

Why did they think he was dangerous to them? Why hadn't they interrogated him? He had several guesses of varying credibility, but since no one had questioned him, he wasn't certain which answers they needed.

Colter didn't think that they would just forget about him, once he was back on Bora. No, they would send people out to see him, more than one this time, once they realized that he was back home again. Colter had stopped reading cables from anyone "official," they knew that. They would send some men to see him. Colter hoped one of them would be Bishop. Colter had some questions of his own.

There had been a wonderful connecting flight from Hawaii to Tahiti via Air New Zealand, and Colter had had not one moment's further trouble reaching home.

Now, as he sat on the terrace of the Hotel Bora Bora, Arthur White was asking him a question.

"Sorry," Colter said, "my mind just drifted off, there. What did you say?"

"I asked you when you were going to give up playing at spies and come into the hotel business with me."

"No, you didn't."

Colter's friend smiled. It was a sincere, oft-repeated suggestion of White's, but no longer a hopeful one. "No, I didn't. I asked you when you think they might be coming."

"Who?"

"Whoever you're expecting. The word is out, Mitch. You're expecting men to come looking for you."

Colter looked around, his eyes taking in the brilliant blue-green iridescence of the lagoon, the deep green of the island's jungle and forest foliage, and the bright cobalt blue of the sky.

"Two or three days, I think."

CHAPTER SEVEN

Derek Taylor had been living under the name of Klaus Brecht for almost six months, running three agents back and forth across the Czechoslovakian border and maintaining a love affair with a busty ex-nun named Marta who lived in a tasteful flat in Budapest.

He was not a tall man, but he gave the impression of height due to the fact that he was skinny. Not lean, skinny. At five-foot-ten, Taylor tipped the scales at 131 pounds, soaking wet. He had never weighed any more than that in his life, despite sporadic indulgence in enormously fattening foods, especially pastries.

He was hurrying on foot through the rain-splashed streets of Budapest under a gunmetal sky, tingling with anticipation at the thought of Marta waiting for him at the apartment. Among other things, she had for him a stock of Bavarian cream puffs. Two of his favorite indulgences at once, he thought greedily.

He had earned them, he felt. He had been in the field for three weeks, and instead of his usual skimpy report for the experts at Langley, this time he had managed to recruit a very promising young engineer who had a good start in the

Party hierarchy. He also had confirmed data on a Soviet operation heretofore unknown involving redeployment of missiles listed as destroyed in practice firings. He had been border-busting, as well, and had brought out two soldiers to be with their families in the West.

Taylor had been with the CIA since graduate school at the American University in Washington, D.C. He had been recruited out of an esoteric Theory of Western History seminar by his own professor. He liked the CIA. He got to travel and do exciting things as well as use his brain, which was an excellent one. And he performed well. His file was marked for advancement.

He hurried past a row of shops at the edge of the Old Quarter, turned the corner, and entered the old apartment building where Marta lived. As he climbed the well-worn stairs, his excitement rose again. Marta was a wild one.

He had met her at a movie theater late one night in a heavy rainstorm. The theatre had been showing *Emmanuelle*, the French film. After one particularly erotic scene, Taylor had gone out to the lobby for a cigarette. Marta had followed him, and had asked him for a cigarette, looking darkly into his eyes. He had asked her if that was really what she wanted, and she had shook her head no.

They had gone to her flat, right then. All her years of sexual repression as a sister of the order of something-or-other were finding expression in every way, at every chance, with Taylor. She was avid, hungry for sexual experience. Taylor was so delighted at their meeting that he had her thoroughly checked out to make sure she wasn't being planted on him by the other side. She wasn't.

He remembered the last time he had come home to her like this. Marta had greeted him with a smile and a kiss at the door, then turned to introduce him to a kittenish Dutch girl of about nineteen or twenty named Ilka. Ilka had been wearing a bathrobe open all the way down the front, and had had nothing on underneath it. Absurdly, Taylor had offered to shake her hand, but the girl had stepped quietly into his arms, with an encouraging exchange of looks from Marta, and kissed him longingly on the mouth. Marta's approving gaze changed to one of excitement. Taylor flushed and his blood raced even now as he thought back to those forty-eight hours. He loved Marta's surprises.

And he got a big surprise as he unlocked and opened the door of the flat. Marta, white as a sheet, was lying on the daybed in the front room, and a strange man was sitting next to her, taking her pulse. Taylor rushed over to her, closing the door behind him.

"What is it? What's the matter with her?" he asked.

"Herr Brecht?" the man in the dark suit inquired.

"Yes," Taylor snapped, "what's wrong with her? She looks cyanotic! Have you given her adrenalin?"

"No, I haven't. I'm sure it's too late."

"Jesus Christ! I'll call the hospital!"

"Never mind," said the man, whose hand now contained a 9mm, silencer-equipped Webley revolver pointed straight at Taylor's face, "I'm a doctor."

*   *   *

Colter was sitting under the thatched roof of the bistro at the Bora Bora Airport, a verandah-style bar which was more or less open to the air, and the warm, salty breezes were tugging at his fair hair as he talked with the uniformed Polynesian man who sat next to him. They both heard the faraway drone of the Air Polynesie Dakota at the same time, but they sat there for a moment more, exchanging smiles and nods, before the uniformed man rose and strolled out toward the arrivals gate.

The man in the uniform was named Rene Iatape and was native-born to the Leeward Islands. He was an Air Polynesie captain who flew the island routes four days out of seven, and he was a vital part of Colter's Distant Early Warning system. It was Rene who had helped discover that the Langley agents were coming in today, and he had come along himself, with Colter's blessing, to join in the fun.

Rene owed Colter a favor. Last year, Rene had stumbled into the Pitate Restaurant in Papeete with the sleeve ripped off his jacket and blood pumping from a gash in his arm, mumbling about three *mahoos* trying to kill him. Colter had scooped up the injured man and halfcarried him outside before the management of that elegant restaurant could recover from its shock sufficiently to even get Rene's name.

There had, indeed, been three men waiting outside. They were Australians, they were drunk, and they were dangerously angry. Rene, who in all fairness had had a drink or two himself, had called them *mahoo*, the Tahitian derisory term for homosexual, or queer, and they had decided to kill him, to prove that they were not. There's something in the water in Australia that causes reactions like this.

All three were armed with fishing knives. Colter had helped Rene around the corner, away from the waterfront crowds, and set him down gently. He had turned to talk with the attackers, to reason with them, but one of them, clearly beyond reason, had gone for Colter with his knife.

Afterwards, they would tell their friends that they had been ambushed by a gang of tough longshoremen, maybe as many as ten, they couldn't be sure. The truth was, they had simply never seen anyone move that fast. Colter was like a hurricane, a force of nature, inflicting black eyes, broken noses, fractured fingers and arms, and internally traumatized scrotums in a shower of surprising, blinding pain. When they awakened, they had been taken by the *Constabulaire* to an emergency clinic nearby. And on top of that, they all would have hangovers.

So Rene had been grateful to Colter, but that might have been the end of it, had not the two men discovered that they liked each other. They both liked to sail, and Rene had a forty-five-foot Morgan which he kept in Papeete Harbor. Over the course of several intra-island cruises, Rene had learned enough about Colter's past to make him the offer of his assistance with information about incoming travelers of special note, and Colter had cheerfully accepted. Rene had sources one is born into.

It had been one week to the day since Colter had escaped from the complex at Langley. One week of wondering and waiting and watching.

Looking out across the tarmac, Colter saw the increased activity among the baggagehandlers, so he rose and walked out to the gate in time to see the old Dakota sweep into its short final approach to the airstrip. The sun flashed off its white-with-red-and-gold paint scheme, and its reliable old landing gear dropped down from their hiding places in the engine nacelles only moments before it touched down at the eastern end of the runway. Not long now.

As the airplane taxied in to the gate, Rene and Colter stepped out past the gate onto the tarmac, waiting quietly as the service crew prepared to offload mail, freight, and the tourists' luggage. The aircraft came to rest on its marks, and as the throttles were cut and the engines' noise died away, the Air-Stairs door to the cabin was lowered and people began to get out.

Bishop was the fourth person out, followed by another Agency type who Colter didn't recognize. With a glance to Rene, Colter strode directly over to confront Bishop. Bishop stopped in his tracks as soon as he saw Colter. He gawked, open-mouthed. Colter had never met the plane before.

"Hello, Steve. I'm glad it was you they sent."

Bishop struggled to regain his balance. "Oh, yeah . . . Mitch, hi," he managed, "we didn't . . ."

Colter turned toward the man with Bishop who had stopped behind them, close enough to hear any conversation but not obviously intrusive. "You. What's your name?"

"Me? I'm just. . . I'm not . . ." the man stammered.

"Yeats," Bishop put in quickly. "Alan Yeats."

"Alan Yeats? That right?" Colter asked the man. The other nodded, reluctantly. "Well, Mr. Yeats, I'm Colter." Neither man offered to shake hands. "You were sent to see me, and now you have. But you'll be going now. You can just turn right around and get back on that airplane. It'll be leaving in just under half an hour."

"Come on, Mitch," Bishop interceded. "You can't just go giving orders like that."

"Shut up, Steve" Colter's tone was new to Bishop, and it threw him off balance. "I haven't decided if *you're* staying, yet."

Bishop was shaken. Colter had never talked that way to him before, and his first reaction was hurt feelings. The two men had been friends.

Yeats said, "I'd like to know who died and made you king of Bora Bora, Colter."

Colter glanced at Yeats, then back at Bishop. "Is he serious?"

"Come on, Mitch, Fairbanks himself gave us orders,

he has to stay or else . . ."

Colter was shaking his head, as if in disbelief. "I'm not the king of anything. But I've received your brand of hospitality in Virginia, and I'm offering you better, now that you've come - uninvited - to my home. Now, that man over there," and Colter pointed to the smartly uniformed Rene Iatape, "is an official here. Suppose he spot-checks your luggage and finds illegal firearms? Or drugs?"

"He won't find a thing," Yeats began, and then began to see it.

"He will if I tell him to," Colter purred.

Yeats was in a box, and he knew it. He decided to be more direct. "Listen," he began, "what's all the fuss? I'm not here to hurt anybody."

"That's good," Colter answered, "because you're definitely not going to hurt anybody. You won't be here long enough."

Bishop blurted, "God damn it, Mitch, we just want to talk to you!"

Colter sighed, and stepped back a pace. The other passengers from the flight had all gone inside now, and Colter raised the intensity in his voice a notch.

"I'm only going to say this once more. Yeats, I don't know you. You can't stay. You're getting back on that plane, I give you my word. Bishop, you and I will take a little walk, and then I will decide if there is any need for further conversation. That's what's going to happen. You should just start getting used to the idea right now."

As he finished talking, Colter gave an all but undetectable handsignal behind his back. On the instant, Rene Iatape sauntered over to where the three men were standing.

"Is there something the matter here, Mr. Colter?" Rene inquired respectfully.

Colter raised his eyebrows. After a brief hesitation, Yeats lowered his eyes and gave an almost imperceptible shake of the head.

"No, thank you," Colter answered politely, "we're just seeing our friend off." He turned to Yeats. "Have a pleasant trip. Love and kisses to Uncle Paxton."

Yeats winced and turned away, dutifully proceeding back up the steps and into the aircraft's passenger cabin. Rene spoke up, obviously enjoying the whole thing enormously.

"You needn't worry about your friend, sir. I'll personally see to it that he gets off safely."

"That's very kind," Colter responded. Then, to Bishop, he said, "Shall we take a walk?"

* * *

"I swear to God, Mitch, I didn't know."

Colter had led Bishop through the airport buildings and past the bar, down by the slip where the launch was taking on its regular diet of giggling, camera-happy tourists, and out onto the beach, facing the island. Only then had he turned to look at Bishop, his face a cold, unreadable mask.

"Really. I swear to God."

"You have something for me, I think?" Colter drawled.

"What? Oh. Yes." Bishop rummaged in his carry-on bag and came up with a vinyl-wrapped package, which he offered to Colter. Colter stepped away smoothly, to a distance of about ten feet.

"Put it on the ground, and open it up."

"Oh, come on, Mitch, for God's sake," Bishop protested, but Colter wasn't taking one single chance with him. It was still within the realm of possibility that Bishop and Yeats had been sent on a "snatch-and-grab" operation, that the packet might be wired for a quick spray of nerve gas, after which Colter might awaken somewhere less pleasant under other than comfortable circumstances. It was also barely possible that it was lethal. Perhaps the Agency had grown tired of him altogether and was setting him up for the final fall. Colter had made the mistake of trusting Bishop the last time, and had ended up a prisoner.

"Have you opened it before? During the trip here?" Colter asked the younger man.

"No, why should I? It's just your money and ID, Mitch," Bishop said reasonably "You, ah, forgot to collect them on your way out."

"If you haven't opened it, how do you know that it contains what you say it does?" Bishop looked blank for a second. "Because they told you that's what it contains, and you believe them. That's the difference. I'm not believing the things they say right now. Put it on the ground and open it up. And if I were you, I'd do it kind of carefully."

Bishop knew there was no point in arguing about it; Colter had made up his mind how things were going to be. He placed the packet gently on the ground and started to open it.

Suddenly, it occurred to Bishop that Colter might be right. Given the mentalities of some of his superiors, and the fury Colter had caused upstairs by just walking out and going home, some lunatic might indeed have prepared an unpleasant surprise for Colter in the innocent-looking packet the Property Department had given him to return, almost as an afterthought. Bishop slowed down his movements and began to take the process very slowly and very seriously indeed. He searched painstakingly for a telltale wire or strip of magnesium foil, and prodded gently for any shape that might be suspect, such as a battery, or a small metal canister suitable for gas.

Colter noticed his increased caution and smiled. The man wasn't stupid, after all. "Not so sure now, are you?" Colter inquired gently.

"No," Bishop replied tersely. "Be quiet, please."

Colter grinned but remained silent until, finally, the entire packet and its contents were laid out innocently on the volcanic sands. Bishop dutifully examined each bill, and flipped through the passport and cardfolder before declaring the job done.

"No bombs, no black widow spiders, nothing." But he was breathing harder than normal, for all that.

Colter stepped in and retrieved his possessions, keeping close watch on Bishop as he pocketed them.

"What about my bag? Clothes, shaving kit, like that?"

Bishop smiled innocently. "Yeats has all that stuff in his checked luggage. But Yeats can't get off the plane."

"Don't be a smart ass," Colter scowled at Bishop. "It's all replaced anyway. All right, empty your pockets."

In a few minutes more, Colter was certain that Bishop was unarmed, so he turned the conversation to its primary direction. "All right. Why are you here?"

"To apologize. I'm supposed to say lots of other things to you besides that, but that sort of sums it up."

"You personally, or you the Agency?"

"Both, but - just let me tell you, explain the reasons for what happened, you'll die, Mitch - " and, in response to Colter's look, "sorry, didn't mean that . . ."

"Why should I believe anything you tell me? You set me up once . . ."

"Mitch, I swear to you. I didn't know they wanted to grab you."

"So you tell me."

"Yeah, so I tell you. I can't prove to you that I didn't know. There's just no way to do that. But I didn't. If I had, I would've found a way to warn you off. The Agency sent me here to apologize to you because they made a bad mistake. But because they used me as the lure man, you're having trouble believing me. I understand that. But you'd have more trouble believing someone like Yeats, right?"

Colter studied Bishop. Then he nodded, slightly.

"The most effective lure man is the one who really doesn't know what's waiting at the other end. That's basics. Hell, we've talked about that, you and me." Bishop paused, and squinted at the crystalline water for a moment. "I guess ultimately, you just have to decide whether you believe me or not. It's as simple as that."

Colter felt himself softening. Not only was Bishop so heartbreakingly direct and sincere, he was also right. The lure man in a trap is the classic argument for the "need-to-know" principle. Colter knew Bishop well enough to realize that his behavior up to the time of the snatch had not been either rehearsed or forced. Further, Langley would not be inclined to let Bishop, a known friend of Colter's, in on the whole plan at the outset. It would have been an unacceptable risk.

"All right, Steve. I believe you."

"Then I can stay?"

Colter smiled. "Yes, you can stay. You have luggage?"

Bishop nodded. "It's still on the plane. Can Rene get it off for me?"

Colter blinked. "You know Rene?"

Bishop laughed. "I wondered if you remembered. The three of us drank all of the claret at the Yacht Club last year and then made the very sound decision to sail his boat to Australia, leaving right then."

Colter remembered, then. There had been something about the Beauties of the Aussie Beaches in some magazine and the encouraging man-woman ratio statistics of the cities there, one in particular. Melbourne, or Sydney, Colter didn't remember which. They had been provisioning the boat with case after case of Hinano beer when they had become very sleepy. The clearest memory from the evening was the Olympian proportions of their hangovers. It was the only time that Rene and Bishop had met.

Colter was pleased with Bishop. Steve had known, then, that Rene had no actual authority to search Yeats' person or luggage other than as captain of a flight, yet Bishop had remained silent so that Colter could pressure Yeats back onto the airplane.

"I remember now," Colter said, "and yes, Rene can get it for you." Colter indicated with a movement of his head that they should stroll back toward the ramp, and the two men started walking.

"Rene looks good in uniform," Bishop offered "Very impressive."

"He thinks so too" Colter grinned at Bishop. "Make sure you tell him that."

* * *

Michelle greeted Colter with a kiss on each side of his face, and Bishop with the most furious-looking scowl she could muster.

"You! You are naughty, naughty, bad!"

Bishop turned to Colter, who was solemnly engaged in studying an imaginary sliver in his thumb. "What did you tell her?"

"Hah! He never tells me! He tells me *rien de tout*!

But I can see with my eyes. You come here, you take him away, back to your stupid country, and something goes wrong, yes? I think so, yes. He comes back all angry. For a week he is worse than a Sicilian. Moods. His eyes are dark. He doesn't eat. Then he hears you are coming again, and his eyes become bright again, but he is not happy. He is eager." She was unsure that this was the perfect word, so she turned to Colter. "Eager. Yes?" Colter shrugged, nodding, deadpan. "Yes. He goes to meet you at the plane, but he doesn't know if you're coming onto the island. Alors, that means he might push you back on the plane. You did something. Yes. I know."

"Michelle," Bishop inserted as she took a breath, "you're right." She had been ready to argue with him, and this simple admission stopped her cold. "I'm not going to tell you all about it, but I'll tell you this: something did go wrong, but nobody was hurt, and it's all right now, and it wasn't my fault anyway. Mitch believes me. I mean, he let me come on the island, yes?"

Michelle, who didn't really want to be mad at Bishop, gave him a shrug.

"I've come back to Bora Bora to apologize to Mitch," he continued, "but if he's been running around kicking dogs and swearing at children for the past week, you take it out on him, not me. Okay?"

Michelle was still sulky, her dark eyes moving back and forth between the two men. "Couple of big stupid boys," she muttered.

There followed a silence, which was just coming to the point of being uncomfortable when Colter said, "Worse than a Sicilian? How was I worse than a *Sicilian*?"

He looked so confused, so genuinely perplexed and wounded by such a horrid description of his behavior, that Michelle and Bishop broke out in laughter, and the camaraderie among the three became instantly whole and healthy again. They all sat down at one of the patio tables, and Michelle called to a girl working inside to bring them three beers. They chatted for a while as they sipped the good cold Danish Tuborg, and then Michelle arose, preparing to leave the two of them alone to discuss whatever it was they discussed.

"*Alors*, Stephen. How long will you stay?"

Colter replied before Bishop could open his mouth. "He doesn't know yet, Michelle. He'll tell you in the morning."

Michelle and Bishop exchanged a quick glance, deciding at the exact same moment not to ask further questions. Bishop was merely curious, but Michelle had to bite back a sharp remark involving her feelings about overgrown children and their secret games. She wheeled and disappeared into the inn.

"So?" began Bishop, as the silence settled around them.

"So," Colter responded. "Here we are. I admit to a certain curiosity. Why don't you tell me about it? *All* about it."

With a sigh, Bishop prepared himself to tell Colter the whole story.

"It was all Einstein's fault."

* * *

Bishop laid everything out for Colter. When the super-sophisticated computer was confronted with the systematic killing of CIA agents, which were all too real, it was instructed to deliver a name, a suspect. One name. The name of any man in its memory banks who had the training, experience, and opportunity to physically carry out such an extensive program of assassinations. Motive had been held in reserve as a factor, initially, because they were merely narrowing down the field. Half a dozen names eventually came up. The Libyan lunatic and the Iranian fanatical old man and their people were reluctantly eliminated from consideration, due to the fact that whoever was behind the killing had access to really first-class information. That single fact helped to eliminate all but two names. It was the stopping-block in the logical process; somebody out there had "The List." The computer then considered motive, and the same two names appeared: Colter's, and that of an Israeli agent named Lasker. Lasker's files were pulled and surveillance was sent out on him, but he had ultimately been eliminated from suspicion due his physical location; he had been continuously, provably on assignment in North Africa during the entire operative period.

That left Colter. The possibility was suggested that he had become paranoid, or obsessed, or maybe just plain island-happy. No one could positively account for his whereabouts during most of the actions, except for the killing of Forbes, where chance had placed a positive sighting of him at the casino at Vina Del Mar, actually in the company of Forbes just before he died.

Colter certainly had the required means, in the form of his Agency-taught skills. He had a plausible motive, and as far as could be determined, he had had opportunity as well. Ergo, according to Einstein, it must be Colter.

That was all Fairbanks had needed, naturally, to start the ball rolling. He had never liked Colter, and he let this personal dislike cloud his judgment of the overall likelihood of such a thing. He ordered Bishop to Bora Bora with a story to tell Colter; CIA agents were being killed all over the world. It was a true story, but it was incomplete, in that it left out the fact that Einstein had singled out Colter as the only possible suspect in the world.

The only problem was, it wasn't Colter.

There is a term often used in computer science which has the acronym GIGO - Garbage In, Garbage Out. If you ask a computer to select a name from all the names that were programmed into it, it will. But if the correct name has never been entered into the system, it is a physical impossibility for it to be printed out. Information retrieval is only as good as the programmed input. Garbage in, garbage out.

Apparently it had never occurred to the "experts" at CIA Langley that the man they were seeking was unknown to Einstein. However, this fact became more and more apparent as the killings continued, in spite of the fact that the supposedly guilty party was in custody at Langley. They went back to Einstein, feeling confused and slightly betrayed, and began to ask the same questions all over again. They continued to get garbage.

Meanwhile, Fairbanks had come to his senses somewhat. After indulging himself in an apoplectic rage over the disappearance of Colter from Detention One, he had realized that he was back at square one. No suspects. Einstein had let him down. His mind drifted back to the idea put forward by Harold Miles moments before they discovered Colter's escape. Although it now seemed impossibly unlikely that Colter would be willing to assist in the effort, he felt that he had to try. Colter had a good mind for this kind of thing and an unusual knowledge of covert operations on both sides. He also had a fresh, outside point of view; Fairbanks knew that he himself was too close to the thing. He must be missing something obvious.

So the CIA Director called Steve Bishop back in and sent him again to Bora Bora - this time briefed fully and honestly on the scope of the entire situation and provided with documents and field reports to back him up. He had sent Yeats along for Bishop's protection — God only knew what kind of reaction Colter would have to immediate further contact with the Agency — but Bishop was the agent entrusted with the mission: Get Colter to help us.

* * *

Colter listened to Bishop in silence as the younger man laid out the explanation. He was no longer even angry. He was, in spite of himself, intrigued. On top of which, it had all the classic marks of CIA truth about it; it was exactly the kind of balls-up mess the Agency was famous for.

He remembered someone commenting, some years back, on the CIA-engineered assassination attempt on Sukarno, which had turned into a massive, lethal shootout with a shockingly high bodycount. The agent reported that "It had all the earmarks of a typical CIA operation; Sukarno was the only one left alive in the room."

The temptation to rely heavily upon the amazing abilities of the state-of-the-art hardware and software available these days was almost irresistible. Unfortunately, it was also a mistake.

Colter suppressed his natural resentment over the fiasco of trying to bring him in and hold him. It would be pointless to dwell on it or even express it. Any sentence beginning with, "Why didn't they . . .?" or "They should have . . ." or "Didn't they know . . .?" would be futile. It would serve only to feed his resentment and to clarify and solidify his dislike and mistrust of Paxton Fairbanks. Pointless.

Not that he hated Fairbanks. Fairbanks wasn't a bad man or an evil one, necessarily, but he *was* a necessary evil in a system which was run by bureaucratic committee. Someone had to make decisions, right or wrong. Fairbanks had been wrong, this time. Too bad, and a damn nuisance, but sometimes he was right, too.

But at the top of all the factors in Colter's decision-making process was a nagging sense of excitement. It began as a tingle he felt in the base of his spine. There was a minuscule contraction of the skin of the scrotum. His heartrate pushed up just a tiny bit. Any of these symptoms alone could have been dismissed, but by now Colter knew himself, and he knew that he was going to involve himself in this business. The only remaining question was, on what terms?

Bishop had paused for breath and to let Colter think, which was patently what Colter was engaged in. Presently, Colter leveled his eyes at Bishop and spoke.

"Suppose I decided to help. Are you authorized to discuss a fee?"

Bishop hesitated, thereby telling Colter all he needed to know. Colter could imagine the conversation in the Secure Briefing Room, with Harold Miles telling Bishop, "And for Christ's sake, if he says yes, don't tell him what we're willing to pay right off. Start him off with the assumption that we'll stand still for his regular fee, and that's all."

Bishop said, "The Agency is willing to go much higher on this one. You and I will have to agree that you threatened to roast me over an open fire, but I'll tell you right now that your hundred thou is guaranteed up front, plus expenses in any amount, transportation, documentation, armaments, whatever. In the event of a successful conclusion, there will be a bonus bringing the total amount up to two hundred and fifty thousand dollars."

Colter smiled. He liked it that Bishop didn't try to give him story to make him negotiate for his own services. "That sounds about right. With the proviso that I can drop it at any time, and the first hundred is still paid."

"Done." Bishop couldn't have been more relieved. It was as far as he was authorized to go.

"All right, then. Why don't we get to work?"

PART TWO

THE DANCE

CHAPTER EIGHT

"Jesus Christ, Mitch! Be reasonable!"

"Let me put it another way. No."

It was well into the night on Bora Bora, and the two men sat in Colter's living room, surrounded by the wreckage of a long afternoon's work which had turned into a long night's work. Bishop had brought out the files, records, and follow-up reports concerning the murdered agents, including the latest information on Derek Taylor and his girlfriend Marta. He also had several masses of computer printout synopses Colter had painstakingly read every piece of information, read it again, and then gone on to the next.

This was not due to a lazy memory on Colter's part; he read the material once simply to get the information, and the second time from the point of view of the assassin, considering each man as a target to be eliminated.

At sunset, Bishop had gone into the kitchen and constructed a pick-up supper of meats and cheeses, which they washed down with a bottle of French Cabernet Sauvignon which was much too good for the occasion. Colter continued to absorb the information without a break, and the moon had risen high in the tropical sky by the time Colter tossed the last file folder on the table and leaned back in his chair, rubbing his eyes.

"Well," Bishop began, unable to remain silent, "what do you think?"

Colter turned to Bishop, and looked at him as if he had only just appeared in the house. After a brief hesitation, he said, "I think somebody's making Swiss cheese out of the CIA." He rose from his chair, stretched out his joints like a cat awakening from a nap, and walked over into the kitchen.

"Great. I'll cable Langley right away."

"You know that's the effect it's having," Colter said, peeling a banana absently, "but I'm talking about the intent."

"What?"

"It seems to me that the Agency may be a bit blinded at this point. Agents are being hit, and the effect is to disrupt operations worldwide. CIA Langley seems to be looking for a pattern that will tell us why it's being done; I think we know why, by now."

Bishop just stared. "Why?"

Colter looked down at his bare feet and shook his head. "Steve," he began, "let's take first things first. We need more information, and we need current stats on every KGB agent now known to be in the field."

"Right, well, when we get back to Langley . . ."

"Oh, I won't be going back to Langley."

". . . we'll be able to . . ." Bishop blinked. "What?"

"I'm not going back to Langley."

There followed a brief argument in which Colter triumphed through the simple technique of not participating. He was not returning to Langley under any circumstances, period.

"I will agree, however," Colter consoled Bishop, "that we need better communications than we'll be able to find here on the island. I'll go with you as far as Papeete."

Bishop sighed. "When?"

"In the morning."

"Where, exactly?"

"Where's your friend Yeats likely to be?"

Bishop didn't hesitate. "The Taharaa"

"No, that's no good. We'll have to be closer in, anyhow. Call him in the morning and have him get us a big suite at the Maeva Beach. If there's any hassle, tell him to talk to Monsieur Barrault, B-a-r-r-a-u-l-t, and mention my name."

"Right."

"Right. Let's get a little sleep."

"Mitch?"

"Yes?"

"What's going on? Do you know?"

Colter paused for a moment, reflecting. Then he said, "Tell you what. I'll walk you back down to Michelle's and tell you what I think on the way. All right?" He moved to the door and opened it. Bishop hurriedly assembled the printed material and, while he was stowing it in his bag, comforted himself that Colter had been saying *we* as he talked about the steps to come. That was good.

As Bishop stood up, ready to go, he asked bluntly, "You know who's behind the killings, don't you?"

"Yes, I think so," Colter nodded soberly.

Bishop stood there, waiting.

"It's the Russians," Colter said.

*   *   *

"It was too simple, so everybody ignored it," Colter was explaining to Bishop as they walked down the moonlight-dappled road. Now and then the sound of a breaking coconut-stalk was followed by a loud but muffled crashing noise as a coconut fell from a tall palm tree. The men's eyes would shift instantly to the source of the sound, and once it was identified and classified non-dangerous, return to the conversation. As absurd as it may sound, falling coconuts were a real and present danger in this tropical paradise. Every season, two or three unsuspecting tourists were seriously injured if not killed by the falling fruit.

"The key, of course, is in the information," Colter continued, "and the fact that Moscow is the only place it would logically be coming from. Moscow keeps pretty close tabs on our people, and the assassin, or assassins, have that caliber of information. Assuming the the CIA is not itself responsible, that leaves Moscow."

"The Agency itself? You mean a mole?"

"Yeah, but it doesn't feel like that to me. The timing is wrong, because a mole has to work through so damn many cut-outs. This guy is faster than that."

"But for Christ's sake, it's impossible! The Russians just don't operate that way!"

"I can hear Fairbanks saying those same words at the biweekly meeting," Colter mused. He regarded his young friend in the pale darkness. "One thing you should have learned by now is that just because the Russians haven't operated that way in the past, doesn't mean they aren't operating that way now."

"All right, but *why*?"

"Look at the results. The CIA is the principal opponent of the KGB, and the CIA is now effectively hamstrung, and running scared. It's the same thing as a cop looking around for a murder suspect; the first question you ask is, *who benefits*?"

"Well. . . why just us? The KGB could benefit from the same result happening inside MI-6, or Mossad, or SDECE . . ."

"Yeah, and that gives us hope. It could be that this kind of a harebrained scheme doesn't have the official backing it should. On the other side, those guys may well be next."

"Next? My God, I hadn't even . . ."

"But it's the List that's the clincher. Nobody else has that kind of information on us. I don't know who in Moscow, yet, but Moscow's the place to look."

"You're sure?"

"Not sure, really, but I'm betting on it."

"Are you going inside Russian territory?"

"I don't know yet. I don't have enough information. You asked me what I think, and I'm telling you."

Bishop was silent for a bit, thinking. "I wish you'd reconsider about going back to Langley," he offered.

"Oh, well, we all wish a lot of things, I suppose."

"No, really."

"Forget it."

"But why? Is it because you're still mad?"

"Yes. It's because I'm still mad."

"Holding a grudge?"

"Nah. Learned a lesson." And after a moment, "And holding a grudge, too, I guess, but that's not really it. There's no operational reason for me to go there. And the operational rules are already in force. Make no mistake."

They walked in silence the rest of the way to Michelle's Inn. When they got there, Michelle was in the process of convincing one of her regular customers to go home. Claude Levalier, the most often married man on the island, was having trouble at home - again. He had been a seafaring man in a variety of navies and had now, unaccountably, reached his early sixties. He always made Michelle throw him out of the inn's bar when he came in to drink. It reminded him of the old days. Levalier had been thrown out of some of the best bars in the world, and some of the worst. Being thrown out convinced him that he had had a good time. Michelle knew this, of course, and a ritual had developed between the two of them involving a crescendo of insults and abuse in the true French manner, climaxed by Michelle tossing a close-at-hand empty whiskey bottle at the old man. She always missed, but she came close enough to provide the old man with an honorable excuse to run for his life — his time-honored method of leaving a drinking establishment.

Colter had seen the show before so he explained it to Bishop, whose first impulse had been to go lend a hand. From the volume and tempo of the hard-bitten gutter French being shouted back and forth, Colter estimated aloud that it was nearing the conclusion. "Bottle minus ten, I'd say."

And sure enough, about ten seconds later Michelle's hand wrapped itself around a nearby empty vodka bottle and she went into her wind-up. Levalier shrieked and Michelle threw, missing him by two feet but sending him on his way. As he ran past Colter and Bishop, who had been watching from the roadway gate, the old soldier winked at Colter.

"*Ca va* Claude?" Colter called out.

"*Bon. Bon*," the old man threw back over his shoulder as he high-stepped down the road.

Michelle saw them then, and came running over to greet them, her great dark eyes shining. Bishop showed her his bag and asked if she had room for the night for *un pauvre Americain*, and she laughed.

"*Oui*, yes, you come crawling back here to me, always!"

Bishop placed his hands over his heart. "She didn't mean anything to me, and besides she's out of town."

She slapped him on the arm, and the three of them went inside and sat for a while, just chatting in the soft night air. Presently Bishop got up and took his bag into his room, saying he'd be right back. When he was gone, Colter leaned in closer to Michelle and whispered, "I'm going to be in Papeete for a few days. Can I bring you anything?"

Michelle's face darkened. "You're going away?"

"Not like that," Colter soothed. "It's just to spend a few days in Papeete. I'm not even leaving the islands."

"So leave, who cares?" She shrugged. "For how long?"

"I don't know, a few days."

"Where will you stay?"

"The Maeva Beach," replied Colter, with a nod of his head to indicate Bishop's room. "He's paying."

"Maeva Beach" Michelle nodded suspiciously "Oh, yes. Stewardesses. American tourist girls. Japanese teenagers. Oh, yes."

"And room service."

"Pig!"

Ever since Michelle had gone to Bishop's room that one night, Colter had teased her about the great "room service" here at the inn. She pretended to be offended, all the while fighting back the giggles of a naughty little girl. In time, "room service" had come to be synonymous with "casual sex."

"Anyway," Colter continued, "can I bring you anything?"

"Do not derange yourself, M'sieur," she answered primly. Then she appeared to consider for a moment. "Perhaps you are bringing back diamonds?"

"It's. . . possible."

Michelle knew that Colter had a secret supply of diamonds hidden somewhere, and that he periodically traded them to *les Chinois* for the cash to live on. She thoroughly disapproved of *les Chinois*, but she was intrigued by Colter's seemingly inexhaustible supply of diamonds. She teased him about them and tried to guess where he had them stashed, but he would never even give her a hint. She suspected that whatever he did when he worked, he was paid in diamonds, and her question about bringing precious stones back to the island was the closest she wanted to come to a flat question. She was not a wife, for God's sake. But she did want to know if he was going to work.

"In fact, it's probable," and he grinned at her. "Just have to wait and see."

* * *

The Maeva Beach Hotel is situated about three miles west of the main harbor of Papeete, on elaborately designed grounds including palm-lined walkways, floral gardens, swimming pools, and a beautiful white-sand beach facing the bright water of the lagoon and the reef beyond. Part of the UTH International chain, it could claim sister hotels in Zaire, Senegal, the Ivory Coast, and all over Caledonia. It boasted 230 rooms, airconditioning throughout (which, in the big tropical hotels, means the same thing as refrigeration), Le Restaurante Gauguin, the Cafe de Paris bar, banquet rooms, a fresh-water swimming pool with poolside bar, private beach with boating and water sports from board-sailing to scuba diving, a nearby golf course, boutiques, newsstand, hair salon, tobacconist, and most of the other amenities, including, of course, room service.

Colter was sitting at the poolside bar having a beer with Lucien Barrault, the resident manager of the hotel. He had sent Bishop and Yeats on up to the suite, to get unpacked and to routinely sweep the room for listening devices. There wouldn't be any, but that didn't matter; there never were any, until the time you didn't look.

Colter let his eyes rove around the poolside area, taking in several elegant European women clad only in the bottom halves of their already brief bikinis. Even without admiring the even, overall quality of their suntans, Colter knew that this was the custom, here and throughout the islands. Here, even the occasional normally conservative American woman felt comfortable, free, going bare-breasted. No one thought it was a big deal, except for the infrequent leering foreigner, usually an American in his middle years, often fresh from his own brand of big-city pressures and inevitably waving his newly signed divorce decree around as if it were a first-class ticket to licentious excesses of the flesh. These idiots were politely turned aside, and very rarely caused any trouble. On the odd occasion that one of them proved troublesome, Lucien Barrault was never very far away. One of his departments at the Maeva Beach came under the official title of Guest Relations; or, as Lucien put it, "asshole control." He had been raised around the docks of Marseilles, and although he presented the outward image of a suave, sophisticated resort executive, he was not a man to be taken lightly.

Some months ago, Barrault had been summoned to the hotel beach to deal with just such a problem: a dentist from Chicago who insisted on pawing the daughter of the French consul-general as she lay sunbathing with a girlfriend visiting from Paris. The man whined that he was trying to "rub some suntan oil on her" as a favor, and while Lucien had been arguing with him, Colter had looked up from his conversation with a certain Danish stewardess to see another man trying to sneak up on Barrault's blind side.

It may have to do with the heat. Or the aroma of

the tropical vegetation, or even the water. But sometimes a man who behaves perfectly rationally in a
metropolitan city like Chicago comes to the islands and
loses his judgment. He loses the ability to think clearly.
Sometimes, as in this case, it happened to two men at
once. The second man turned out to be a friend of the
dentist's who had come out to Tahiti on the same package tour.

Colter had reacted instantly, and just in time. Barrault had become aware of the situation just as Colter
took the dentist's friend out of play. Lucien wrapped up
the dentist in an extremely painful come-along hold,
then turned to find Colter sitting on the other man's
chest, quietly pouring handfuls of soft, white sand into
the man's open mouth.

When the two tourists sobered up, Barrault had
explained the facts of life to them, and they had apol-
ogized like men and been sent on their way. The incident was closed, except that it had served to introduce
Colter to Barrault. It wasn't so much that they got to
know and like each other, but more that they recognized each other. They were both men of action and of
experience, the experience that is hard to come by
without being tough, quick, and smart. The two men
developed a cautious friendship, an uneasy alliance.
They were almost too much alike.

A particularly striking stewardess from UTA French
Airlines came into the open deck area of the pool and,
disrobing down to a monokini consisting of a black
string and a triangle of black satin, revealed a truly
remarkable pair of young breasts. She proceeded to
apply a thin layer of coconut oil all over her smooth
skin.

Barrault looked at Colter. "Yes, but can she type?"

"Careful what you say about my fiancee," Colter
answered.

"Daughter, more likely."

"I'm younger than you are."

"You don't look it."

Just then, the young stewardess was joined by her companion, a very muscular man of about thirty, unreasonably handsome, with the build and carriage of a professional boxer. She asked him in French to please help her apply her suntan lotion. Lucien sighed in disgust.

"I'm getting too old for this job."

"Yes, you are. You ought to get a wheelchair and a shawl."

"Stop trying to cheer me up. Did I tell you I've been offered a hotel of my own?"

"No! That's wonderful, Lucien! Where?"

Barrault made a face. "The Ambassador. In Djakarta. Indonesia, for God's sake."

"As managing director?"

Barrault nodded, trying not to let his pride and pleasure at the offer be too visible. "It's too good an offer to pass up, but I'd been hoping that the space at the top would come available right here. Fah."

"The islands won't be the same without you, Lucien." "Don't be in such a hurry. I haven't accepted yet."

"Ah."

"The question is, would I be the same without the islands?"

"Ah."

"Anyway, shut up. What are you doing here? Why do you rent that big suite, with two other *men*?"

"Some business to take care of. They're paying, so what do I care how much you overcharge them?"

"What business, Mitch?"

The banter had abruptly stopped. Now Lucien was working, protecting himself and the hotel from anything dangerous happening on its property. His tone of voice had that soft, expectant quality which said, "Tell me the truth, the first time."

Colter paused to construct his response. He wasn't going to lie to Barrault, but he wasn't going to tell him the whole story, either. "We're using the suite as a base for purposes of communications. We'll be running up phone bills and doing some cable-sending back and forth to America. That's all."

"You're not interested in someone who's here? Or arriving here shortly?"

"No" Colter shook his head "There will be no operations of any kind while we're here, you have my word. Just phone calls and cables, and maybe a package or two to be delivered. Chrissakes, you know what communications are like on Bora."

Barrault nodde, "One of its charms." Then: "You are not in danger? Someone is not going to come looking for you in the night?"

That was a tougher one. Was Colter's name on the hit list?

"I doubt it," Colter replied after a pause.

Barrault searched Colter's eyes, which did not waver. He gave a short nod. "*Eh bien*. Welcome to Maeva Beach." Lucien shook a finger at Colter, warning, "But if you make a mess in my hotel, I'm going to be angry at you."

"Fair enough."

Lucien Barrault nodded again, rose, and with one final look around at the inhabitants of the sun-drenched poolside, strode off in the direction of the boat ramps. Colter sat for a moment longer, finishing his beer and watching the UTA stewardess and her friend splashing water on each other in the shallow end of the pool. Then he rose to his feet, and headed for the hotel door.

It was time to go to work.

* * *

Krasnevin scanned the summary-sheets which were always delivered to his desk along with the morning report. The news was good, very good. Not only were the Voices well pleased with the Doctor's successes, CIA operations were grinding virtually to a standstill as they frantically tried to recruit new operatives to replace the broken links in their chains of information. In response to this, Krasnevin had been able to successfully launch new KGB operations all over the world. As long as no one could connect him directly to the Doctor, he was safe. In the meantime, he was merely doing his duty to take advantage of the CIA's momentary weakness.

Krasnevin had made sure that no one could directly connect him with the Doctor. When the Doctor had successfully completed an assignment, he had merely to ring a telephone number in Moscow to learn how the money had been paid, and into which of his numbered accounts. At the same time, he would receive the necessary information regarding his next target. He was being connected, on these occasions, with the ultrasecret KGB computer lines of Moscow Center. Krasnevin had written the program himself, and classified it "KGB Director Only-Ident 99." Mechanically, it was foolproof; only he and the Doctor had any idea of the access codes to the program, and it was further secured with the help of voiceprints, codephrases, scrambled burst transmissions and auto-erase. Krasnevin was not worried. For any agency to find out what was really taking place, either the Doctor or Krasnevin himself would have to tell them. Krasnevin knew that *he* wouldn't talk to anyone, ever. That would be suicide. The same held true for the Doctor. He, too, knew the dangers of exposure; his life would end mere hours after he was discovered. But the man was a thorough professional, and took every precaution against such a catastrophe. Both of them were, Krasnevin assured himself. No one would be discovered. He had every intention of living for a long, long time. And in very great luxury indeed.

As head of the entire KGB, Krasnevin controlled access to enormous sums of money which would never, *could* never be accounted for. In fact, huge sums of money in the KGB organization fell into a category which made the act of inquiring what they were used for a virtual act of treason.

These amounts of money were gradually insuring the Doctor's future. The assassin was very much aware that he would have to retire as soon as this series of assignments was complete and paid for. The job he had been doing was too big. He could never work again if he wanted to remain obscure and alive. The search for him would never end, he knew, so he had already begun to make his preparations for a completely new identity.

He had been born Yuri Turpenov, the only son of a minor bureaucrat in the Ministry of Foreign Affairs. He had been educated in Moscow, and had progressed through his entire course of mandatory schooling without any particularly impressive demonstration of aptitude for any area for further study except languages. The boy had an almost eerie knack for picking up foreign languages; in this he had been secretly tutored by his father, who had learned fluent German, English, and French in the course of his career. When the time came for Yuri's military service, this language aptitude was noted and Yuri was taught Vietnamese, which he picked up with astonishing speed. He was politically indoctrinated, combat trained, and sent to Hanoi as part of a team whose assignments would include guerilla organization and support, disinformation, and sabotage. While in the field on their second mission, the team lost its medical expert, whose second specialty was interrogation. The luckless man had triggered a claymore mine which had been manufactured in Connecticut.

Yuri had assumed the job of medic for the team, and it was in this area that his natural talents began to come to light. He had a genuine ability in the field of medicine, undiscovered to that point, which he developed at every opportunity. During the time that his team was on "stand-down" in Hanoi, he raced through medical texts, talked with the combat surgeons, and all but haunted several local clinics. He managed to learn a great deal, and in an amazingly short period of time.

His comrades encouraged him, naturally, and gave him the nickname which would stick with him, although taking on a more sinister flavor in the future: the Doctor. They could see only that a young man was becoming a healer. They had no way of knowing that, like Krasnevin, there was something missing in Yuri.

There was a secret heartlessness in Yuri, a void where compassion and human warmth normally resided. From his first encounter with armed combat, Yuri had been fascinated with sudden death. Not horrified, not sickened - fascinated. He was not moved by the sight of a wounded comrade, he was curious. Rather than tragic, death in battle became rather exciting to him.

Over the course of many of the team's long-range penetration missions, Yuri became familiar with and expert in the use of virtually all of the various arms available to the unit, and used them with deadly accuracy. He performed with disinterested heroism in a firefight, calmly taking up whatever weapon was at hand. The American Special Forces put a price on his head, and his Soviet masters began to take notice of him. Krasnevin was one of these.

Then came the Tet offensive. Yuri and his team were operating in the Mekong Delta, far into the south, when they were betrayed by an NVA captain named Van Minh. The team was carefully ambushed, and every member of it died in a few nightmarish, interminable seconds of automatic-weapons fire.

All except Yuri.

Although badly wounded, he managed to drag himself into the spiderweb of escape tunnels which provided him temporary cover. The ARVN troops which had carried out the ambush were delighted with their work, but Van Minh screamed at them that one had gotten away. They didn't listen to him, so he himself began a search of the tunnels. Yuri heard him coming, and quickly emptied a combat hypodermic needle full of morphine which had remained intact in a pouch on his web belt. As Van Minh cautiously peered around one curve in the tunnel, Yuri reached quietly out and injected a 10cc air bubble into the traitor's jugular vein. Instants later, Van Minh was dead.

Yuri found himself wounded, alone, and cut off from any hope of rescue. Methodically, he applied his medical skills to his own body, and set about surviving; water, shelter, food.

Van Minh's disappearance was unmourned and soon forgotten; no one was much interested in what had become of the NVA traitor in the aftermath of the midnight firefight. Since the ARVN commander reported a complete success, Yuri's name was automatically added to the CIA's "Confirmed Dead" rolls, and the CIA and MAC-V turned their attentions to their other, more pressing problems.

Meanwhile, Yuri had found shelter and support with an isolated unit of irregular Viet Cong. His wounds healed, and he became fit again. He heard the reports of the success of Tet, and surmised that his own death must be a given as far as the American military was concerned. So he decided not to return to the North. He reasoned that he was of more use right where he was, so he stayed.

In the end, he stayed in the Delta three more years, running operations of sabotage, intelligence-gathering, and assassination, the latter being his specialty. When the Americans finally abandoned the country altogether, Yuri presented himself to the Russian Advisory Headquarters for routine repatriation. He had been long forgotten, presumed dead, and his appearance in the melee of Ho Chi Minh City caused more surprise than celebration. He was routinely sent back to a processing battalion in the USSR, where he was duly informed that his parents had died of cancer two years before. He was utterly alone.

In the shuffle of paper, no one took much notice of Yuri Turpenov until his name appeared on a list which had to cross Krasnevin's desk. At first, Krasnevin had been suspicious. How had this man survived? What had he been doing all this time? Had he collaborated with the Americans? Krasnevin made a few discreet inquiries, and refreshed his own memory with the glowing reports he had taken note of years before. This man did not have the earmark of a collaborator. What, then?

Krasnevin sought Yuri out at the processing station and engaged him in conversation. Yuri gave Krasnevin a truthful, straightforward account of his activities, neither omitting nor embellishing any of the facts. Krasnevin was very impressed.

Ordinarily, Krasnevin would have brought the man

to the KGB for closer attention and further training, had he needed any. He didn't, of course. The man was already a trained *and experienced* world-class saboteur and assassin. Some feral instinct in Krasnevin compelled him to keep Yuri to himself, a "special" of his own. Off the books. Unrecorded in the KGB computers. For Krasnevin's use only, should the need arise.

Krasnevin set about the process of making Yuri loyal to himself and himself alone. Even then, in those early days, Krasnevin knew that he would be rising high in the organizational structure of the KGB, and he understood the need to "distance" himself from Yuri, as far as could be seen. Later on it would be all but impossible to trace any positive linkages between the two men; but at the moment, Krasnevin acted swiftly.

Within days, Yuri found that he had been promoted to the rank of army major, jumping several grades upward from his old rank. He received all his back pay, a process which normally took months, plus combat bonuses. To Yuri, it seemed like all the money in the world.

Along with his honorable discharge papers, he received a letter of acceptance from the Medical School of Moscow University, an honor for which he had not even applied.

Yuri was no fool. He knew that someone in a position of importance was taking an active, benevolent interest in him. It could only be the quiet, cold-blooded KGB officer he had talked to at Repatriation, the one called Krasnevin. He sought to get in touch with the man, to express his gratitude, but his letters and calls went unanswered.

It was at that point that Krasnevin appeared suddenly on the campus of Moscow University. He merely fell into stride alongside Yuri as the younger man was leaving the classrooms for the day. They walked and talked for a long time, through the cold, blustery streets of an October Moscow. At the end of the evening, Yuri finally understood the arrangement. Yuri would never attempt to contact Krasnevin again. There would be a job for him to do from time to time, but these would always be paid very well, in untraceable KGB money. Meantime, Yuri would complete his studies and live the life of a normal, if privileged, Soviet citizen. He would keep his special relationship with Krasnevin absolutely secret, in return for which he would be assured of the benevolence of the State. And in the Soviet Union, where everyone was afraid of the merciless, all knowing KGB and the knock on the door in the middle of the night, this promise was the equivalent of a magical suit of armor; Yuri, now officially if secretly designated "the Doctor," was well pleased by the arrangement.

Over the years, there had been many "jobs" for him to do, and they had all gone perfectly. He had traveled to foreign countries, learned new languages, and secretly become skilled with new weapons. He had stayed fit, and he had stayed remote, never feeling the normal longings for the basic security of wife and family, and this helped him to keep his secret. Which he had kept, absolutely and totally. His life was very good, by Soviet standards; he had even managed to acquire a small dacha in the country, an amazing achievement for a private citizen.

When Krasnevin had come to him with this last, enormous assignment, Yuri had known instantly that it would be the end, the final task he would undertake for his old mentor. He could see the cold lights of madness burning in the man's eyes as he talked, revealing the scope of his insanity and hatred of the West. Yuri felt sure that Krasnevin would not be able to last much longer as head of the KGB, but he had accepted the assignments, which amounted to a virtual crusade, willingly and for two reasons. One, he had no choice; if he refused, he would not live out the day. Two, he desired to leave the Soviet Union forever, and this series of assignments would make that dream not only possible but inevitable.

Yuri had grown tired, over the years, of the continual yammer about the glorious revolution, the glorious advent of world socialism, all the while watching the economy of the country bringing its people closer to chaos and darkness. He was also tired of the obvious lies and propaganda about the evils of the Western decadent imperialist et cetera. He had traveled extensively in the West, and each time he returned Russia had seemed colder and more dreary than the time before. With the money he had saved over the years, which had ripened considerably in its numbered accounts in Switzerland and Nassau, Yuri could live out the rest of his life in leisure and comfort.

Besides, this set of assignments was too big; he would be forced to disappear from the face of the earth, even if he had not wanted to, in order to survive. If everything went smoothly during the course of these assignments, as Yuri was certain that it would, Krasnevin could not possibly leave him alive at the end. He would have become far too dangerous to Krasnevin, and Krasnevin was, after all, the head of the KGB. Despite any promises to the contrary, Yuri knew that Krasnevin would have him eliminated the instant he felt that Yuri had outlived his usefulness.

But first, Krasnevin would have to find him.

CHAPTER NINE

"Krasnevin?" Mitch Colter inquired. "Who the hell is Krasnevin?"

Bishop looked at him, surprised. "Oh. I thought you knew. Well, when the old Premier died . . ."

Colter shook him off. "I read the papers. I mean where's his file? We've got all these miles of computer printouts and nothing on Sitting Bull himself? And what happened to Leonov? Wasn't he the one the Kremlin-watchers had all picked out to be the new boss?"

"That's right, but Leonov disappeared in the reshuffle, and this man Krasnevin wound up with the top job."

"Really. What's Leonov doing these days?"

Bishop raised his eyebrows at Yeats, looking for help.

"I don't think anybody knows," said Yeats, "but there was some talk about him having a stroke, I think. Is it important?"

Colter got to his feet, walked over to the floor-to--ceiling sliding-glass door which led out onto the suite's spacious patio, and opened it wide. He swept the distant horizon with his eyes, as if watching for the approach of a storm.

The three men had been hard at work, going over

each of the killings again, minutely, looking for something, anything, which would lead them closer. It had been a fruitless effort so far. The beautiful suite was beginning to look like a large, untidy office. There were remains of room-service sandwiches on platters, a few empty beer bottles, and several empty thermos bottles, now devoid of the rich island coffee, scattered around. A half-dozen long, Telex-type cablegrams lay open on the coffee table.

Colter returned his eyes to the room, focusing on Yeats. "I don't know if it's important until I know the answer. We need to find out, all right? What caused the stroke, is he dead yet, when exactly did it happen, you know the kind of thing."

Yeats was writing quickly on a message form, phrasing Colter's request for information in Agency language (REQUEST FURTHER UPDATE AND CLARIFICATION, ALL ANCILLARY DATA, NATURE AND TIMING LEONOV ILLNESS, etc.) and Bishop was watching Colter's eyes. For the first time, Colter seemed to be following a specific trail.

"While you're at it," Colter continued to Yeats, "have them send everything they've got on this Krasnevin. Personal history, military records, everything. Dental charts. The works. As much as the courier can carry, even if we have to go to microfilm. Right?" Yeats nodded and kept on writing. Colter turned to Bishop. "While we're waiting for that, you can tell me about him, as much as you know. Who is he?"

"Krasnevin, Pyotr. I don't know much at all, except that he's a career KGB officer, went through all their schools, including America-town and that secret laser-shop they think we don't know about up near Murmansk. He was head of Department Five for a while; that's where I first started coming across his name. Not married, no family. I think he was an orphan, or something. Been decorated a few times. A lot, really. He's only fifty-six, according to the newspapers. That's young to be head of the KGB, so he probably knows where a few important bodies are buried."

"Oh, yeah . . ." Colter drawled.

Yeats finished writing the cable and tore it off the pad. Standing up, he said, "I'll go downstairs and send this off. Anyone want anything?"

They shook their heads, and as Yeats closed the door behind him, Bishop asked Colter, "What is it, Mitch?"

Colter grimaced. "I don't know. Maybe nothing."

"Come on. What are you thinking?"

"Well," Colter began, "we may be going at it the wrong way round. We're all trying to find the killer. The assassin himself. We seem to be hoping that we're going to finally catch the asshole standing over one of our guys with a smoking gun and a silly expression on his face. Or maybe discover his next target in time to get there and stop him. But I don't think that's going to happen."

"We've got to try," Bishop defended.

"We'll never do it, not like this. This guy is too good. He hasn't left a trace, at any of the sites. There's not one single witness. Not one clue. No pattern, even. He uses different weapons and different methods of getting close to the target. He hits quickly and quietly and carefully, and by the time we're fully aware of what's happened, he's all set up to do it again, somewhere halfway around the world from the last place. And if he's smart, which he is, he also knows by now that virtually every intelligence man in the Western world is holding his collective breath, waiting for him to make one little mistake. So he's extra cautious. He'll be just about impossible to surprise."

"Very encouraging."

"Yeah. But the good news is, I think it's just the one guy."

"Why? Anything specific?"

Colter shrugged "The flavor, the style. There's a certain economy to all the hits. He's quick and he's quiet and doesn't use any more firepower than the job takes. He always sets it up so that he'll have some lead time before anybody actually discovers the hit."

"That doesn't prove he's working alone."

"No, just a feeling - and the other thing is, I doubt if he is alone, not really."

"What?"

"I think this guy, this killer, is a weapon. And I think he's being aimed by somebody else."

"What makes you think that?"

"The information. The so-called List. That's always been the tricky part about this whole mess. Somebody has direct access to, or a copy of, the List. Right? Well, it just doesn't seem to me that the killer himself is that person. I think that the killer is a professional, one of the best in the world, probably. But it doesn't follow that a guy like that thinks up his own assignments."

"Okay, I'm beginning to see . . ."

"I think we have to proceed on the assumption that he's being run by somebody else. And given that, I think that it's the somebody else we ought to be concentrating on."

"Helluva lot of guesswork in there, Mitch," Bishop contributed.

"Yeah, well. This isn't algebra." He snorted. "There's more, besides. I'd be willing to bet that the guy who's pushing the buttons, call him X, is only giving our killer one target at a time. He gives the shooter all the detail he needs, but I bet he only gives him one at a time."

"Why? Unless it's the old need-to-know," Bishop asked.

"Sure. It's classic. And that means," Colter connected, "that if we can find X and isolate him, disclose him, liquidate him, whatever, there's an excellent chance that the killings will stop immediately."

"What if X has given the killer the whole List?"

"Then we're shit out of luck. But this makes more sense. It's the way I'd do it. If not, then the chances are that a whole lot more agents are going to die pretty soon."

"Stop trying to cheer me up."

"Don't worry," Colter soothed "If we're right about X in the first place, it's fairly certain he's assigning the targets piecemeal. That way he stays in control."

Bishop was thoughtful for a long moment. Colter left and went to the bathroom, washed his face and hands, and came back into the room.

"It's amazing to me," Bishop began, "that we have no idea who the actual assassin is."

"I don't see why you find that so surprising," Colter said disinterestedly "You guys are so proud of your computers, with their microchips and their bubble memories. You start assuming that just because you don't have a certain piece of information, it doesn't exist."

"Yeah, but if this guy is really a top-grade Russian assassin, then he damn well *ought* to be in the machine."

"I agree," Colter said, "but don't blame it on the computer. Personally, I'm not surprised that this guy doesn't have any file. We've probably seen his work before, and not known it. I wonder how many top-level Russian hits we've got on the books marked *Assailant or Assailants unknown*? Just like any major police department . . ."

"You want me to find out?" Bishop asked.

"No, no. That's what I mean by the wrong approach. Even if we did find out who he is, I doubt if we'd be able to stop him. We wouldn't know where to look, and we wouldn't know what to look for. Anyway, suppose we got lucky and even took him out? What's to prevent X from finding himself another shooter? Then you're right back at the beginning."

"All right, all right. I see your point. Okay then, we'll go on the assumption that there is an X, and make him the focus of our effort. Right?"

"Right," Colter agreed "At least, that's my recommendation."

The telephone rang, and Bishop moved to answer it. Colter walked out onto the patio of the suite, rubbing his eyes and flexing the muscles of his neck and shoulders. He stood at the balcony railing, looking across the lagoon and the sea beyond the reef at the outline of Moorea, the beautiful volcanic island only ten miles away, now dramatically backlit by the setting sun. The island wore a crown of thick, soft clouds which refracted the sun's departing rays into a glorious aura of deep golden light.

The air was just pleasantly warm, and the underwater lighting had just been turned on in the hotel swimming pool.

It looked refreshing and inviting, and Colter decided to take a break. He went into his bedroom and stripped off his clothes, donning a black bathing suit which was cut in the racing style. Grabbing up a towel and one of the hotel-furnished robes of thick, absorbent white terry cloth, he reentered the main sitting room, where Bishop was still on the telephone, struggling with an overseas connection.

Bishop looked up, covering the mouthpiece. "Where you going?" he asked.

"To the opera," Colter replied, not even slowing

down to see Bishop's reaction to his own stupid question. Colter left the suite and summoned up an elevator. Pressing the button marked Piscine-Plage, he descended to the level of the Guests' Exit to the outdoor facilities.

The pool area was deserted in the fading light, and the water was perfectly still as Colter dropped his robe and towel on a nearby chair. He took the last three steps toward the pool at a run and hit the water in a flat racing dive. It was just as refreshing as it looked. Exhilarated, Colter did his first three laps at a sprint, and then settled into his working pace. As he dissipated the tension which had built up in his shoulders, neck, and back, he brought his mind into a relaxed, meditative state. He did not count the laps he swam. He swam back and forth, back and forth, using every muscle in his body and executing a neat kick-turn each time he came to the wall.

His body began to protest, but his pace did not vary. His shoulders began to ache, and his lungs started to burn.

Back and forth, back and forth. Just at the point when his body demanded that he rest, Colter kicked himself back up into a sprint, going all-out for speed for two more laps, and then stopped. He stayed in the water, though, gliding lazily and aimlessly, feeling the blood pound in his ears, his chest, his arms. He was heated from the workout, and the water felt cooler now. He looked around, his eyes smarting slightly from the chemicals in the pool, and saw that the swift island night had arrived while he had been swimming.

Many of the rooms in the hotel were lit up now as their temporary occupants dressed for dinner. Music was coming from the Cafe de Paris bar, and the island seemed strangely alone in the immense Pacific. Colter fought off a brief temptation to feel lonely and sorry for himself. He had given up his rights to feel sorry for himself long ago, on the day he had selected this way of life.

And, on balance, Colter loved his life. He was not alone, despite the occasional pang of homesickness. He had friends, he had money, he was healthy. He always seemed to be busy. Eventually, he supposed, he would grow old, and he had found the best spot in the world for that. Growing old was something he had never bargained for. It had never been promised him.

Colter's mind returned to the work in which it was engaged. Perhaps he would die before it was over, before they were able to isolate X. He was briefly very aware of the amazingly easy target he made just at the moment, paddling around in a brightly lit swimming pool in full view of over an hundred hotel rooms. Instinctively, he swam to the side of the pool and got out, drying himself in the darkness beneath a nearby palm tree. He was in no danger yet, he felt sure. But Bishop and Yeats were, after all, CIA agents, and who knew but that they might be next on the List. It was never too soon to begin taking precautions. Colter slipped into the soft robe and made his way back into the hotel.

In the suite, Colter found Bishop and Yeats going over a long Telex at the coffee table. He nodded to them as he went on through to his bedroom, where he peeled off the robe and swim suit. Naked, he walked to the bathroom and stepped into the shower, running hot water, then cold over his body.

He dried himself again and dressed in blue jeans and a favored old rugby shirt. Back in the main salon, he walked over to the Frigo-Bar and made himself a short Beefeater's Gin over ice, with a splash of tonic water. As he took the first sip, he turned to the others, to find them both watching him with peculiar expressions.

"What's the matter?" Colter asked, surprised by their obvious attention to him, "Was I supposed to fix you guys a drink?"

"I think maybe you hit it, Mitch," Bishop said.

Suppressing the tingle of excitement, Colter muttered, "What do you mean?"

"We've just decoded this damn great epistle from Langley. They're very excited there. They agree with everything you told me before you left. About the suggested approach to the problem, I mean."

"Good."

"That's not all," Bishop went on "It seems this Krasnevin guy you wanted to take a closer look at. . . might be worth taking a much closer look at."

"Oh?"

"Mitch? I think he might be X. . . and so does Langley."

* * *

Langley had not been asleep. Section Six, to which almost everyone applied the label "Kremlin-Watchers," was tasked with the hideously difficult job of evaluating the moves and strategies, powerplays, and political in-fighting which were a daily feature of Kremlin life. Comprehensive analysis was always difficult, but the experts in Section Six were fanatics, and their intelligence sources, especially in the last year, had proved remarkably good. Section Six had been interested in Krasnevin from a time even before his installation as head of the KGB, and when the old "heir apparent," Leonov, had gone missing just as the death of the old Premier had precipitated the newest power struggle,

Krasnevin became a subject of the most intense scrutiny Section Six could devise. Insofar as it was possible, Krasnevin's life from the day of his birth to the present had been laid open for examination and analysis.

Section Six found that Krasnevin was a dangerous man to be around. An unusually high number of his coworkers had fallen victim to accidents of one kind or another, and Krasnevin invariably seemed to be the better off for their demises. Gradually the assumption was made that Leonov would never be heard from again, and that Krasnevin was to blame.

This was not an enormous surprise; in fact, it was virtually "politics-as-usual" in some KGB circles. However, when the experts projected the psychological profile of the man through Einstein, the circumstances of Krasnevin's father's death set off an alarming series of corollary hypotheses, culminating in a blue flag being attached to Krasnevin's file folder. The blue flag was rarely seen.

So rare was it that when Paxton Fairbanks was presented with the file in order to okay it for transmission to Bishop and Colter he had to call Harold Miles into his office to find out what it meant.

"Psych Profile Alert, if I'm not mistaken," said Miles, glancing through his desk-reference booklet. "Yes. Here it is. Dangerous or unusual psychological characteristics; consult program two-one-oh-one."

"What the hell? All right, go get it."

The two men read Section Six's Blue Flag report together, with a sense of chilled excitement. The man Krasnevin was portrayed as having a high-probability factor for being dangerously unbalanced, due to some emotional miscue in his past, most likely his early youth.

> SUMMARY: SUBJECT CONFOR-
> MS TO PROFILE OF SCHIZO-
> PHRENIC/HOMICIDAL. PROBA-

BLY HIS TENDENCIES UN-
KNOWN TO THOSE AROUND
HIM. POSSIBLY UNASSAILABLE
NOW DUE TO NATURE OF
PRESENT POSITION. DANGER-
OUSLY UNBALANCED. MAY
HAVE DEVELOPED SEPARATE
PERSONALITIES. NOT DEEMED
THREAT TO NATIONAL SE-
CURITY. PROGNOSIS: POOR.

But Fairbanks didn't care about the long-term prognosis for the man's career in the Kremlin. He didn't care if he suffered some kind of breakdown next year. If Krasnevin was behind these killings, and it was still a big *if*, he had to be stopped *now*.

*   *   *

CIA field agent Lawrence Archer was operating his string of sources with very great care indeed. He was spooked by the rash of recent CIA losses. He wasn't supposed to know about them, of course, but the CIA's rumor mill was difficult to silence. Everyone he knew in the Agency was spooked.

He was operating under the cover of the assistant to the managing director of the Savoy Hotel, one of the greatest hotels of Europe, if not the world. It was a landmark on the banks of the Thames River, in the heart of London. It was an excellent cover, giving him plenty of room for movement while providing almost limitless concealment. Still, he was spooked.

Until Langley advised him that the unknown assassin was either in custody or dead, preferably the latter, Archer was going to remain constantly on his toes. He knew from his training courses that virtually anyone could be hit; this he accepted. If he, Larry Archer, was next on the killer's lethal list, he knew his chances were not good. But he'd be damned if he was going to make it easy for the bastard. He double-checked for a tail every time he went outside the Savoy premesis. He avoided crowds of people. He never took the lift from floor to floor. He had even stopped eating or drinking anything he hadn't prepared himself.

Which is a shame if I'm overreacting, he thought grimly as he studied the sloppy, bland omelette he had fixed for himself in the small kitchen of the apartment he had taken in the hotel. The food from the hotel's kitchen was famous. *But*, he consoled himself, *one can't be too careful*.

He had just under an hour to live.

Three floors below, the Doctor was opening the door of his own room to admit the room-service steward, a young man named Michael Chaverin. Chaverin wheeled in the service cart, nodding to the lean, somewhat sallow-complextioned man who held the door. He went about setting up the meal, removing the silver covers from the dishes and storing them under the table, as the Doctor made sure that his nose plugs were in place.

Suddenly Chaverin felt very tired. Turning toward the Doctor, he started to say, "If that will be all, sir . . ." and then he saw that the room's occupant had moved right up behind him and was fiddling with some kind of spray bottle.

The light in the room had gone all funny. Chaverin felt dizzy, and tried to speak, but all at once he was much too tired. The man was smiling at him, so it must be all right, but. . .

The Doctor helped the young man over to the bed, just in time to see his eyes unfocus and roll back in his head. Chaverin collapsed on the bed, unconscious.

Yuri examined him briefly, then went to the windows and opened them wide, helping the quickly dispersing nerve gas to become harmless even more quickly. Satisfied with his progress, he sat down to table and ate a hearty breakfast.

When he had finished, he turned his attention back to the room steward. Chaverin's uniform consisted of black tuxedo trousers, a red military-style mess jacket, white boiled shirt, and black tie. Yuri was wearing his own black tuxedo trousers, white shirt, and black tie, so he was concerned only about the jacket. If it didn't fit well enough, he could fix it very quickly, but it looked as though it would serve.

Archer still had several more minutes before he had to go down to the lobby to begin his chores, so he busied himself with the newspaper crossword puzzle. When the knock came at the door, he was trying to think of a six-letter word, for a river, a tributary to the Seine. He was halfway to the door when the need for caution came rushing back into his consciousness.

"Yes?" he asked through the door.

"Mr. Archer? Packet for you, sir."

Archer peered through the peephole, to see one of the room-service stewards standing in the hallway, holding a package in his hands.

"Packet? I wasn't expecting any packet. Who's it from?"

"Mr. Griffin, sir."

The general manager. Had to be okay. Still. . . Archer was unaccountably unsure.

"Listen, I. . . I don't know you, do I? Would you say your name, please?"

"Chaverin, sir. Michael Chaverin."

"Yes, well, look, Chaverin, I know this'll sound a bit odd, but. . . would you mind just slipping your employee identification Card under the door? Sorry to bother you. . .   Archer was getting embarrassed now; this was really going too far. There was silence from the other side of the door. *Probably thinks I've gone daft*, Archer thought. Silently, he actually *willed* the man to be who he said he was, just so they could get on with it.

"Er. . . Yes, sir. Just as you say."

The card came under the door, and Archer picked it up, saw that it was not a faked card, and with a sigh of relief, opened the door.

The birth date. This steward was ten years too old.

His hand is *inside* the package.

These were the only thoughts that Lawrence Archer had time to think before the silenced Beretta inside the parcel went off, twice. A great white light rose instantly behind Archer's eyes, blocking out his thoughts, his regrets, and his hopes for the future. Forever.

Ten minutes later, the Doctor had left the hotel.

* * *

It was four-thirty in the morning in Tahiti, and Colter, Bishop, and Yeats had gone to bed some time ago. Bishop and Yeats had taken the second bedroom with its twin beds, leaving the king-sized single for Colter. Both the CIA men were exhausted, no doubt suffering a delayed jet lag. So they didn't hear the soft click which had caused Colter's eyes to open and his senses to sharpen.

Colter didn't move. He listened instead, allowing for the possibility that it was nothing to be concerned about. He lay on his stomach on the bed, eyes open, silently making an inventory of his parts; legs ready, arms awake, back okay. He had a strong erection, as he often had at this hour, a product of both the pressure on his bladder and sleeping naked in the wide, soft bed. That was a nuisance, but he could deal with it later.

The click came again.

Colter was out of bed at once, adrenalin flowing. He knew that speed was on his side in a situation like this, not time. An intruder wants to go slowly, carefully. He is trying to be invisible and inaudible, and he is thinking of himself as the only person awake in his surroundings.

Colter was thinking fast. It could be a simple thief, but that was doubtful. Hotel thieves picked older, rich-looking couples, not a suite with three able-bodied men. The killer? Somebody had to be next on the list, and Bishop and Yeats were both CIA field agents. Two at once?

Whoever it was probably knew that Bishop and Yeats were CIA. That meant it was probably a local KGB stringer, a spy on retainer. Possibly even a KGB professional. That would be a lot to hope for; they could squeeze such an agent and get a direct lead back to Krasnevin, or to his cut-out. Maybe.

First things first. To make a rabbit stew, you had to catch a rabbit.

Colter was at the doorway. He waited, tensed. A shape moved toward him, paused, and turned away. Colter made his move, silently and swiftly. He extended his left arm around the intruder's waist, pinning the arms into the body. He clamped his right hand over the shadow shape's mouth, pulling back and lifting with his back. Within instants, he had carried the surprised intruder back into his bedroom and tossed him on the bed. Before the victim could react, Colter's hands were all over his body, searching for any weapon.

Her body.

A fine, firm, woman's body, Colter automatically categorized. But he did not make the mistake of pulling back in embarrassment. This was still an intruder. More than one man had been surprised to find that a woman could kill him just as dead as a man. Colter methodically searched sleeves, legs, chest (no brassiere, he noted approvingly), armpits, crotch, back, and hair. When he was satisfied that she was carrying no weapon, he turned her over on her back and threw on the light.

"Don't you want to talk first?" She was out of breath, her hair was mussed, and she was absolutely beautiful. Dark hair, huge dark eyes the color and shape of almonds, high cheekbones, and full, sensual lips which were arranged at the moment in a lopsided grin.

"Who are you?" Colter asked her.

"Samantha Sandri. CIA courier," she responded breathily. With an amused glance at Colter, she added, "And from what I've heard, judging by appearances you must be Mitchell Colter."

Colter had forgotten that he was naked. Simply forgotten. He still had a painfully large erection, and was suddenly quite aware of himself.

"I've heard of Polynesian hospitality, but this is not to be believed," she teased him, sensing his discomfort.

Muttering, Colter grabbed the first thing at hand to put on, which was the swimsuit he had worn earlier that evening, still slightly damp. He winced as he covered himself with the cool, clammy material. His penis made an enormous lump in the swim-suit material.

"I assume you can prove that you are who you say you are," Colter asked the girl. She had not moved.

"Steve Bishop knows me by sight."

"Don't move."

"I haven't," she argued.

"Well. . . don't," Colter responded lamely. He

turned to to the door of the bedroom and stepped out into the larger room, never breaking his line-of-sight contact with the beautiful nocturnal visitor. "Bishop!" he called out.

Instantly, Bishop appeared, puffy-eyed but alert and ready for action. "What?" came his whispered response.

"Come in here a minute," Colter said, as Yeats appeared over Bishop's shoulder. "Just you. Just for a second."

Bishop and Yeats exchanged puzzled looks, and as Bishop stepped forward to comply, he grumbled, "What the hell time is it, anyway, Mitch?"

"Four-thirty. We have a guest."

"A guest?"

"Yeah. C'mere," Colter said as he pulled Bishop's elbow, placing him in the doorway, facing the immobile female on the bed.

"Hi, Steve," intoned the girl wryly.

"Sam! What are you doing here?"

Colter relaxed. Bishop obviously recognized the girl, and Sam was the natural contraction for Samantha. So she was CIA, a courier, and probably guilty of nothing more serious than trying not to disturb sleepers at this ungodly hour.

"I'm not doing a damn thing," Samantha Sandri answered, "until the big guy tells me it's okay."

Colter laughed, the tension escaping. "It's okay."

"Thank you," she smiled, lighting up the world, "and as for what I'm doing here, if you'll look in my bag, which I set down beside the door as I came in, you'll find a Blue Flag file on a joker named Krasnevin marked Courier Delivery, Signature Required."

"What the hell, Mitch?" Bishop accused.

"She didn't knock. She came in quietly enough to be the kind of person I worry about."

"Well, she's okay."

"So I gather."

"No better than okay? You gave me everything but an insurance physical."

"Better than okay. But I wasn't taking the time to get into the esthetics of things, you know?" Colter countered.

"Practically gave me a Pap smear. . . Which reminds me, is it okay if I use the bathroom?"

The two men stumbled over themselves pointing out the locations of the facilities, and Samantha gracefully closed the door behind her.

"Jesus Christ, Mitch," Bishop said with a grin, "you'll be jumping the room service guys next."

"If they don't knock? You're damn right I will."

"Yeah. You're right. So would I."

"Yeah," Colter agreed, omitting to mention that he hadn't, and added, "No more sleep tonight. Get Yeats together and go start some coffee and maybe some breakfast. If they got her into the airport at this hour, that means a private jet and that means they've got something they think is hot. Did you know anything about a courier?"

"No."

"Okay."

Bishop went back into his room, and Colter went to the doorway and retrieved Ms. Sandri's bag, which was right where she said she had left it. He returned to his bedroom and placed the bag on the bed, for her to use to change, or to "freshen up," or whatever. She had mentioned a Blue Flag file which she had brought in it, but that could wait. He was feeling the adrenalin shock wearing off, so he sat down for a moment, giving his body time to balance itself.

Samantha stuck her head out from the bathroom. "Listen, would you do me a favor? My bag is . . ." And then she spotted it on the bed. "Oh! You already have.

Thanks," she said, gliding toward the bed. As she manipulated the combination-type luggage lock with smooth, deft precision, she gave an inquiring glance in the direction of the door, which Colter had automatically closed behind him.

"They're fixing coffee and things. Everybody's getting up."

"Sorry to make such a fuss," she offered.

"I just don't like surprises much, is all" Colter grinned in apology.

"For a minute there, I was afraid I'd interrupted you."

"What?"

"In the middle of," she smiled, "something urgent."

Colter remembered his state of arousal and, to his horror, found his ears getting warm. He didn't say anything, he just looked into her twinkling eyes.

Samantha looked at her rumpled sleeves and her wrinkled skirt. She began to unbutton her blouse, saying, "I just can't stand these clothes for one more minute, I've been wearing them since yesterday, and I can't bear it any longer." She slipped out of the blouse, revealing her breasts to Colter. They were lovely; her skin was satiny and of a uniform color, and her nipples were erect, of a hue perhaps two shades darker than pink. She was comfortable with them, and stood proudly, not round-shouldered with the attempt to somehow make them smaller. Colter found that he had not taken a breath for more than a minute.

As she took fresh clothing out of her bag, she stepped out of the skirt and let it drop to the floor. Her eyes looked straight into Colter's. She was wearing nothing but the briefest bikini-style panties, and Colter cursed the trained mind which automatically recorded *must have taken off her stockings in the bathroom* and he also cursed his lack of control over his own body, which was once more causing a huge bulge at the front of his swimsuit.

"If you're wondering why I'm doing this," Samantha was whispering to Colter, "part of me is, too." She stepped closer and closer to him, and now he could feel the heat of her body, coming off her in waves. "Partly it's that you're Colter, but it's also that I think one good look deserves another, don't you?" Colter nodded, as calmly as he could manage. "And when the lights went on back there, I took a good, *long* look. Believe me." And she stepped out of her bikini briefs, boldly standing in front of him, willing him to look at her.

Her body was spectacular. Colter didn't trust himself to speak, so he dutifully took the good, long look she had mentioned. Every curve, every fold was pure, ripe Woman. Colter's breath was now ragged in the back of his throat, and he drank deeply with his eyes as this playful, sparkling girl raised her arms above her head, and slowly turned all the way around, as he appreciated her forms and curves. Her buttocks were full, and taut. She was visibly trembling, yet make sure that she took her time, displaying herself fully. When she was facing Colter again, she slowly lowered her arms to her sides.

"And now," she breathed, "I'd like to take another look, if you don't mind."

Apparently Colter didn't mind, for he offered no resistance as she reached out with both hands and peeled away the slick fabric of Colter's swimsuit. She slid it down to his ankles, and tossed it away. As she raised her head to look at him again, his freed penis, fully erect, seemed to draw her hands and mouth to it by a power of its own. Colter closed his eyes at the exquisite pleasure of her touch. Her hands played over him, lightly as a butterfly's touch, and then he felt her hot breath. Then her tongue. He almost cried out when her lips encased him, but held back, merely reaching for her and pulling her up to him, and rolling back with her onto the bed.

"I'm not like this," she whispered urgently, "I don't do things like this." But then Colter's tongue and teeth went to work on her nipples, and her breathing quickened, losing control. "Fuck me," she whispered fiercely in his ear, "fuck me, fuck me, fuck me!"

As Colter entered her, she had her first orgasm. She had to bite the pillow to keep from screaming, and she clung to him hard as he rocked himself in and out of her. She spread her legs further apart and locked them behind Colter's back with crossed ankles. Colter suddenly felt himself coming, and he lifted her hips as it happened to him, and she had her second orgasm as he came in her.

They lay together quietly for a few moments then, as their breathing returned to normal. Samantha raised her head to look into Colter's face, studying him.

"Look, I. . . I'm sorry about that," she began, and then the words began to rush out in a torrent, "I just. . . it's just that seeing you like that, I mean, and I'd heard too much about you, and when you grabbed me and searched me, it's been a very long time since I, you know, had anyone to, you know, and all of a sudden I just couldn't breathe, God! And I mean on top of that it's Tahiti, I've probably been having fantasies my whole life, practically, and I just . . ."

Colter's grey-green eyes sparkled as he cut her off. "Wait. I can't say, I forgive you, there's no guilt here, no blame. We made love. Is there something the matter with that?"

"Oh, no, nothing," Samantha defended, "it's just that normally you know someone for a bit longer before you progress to this stage. . . at least I always . . ."

"Like you said. It's Tahiti. Things are different in

French Polynesia. I think it's something in the air that does it." He smiled at her.

"I'll have to start watching the way I breathe," she said, getting out of bed and slipping into clean panties "I just don't want you to think I do things like this all the time."

"God, no . . ."

"No, I *mean* it," she said, looking so serious that Colter had to fight back a laugh. He changed the subject.

"What did you mean, you'd heard too many things' about me?"

Samantha was zipping up her blue jeans. "Oh, you know, just stories. The famous Mitchell Colter," she said with a shy grin, reaching for her T-shirt. "Superspy, license to kill, only man ever to thumb his nose at the Agency and get away with it."

Colter chuckled, and began to climb into his jeans.

"Of course," she continued, "the talk right now is about your miraculous escape from Detention One. Fairbanks about had a hernia. Very upset. How *did* you get out, by the way?"

"Hypnotized the guard," Colter kidded her as he slipped into a clean white shirt.

From beyond the door, they heard Bishop yell, "Coffee's ready!" and they looked at each other. Playtime was abruptly over; it was time to go to work again. Samantha picked up the file and her courier log. She looked toward the door.

"I guess playtime is over."

"Yes. For now." He stayed locked in her gaze for a bit longer, not wanting to be the one to break it off.

"They'll make snide remarks about this," Samantha breezed, not completely unconcerned.

"About this horrible thing that's just happened, you mean?" Colter seemed darkly serious. "*On government*

144

time, I might add?"

She laughed then, and shook her head. "I'm still not an island girl, I guess, not yet."

"If you were, if you were to live here for just a little while, you'd come to understand that shame and guilt are just plain inappropriate reactions to lovemaking, Sam."

"Well. . . what are some appropriate ones?"

"Hunger. Sleep. Laughter."

She looked at him for a moment, deadpan. Then, suddenly, she giggled. "I'm so hungry I can't see straight."

"Very good. Two out of three. You can sleep later. Now come on. Let's see what you've brought us."

CHAPTER TEN

They sat around the large coffee table, amidst the wreckage of the breakfast Bishop and Yeats had put together. The level rays of the island dawn were filtering through the room as Samantha poured out the last of the coffee into Yeats' cup and rose to go get more. She had already made the obligatory joke about the woman getting the coffee, etc.

Apart from a couple of curious, amused glances, Bishop and Yeats had had no comment on the new and obvious relationship between Samantha and Colter.

They had bigger fish to fry.

Bishop looked up from his second reading of the Blue Flag file, and tossed the document on the table near Colter. Yeats belatedly noticed Sam's courier log on the table and picked it up.

"You need Steve to sign this, Sam, or should I?" Yeats called out in the direction of the kitchen.

"Either one, but all three is better," breezed the reply.

Yeats signed the log and passed it on. He turned to Bishop. "So what's the verdict?"

The discussion had been going back and forth for over an hour, with Colter remaining curiously quiet. Bishop had taken the point of view that yes, Krasnevin

146

might be a nut case, but it was going too far to extrapolate from this one document, not even legal evidence, that he was X. Bishop had never believed in the accuracy of "psychological profiles" that were fundamentally based on computer analyses, anyway. Yeats had simply been horrified to learn that such a man could be in actual charge of the KGB. Colter had kept pretty quiet.

Bishop sat back on the couch, closing his eyes. "I can't give any verdict. If any part of this is accurate, Krasnevin might be X. *Might* be. I don't know." He opened his eyes and gave Colter a penetrating stare. "What about you, Mitch? You haven't said much. What do *you* think?"

Colter returned the stare for a moment, then rose to his feet. Thinking, he drifted over to the windows, looking out at the pale yellow dawn.

"I think," he said at length, "that the CIA asked me to help point it in the right direction. I think that job is done. Krasnevin is either X, or he knows who is. I have thought so from the beginning. The head of the KGB is kept informed in a way that is difficult for us to understand. He hears everything. People fall all over themselves to tell him things. He is placed perfectly to be X. I'm inclined to put credence in this psych report, to this extent; the man is probably a walking psychological time bomb.

"But it raises another, more uncomfortable, possibility.

"The current Premier had long and deep ties with Andropov, the old man, when *he* was Premier, and before. I just can't believe that the old bastard doesn't know everything in this file. He'd know everything there is to know about Krasnevin. I could believe that no one *else* does, hell; Krasnevin himself could see to that. But the Premier must know what kind of a KGB chief he has working for him. So, two possibilities. No, three. Krasnevin knows who X is, and is encouraging the killings to go on. Two, Krasnevin *himself* is X, and the Premier knows it and approves. And three," Colter winced, "the guy we're calling X is the Premier himself."

"What?" cried Bishop.

"You're crazy!" This from Yeats.

"Come on, Mitch!" Bishop again.

"You asked me what I think," Colter snapped. "You figure it out any other way. Go ahead. Anyway, my job is over. No matter who X actually is, you can find out only one way. You'll have to ask Krasnevin."

There was a beat of silence, and then Bishop asked, in a tone of foreboding, "What do you mean, ask him?"

"You'll have to grab him and squeeze him hard enough to make him tell you the truth. Then you'll know who X is. If it isn't Krasnevin, it's the Premier. Glasnost or no glasnost."

"It's not possible." Yeats seemed stunned.

"It has to be. But personally," Colter took a deep breath, "I think Krasnevin is our man. What we've seen in Sam's file here is good enough for me."

Samantha had come back into the room and had been quietly attentive, frightened by the implications of what she was hearing. She wasn't entirely sure she had clearance to be hearing it, but she ventured, "Grab the head of the KGB? And squeeze him?"

"Have to. It's the only way."

"How, Mitch?" asked Bishop. "You know the way he's guarded. . . a full company of hand-picked men, twenty-four hours a day. It's not exactly easy."

"How would you even begin? Where would you make the try; Number Two, Dzerzhinsky Square? The Kremlin? Grabbing the head of the KGB has never been done. It's never been even contemplated, as far as I know. It's impossible!"

Colter looked at the two men with a chill in his eyes. "Yeah, you're right." The sarcasm was not veiled. "We better forget the whole thing. They'll probably get tired of killing American agents soon, anyhow. It's too easy, you know? No real challenge . . ."

"Hey, wait a minute . . ." Bishop began.

"It's a wonder you guys ever get anything done at all, you know that?" He stood up, stalking like a big cat. "Impossible because it's never been done. It's a wonder you guys discovered edged tools. And speaking of tools, why don't we put it to Einstein and see what comes out?"

Bishop and Yeats looked at each other. Samantha had almost none of their career-oriented reluctance, so she asked, "You mean ask the computer how it would go about abducting Krasnevin?"

"Yeah, why not? What's it good for, if it can't answer a simple question?"

"Mitch, it doesn't work that way . . ." Bishop began, but Colter had had enough.

"I sure am hearing a lot about why things are impossible and why things can't be done. Tell you what. I quit. Keep the money. Go home. Have the Agency spend a few million bucks on a feasibility study on it." Colter left the room, slamming the bedroom door behind him.

The three CIA employees sat in the ringing silence for a moment. Then Bishop said to Yeats, "Get Langley on the phone."

"Right," said Yeats. "Who do you want to talk to?"

"Miles."

"What are you going to tell him?"

"I think I'm going to quote Mitch as closely as I can. Because I've got a sinking feeling that he's exactly right, all the way down the line."

Samantha and Yeats exchanged glances. As she

stood up and moved toward Colter's bedroom door. "I'll just see if he's serious about quitting on us."

"Good idea," said Bishop. "In a way he's right, his job is partially done; but I'd sure hate to see him head back to Bora Bora right now."

"Me, too. I'll tell him you're sorry."

"Tell him I'm asking Langley for the moon, and he could at least wait to see if we get it. Tell him anything."

Samantha went to Colter's door and knocked. There was no answer, but she thought she could hear the sound of the shower running, so she opened the door.

"What is it?" Colter called from the shower.

"It's me. Sam," she replied in the direction of the steamy, oversized shower stall. She quickly stripped off her T-shirt and jeans, and crawled out of her panties on the way to the bathroom. "It occurred to me that you might like your back scrubbed, and I could use a shower anyway," she prattled, "I mean, after such a long trip and all."

"Did Bishop tell you to come soothe my ruffled feathers?" Colter asked as the naked girl stepped into the shower with him and snapped the clear-glass door behind her.

"Yeah. Had to twist my arm real bad."

"What's he doing?"

"Contacting Langley. He said to tell you he's asking for the moon."

"Good."

"He thought you were packing."

"I'm taking a shower, first."

"I can see that."

"What are you doing?" Colter's tone of voice changed.

"You don't like that?"

"Yes. I do like that."
"You do wash him, don't you?"
"Yes, I do."
"Like this?"
"Yes. Just like that."
"Can I do this?"
"Yes. Please."
"Just tell me when I should stop."
"You'll know."

* * *

At noon, Colter and Samantha had left Bishop and Yeats in the suite and had gone downstairs to Le Gauguin restaurant for lunch. She dressed in a *pareu* Colter had helped her pick out at a boutique in the hotel that morning, made of the thin native cotton tie-dyed in blues and greens. With her short dark hair and flashing, somehow naughty eyes, she was a vision which drew the appreciative gaze of all who were near. In the tradition of the islands, she wore nothing underneath the wraparound dress, and her secret excitement at this boldness caused her nipples to remain erect through the entire meal, which Colter had ordered with lavish abandon. The CIA was buying.

And Sam was prying. Not that she meant to make him divulge secrets, or to seduce him into betraying confidences. It was just that he was the most exciting man she could ever remember being with, and she was ravenous to know more about him.

They had begun by talking easily, comfortably, Colter telling her stories about Bora Bora and some of the island's lore. She felt wonderful in his company, and was enchanted with his island from the tone his voice took on when he spoke of it. She told him some of her own background, more than she meant to, without even realizing it. She told him about her recruitment into the Agency, her family, her almost-marriage to a fighter pilot a year and some months ago, and found that he had told her next to nothing about himself. When she pointed that out to him, he grew thoughtful.

"I don't usually talk much about myself, Sam. You kind of get out of the habit."

"You mean you won't tell me?"

"No, I don't mean that. I just mean it's not as easy as I wish it was."

Colter gave her an account of his life that she could have picked up from reading his 201 file at Langley, with a few jokes thrown in to make it more interesting. He told her about the schools, the troubles with his father, and the death of his mother and sister. He told her about his military service, as much as he could, and he mentioned some of the training he had received from the Agency, but nothing that would compromise anything or anyone. Then he sort of smiled at her, as if to apologize.

"I know that sounds like I'm reading it. I really had to do a lot of hard work to get rid of some of my past, Sam.

It's that simple, maybe, or that complicated. I used to be very different from the way I am today. But in another way, my nature is what it is. I'm an anachronism, in a way. In another time they'd have given me a horse and a sword and sent me on errands. But I'd still have had to agree that the errand had merit."

Colter turned the conversation back to her, and her lifestyle in the States. "It's not a bad job," she said between sips of mineral water, "especially at moments like this." They smiled at each other.

She loved to travel, she said, and although she didn't really need the money, it was nice to feel that she was having an effect on the world, in her way. She had been educated in the States but born in Berlin, and so she held two passports. She spoke English and German with equal fluency, as well as college-level Russian.

As they left the restaurant, they ran into Rene Iatape, who was fresh from a flight to the outer islands and in the company of a stunning Chinese-Tahitian stewardess from Air France named Bari Lee. After the introductions were made, the four of them decided to meet out at the swimming pool in a few minutes for, as Rene put it, "a splash and a giggle."

Colter and Samantha went upstairs and changed, finding Bishop and Yeats dozing in their chairs over the remains of a room-service lunch. The hotel maids were remaking the beds, and Colter and Samantha slipped into their suits in the bathroom. As Samantha reached behind her back to fasten the hook of her bikini top, she caught Colter's eyes on her, twinkling strangely. She raised her eyebrows at him, and he just shook his head.

"This is Tahiti, Sam. Wear the top if you feel more comfortable. It's up to you."

Sam thought about it for a moment, then nodded in return. She secured the top and put on a smile. "This place may take a little getting used to for a country girl." She picked up Colter's white shirt and threw it on as a coverall, tying the shirttails in front, above her navel. They grabbed fresh towels from the room-service cart on the way out, waving to the two sleepy agents.

They set up chairs near Rene and Bari, who had emerged only a few moments before from the hotel, and ordered drinks from the poolside bar. Bari removed her robe, revealing a lovely, strong body with high, smallish breasts and a stunning pair of legs.

Stephen Johnson

Samantha took off Colter's shirt, and had a moment to herself. Looking around the pool, she felt, she *knew*, that she was in a place that was different from anyplace she had ever been before. She reached back and un-hooked the bra-top of the bikini, and tossed it into the carryall. She smiled at the others, and began to look for the suntan lotion.

Bari noticed and said that if she wanted something for the sun, she had just the thing. She produced a jar of a local cream made with cocoa butter but without the PABA elements that can irritate delicate skin. She began to rub it over Samantha's back. When she fi-nished, she handed the jar to Samantha and turned her back, wordlessly asking Sam to return the favor, which she did. Then they took their turns with the cream, applying it to legs, face, breasts, arms and tummies. It was not a process that the men could watch, dressed as they were.

The four of them lay in the bright, hot sun, chatting easily and sipping the cool fruit drinks which were the specialty of the poolside bar. Samantha slipped into an easy doze, the result of travel, food, sun, and sex, under the appreciative eyes of her three companions. They spoke in hushed tones, protecting her nap.

"She's really lovely, Mitch," said Bari.

"I told you about him, didn't I?" Rene asked her. "I don't know how the ugly great ox keeps grabbing the pretty ones, but he does."

"Such a lovely body," Bari continued, "I think that if I were a *lesbienne*, I would want to make love with her."

"You'll wake her up with thoughts like that," Colter said, whose own thoughts were very much upon the subject.

They lazed about in the sun for another half hour, and just at the point when Colter was going to wake Sam and take her swimming with him, Bishop came out

154

onto the pool deck, wearing an expression of urgency on his face. He waved to Rene and gestured for Colter to come over to him.

"Just had Langley's response," he said when Colter joined him, "and I think you'll want to see it."

Colter went back to the group at the poolside and asked Rene and Bari to look after Sam and make sure she didn't get too much sun. Then he rejoined Bishop and they went up to the suite. When they got there, Yeats handed Colter a couple of sheets of notepaper.

"This is the gist of it. You got the fastest run that track's ever seen, I'd be willing to bet."

Colter looked it over. It was in Agency-ese, all full of "at discretion of Station Matform" and "contact if and only if" and "in no case will Agency personnel be discovered in violation of sovereign Soviet territory" and crap like that. Colter grunted at it.

"What does it say? Or do I have to sit down and go through it myself?"

"It says go ahead and snatch Krasnevin yourself," said Bishop. He couldn't suppress a grin.

Colter gawked at him. "Then I guess I have to sit down and go through it myself." He took it over to the desk and sat down, starting at the beginning.

Presently, he looked up. "Samantha speaks Russian. Did you know that?"

"No," Bishop said, "but it doesn't surprise me. A lot of the courier staff are multilingual."

"Can you get us papers fast? Married couple, business trip, something like that? *Fast*?"

"Yes." It was Yeats. He didn't elaborate, and Colter believed him.

Colter read on. The cable revealed that Einstein had indeed been put to work on it, and that among other arcane bits and pieces of information it fed into the problem was the all-but-forgotten annual trip that

Krasnevin made to visit the grave of his father, in a little town north of Donetsk not far from the Black Sea. Krasnevin's habit had always been to continue on to his private *dacha* for a day or two of rest. It was a personal tradition, a time of retreat.

At the gravesite, he would be invulnerable. The men assigned to him would be a virtual wall of armed guards. But once inside the grounds of his own house on the shores of the sea east of Odessa, patrolled by dogs and wired with the latest in security devices from the West, the personal guard would be relaxed to the lowest point it ever was.

Einstein suggested that as the time to make the attempt.

It was only ten days away.

Colter's first instinct was to reject the assignment as precipitous. You don't go jumping across that border half-cocked with a gun in your hand and expect to get back, no matter what they said they'd pay you. But the cable also enclosed the latest information on the killings, which was the fact that Lawrence Archer had been killed in a room in the Savoy Hotel in London. Colter had known Archer. He hadn't known him well, but he had known him. The killer was continuing with his assassination schedule, undaunted and unmolested. He had to be stopped.

"Call down to the pool, Steve. Have Rene wake Sam up and tell her I need her up here. Never mind his smart remarks, either."

* * *

"When were you field-trained?"

"Four years ago, at the Farm. But I've been in the

field ever since, if you mean can I take the pressure."

"This isn't pressure, it's a wild, irresponsible longshot."

"I don't want to die, if that's what you mean."

"How good is your Russian?"

"Not good enough to pass me as a native, but I can get around. Order a meal, get transportation, have a simple conversation, that kind of thing."

"I'm going to offer you a chance to go along with me on a little trip, Sam. Half of me wants you to say no. The other half thinks you might be a big help. Neither half knows if we come back alive."

"You're a lousy salesman, Mitch."

"You can say no right now. I advise you to. There are lots of ways to get into Russia without posing as a married couple."

"But I don't say no. I say yes."

"Don't say either one yet. Wait till I've laid it all out for you. What the computer has come up with, and what I think will actually happen, and what the think-tank guys at Langley say the stakes are."

"I'm listening."

"All right. To begin with, I think the Soviet Premier has gone crazy."

CHAPTER ELEVEN

Colter was not perfect. He was wrong about the Soviet Premier. The Premier was not crazy. The Premier didn't have any knowledge of Krasnevin's emotional past, in spite of the logic of Colter's deduction. Krasnevin had taken care to rewrite his own personnel file long ago, before the man who was now Premier even had access to it.

The Premier had suspicions, however, of the man who sat at the helm of the Committee for State Security. Krasnevin's appointment had been a political concession to Kropotkin, the foreign minister and one of the most powerful voices in the Politburo. Nevertheless, personally he was uneasy with the man. He kept loose tabs on his movements, and he had assigned a special case officer from the elite Kremlin Guard to inform him of anything out of the ordinary relating to his KGB chief.

The document in front of him now was a precis of the trip which Krasnevin made every year at this time to visit the grave of his father. It was not a request, simply an advisory memo that Krasnevin would be reachable at numbers other than his regular Moscow numbers for the period of his absence. Sentimentalism, of course. A surprise, in such a cold fish as Krasnevin. Maybe there was a woman in Odessa. The Premier was surprised to find that he would strongly *approve* of such a secret liaison. At least it would be human. If it were so, the Premier would find out in due course.

The only nuisance was that Krasnevin would be absent during this damnable period when the killer of CIA agents was still unknown and at large. The KGB would still be functioning at top form, of course, that didn't and couldn't depend on only one man, but still.

Ah, well. The Premier put the memo aside. The new accords with the Americans were shaping up into final form, and a place in the history of the Soviet people was waiting for him. KGB problems come and go, but the era of glasnost was the wave of the entire future of the civilized world.

* * *

Just north of the town of Donetsk, there is a memorial to the soldiers fallen in battle in the Great Patriotic War.

Through his influence, Krasnevin had been able to secure a place in this prestigious cemetery for his father's remains.

Krasnevin and his retinue of staffers and personal bodyguards made their annual descent on the small facility, causing the locals to cluster about and gape openly at the man who was the chief of the most feared organization in the Soviet Union. Krasnevin was not feared on these occasions, rather he was respected. He seemed to the locals to be merely a man who had made it his habit and custom to remember his father, no matter what lofty affairs of state might be pressing for his attention.

159

It was not a long ceremony. Krasnevin employed no cleric to give authority to his observance. He went to the grave and spent several moments there, alone, thinking his private thoughts.

All around him, his staff of elite KGB men were as tense as piano wire. Krasnevin was more exposed here than he ever was. Even if it was only once a year, it was a *predictable* thing, and that is anathema to the professional. Better he should roller-skate through Red Square, as long as no one was expecting him to do it. They kept a very good watch over him.

Krasnevin completed his homage, and returned to his limousine. Only when he was safely back inside the armored vehicle did his men begin to relax. And from that point on, they would indeed begin to relax. They were headed for the Russian Riviera.

Krasnevin could have managed to secure a country dwelling in as remote and pleasant a spot as Yalta, or somewhere less populous in the Crimea, but the dacha he had settled on had attractions beyond the normal requirements for a home away from home. It had been owned by Sergei Ziolkowski, an architect of some renown, and had been built out of the hills themselves, in a very sparsely populated section of Black Sea coastline about seventy miles east of Odessa.

Ziolkowski's dacha had come to Krasnevin's attention through an article published in a magazine devoted to the progressive nature of Soviet thinking in all areas, including architecture. The dacha was comfortable and charming, to be sure, but it was something else that made it most attractive to Krasnevin; it was isolated.

Really isolated.

Unless you had been specifically invited, or had called ahead to let someone know you were coming, you just weren't going to get in. Aircraft were prohibited from overflights by several different sets of retrictions on the airspace. The waters offshore were cobalt blue and inviting, but the dacha itself was set on a bluff some hundred and fifty feet above the beach. There was a funicular car that could deliver people and provisions to the beach and return them to the main house.

It was a fortress. It was a very well done, fashionable fortress, but it was a fortress.

As the motorcade made its way toward the main autoroute to Odessa, the thoughts of every man in the procession turned to the chance to take a deep breath and relax, if only for a day or two. Once Krasnevin was safely ensconced in the dacha, it would take an armored battalion to threaten his safety.

* * *

Colter included Samantha in his deliberations from the beginning of the planning stages of the operation. This was not standard procedure, merely something he had learned was a good idea. Often it was more than merely two heads being better than one. The standard practice of penetration assignments - being compartmentalized so that you know only what you need to know, and the same for your partner - was a two-edged sword. If you were taken prisoner, you could tell only what you knew. But if the partners in the op all knew everything, the chances reduced dramatically that anyone would be taken prisoner.

She was not a wide-eyed beginner, but she had never been on the kind of penetration op that Colter was showing her how to mount, and she was both fascinated and frightened by the skills he was revealing with such nonchalance. As they sat down to their first planning session, for example, he turned to her and asked her a simple question.

"Are you qualified as a scuba diver?"

"Yes, I'm rated by the Agency, but I've got my C-card from PADI as well."

"Good."

"Why?"

"I'm thinking about our extraction from the op, when we've got what we went for."

"Isn't that putting the cart before the horse a little?"

"No. I wouldn't even consider an op I'm not a hundred percent positive I can get out of when the balloon goes up. First, the extraction. And a back door in case the extraction gets blown. Then, when I'm comfortable with those arrangements, I'll start to take a look at the other problems. It makes a difference, Sam. If I'm coming out on horseback, the rest of the plan better include getting me a horse."

Samantha saw the logic, and began to feel better about the accelerated jumping-off time for the operation. She had taken Bishop aside at one point and quietly asked him if it wasn't risky to try to mount this kind of operation this quickly.

"Yes, ordinarily I'd say it was out of the question. And quite honestly, if it was being mounted at Langley, I'd have to try to find some way to get it scrubbed. But Mitch won't go unless he thinks it'll work. And if he thinks it's going to work, it's going to work."

There was also the additional factor in the equation of the "mole" who would assist them once they had landed in Odessa. They would come ashore as a master mariner and his wife being moved into the shipping hierarchy of the port city. They would have the right papers, and the right legend, and they would be met by a man named Ilya Litvak, code-name "Tex." Litvak was in deep cover and had been for years. But Colter had been through his file, and seen the kind of information he had delivered on the rare occasions when he had been activated. Litvak was good. He was also a martial-arts expert and an excellent shot.

The plan, as it developed, was that Litvak would help Colter and Samantha get through the official customs and immigrations tangle of Odessa, and drive them to a safe house. He would provide them with papers for inland travel and a car. He would accompany them to the dacha, and assist Colter in any way Colter required. Colter would make a certain amount of decisions on this once he had met and assessed the man.

Colter would penetrate the dacha and isolate Krasnevin, and get him to reveal what he knew about the assassinations.

He would make the determination on whether or not to leave Krasnevin alive on the spot, partially based on what it took to make him conversational.

Samantha would use the time to get down to exactly the right spot on the beach, with the equipment they would need for the extraction. Litvak would disappear, vanishing back into his cover as a shipyard manager in Odessa.

Afterward, Colter and Samantha would be picked up by submarine. It was a technique Colter liked and had used before.

That was the general shape of the plan. By the time Yeats had documents coming in for the actual passage, it was time to jump off. They were all cutting it very fine.

* * *

Odessa is not a beautiful city. Very few port cities

are, with some notable exceptions. Odessa has a population under a million, but is a principal port in a nation that has gone to war more than once for a warm-water port. Odessa is a center for industry, chemical production, shipping, and machinery production, as well as having a university of note and a famous opera house. Its population lives at the edge of the Black Sea. On the edge of the free world.

The vessel Ronsbovna II was a weathered but serviceable freighter with limited passenger accommodations which plied the waters between Istanbul and Odessa and had for sixteen years. Its master was a Greek named Katselas who knew enough not to ask too many questions when passengers came aboard "fortuitously." Passage *into* the Soviet Union was not an area he was likely to find himself in trouble over. He was extra careful about who he took out of the Soviet Union, because he valued his master's licence and his freedom.

So when the big Czech and his good-looking wife came aboard, he didn't ask questions. Normally there was a waiting list for passage in one of the four staterooms he was allowed to book. There had been a last-minute cancellation, and the normal rebooking process had been bypassed to allow the Czech couple to board. They looked all right to Katselas, and their money was as good as anybody else's, so what's the difference? There were many things in this part of the world that Katselas didn't know about, and he liked it that way.

When the Ronsbovna II docked in Odessa, there was the usual official greeting party waiting at the gangplank, with the usual forms to fill out. There was also another man waiting, with a clipboard in his hand and a plastic badge clipped to the lapel of his coat. It identified him as Ilya Litvak, and if you looked closely enough, you'd see that the badge was endorsed by the

Port Authority. No one looked that closely.

It is a fact of the working life in Odessa that a clipboard in one's hand makes you invisible. Not literally, as in a science-fiction movie, but practically and for all intents. A man with a clipboard is a man with something he's supposed to check on. You hope it's nothing to do with you. So you ignore him. Litvak was seen by everyone in and around the docks as the ship's gangplank was opened, but noticed only by Colter and Samantha.

They made their way over to him easily, and Samantha spoke Russian with him quite naturally, as Colter busied himself looking through his pockets for a nonexistent document. No one would be able to describe what he had looked like.

Even at that, he had changed his looks. His hair was cut shorter, as a seaman of years' service is used to cutting it. They either let it grow, or keep it cut, and Colter's cover was that of a master mariner. Samantha, too, had dressed down for her part, and the shapeless dresses she had been provided with did much to disguise the figure underneath.

There were formalities, but the paperwork was in order, thanks to extraordinary efforts by both Bishop and Yeats and the speed and efficiency of Langley's forgery apparatus. With Litvak to guide them through the process, they were soon in the aging car which drove slowly past the gates to the dock area and into the city itself.

"Welcome to the Ukraine," offered Litvak in English. It was the first time he had seemed to have a personality at all. His persona at the docks had been purely that of a functionary, gray and dull. Now, his eyes sparkled.

Colter noticed, and was pleased with the chameleon in the man. "Thanks. They call you 'Tex' at Langley, don't they?"

"Yes. It got started because I shoot a pistol with either hand. They call you 'Triphammer.' I guess we all know that. And the lady is Pearldiver?"

"Pleased to meet you," offered Samantha. She was fighting off a case of nerves, and the smiles and idle chat came at exactly the right moment.

Colter wanted to see something else. "Your file says you're a Ukrainian?" he asked.

"Yes." The reply was simple, but Colter could see the fire burning in Litvak's eyes. He was not a Russian, he was a Ukrainian. It was a powerful motivator, and it was exactly the right kind of passion it takes to stay in deep cover. Colter was feeling better about the whole operation.

They arrived at the safe house and went through the motions of bringing luggage in, examining the neighborhood, and remarking on the trip, all for the benefit of the neighbors and any onlookers with ties to the State. The house was purportedly clean of electronics, but Colter swept it anyway.

Litvak went to the phone and unscrewed the base plate. He found a note, and called a number. He spoke briefly in rapid-fire Ukrainian, and then hung up, looking sour.

"I hate to give you this even before you get a chance to sit down, but there's word that we may have to go tonight."

"Krasnevin's leaving?" This from Samantha.

"He may be. He's been on the phone constantly with Moscow, and now he's sent his driver for petrol and we've managed to find out that his private plane is coming in to Odessa in the morning."

"Better get a look at the equipment. How good is your contact with the sub?"

"Better than good."

They went over the equipment that was waiting there for them piece by piece, and finally sat down at the dining room table to discuss the next steps.

Colter took charge of the conversation easily, naturally leading them all through the clearest possible summaries of the way things had to happen, what could possibly happen to make them go wrong, and what could be done about it in that eventuality. Samantha was used to the methodical, deliberate pace Colter set as he laid out his thinking on an operation, but Litvak had never been around Colter before, and was beginning to be very enthusiastic about working with the legendary "Triphammer".

"In the end, it's too big to just guess at. If he's called his plane in for the morning, he may or may not be leaving, but we can't take the risk. We'll be going in tonight."

Samantha was struck by the reality of it. Up to now, it had been a plan. Her scalp crawled, and her spine shivered all the way up to the back of her neck. But she set her face, and just nodded.

"The car is ready," Litvak said, agreeing. "I suppose we'd better get it loaded, and then have a bite to eat. Unless you'd rather eat on the road. I know a good place between here and the dacha, out of the city itself."

"I think that's the better idea," Colter said. "It fits the legend better, anyway. If we were just moving in here, we wouldn't be provisioned yet, or we might be out celebrating."

So they loaded the car and attached the small trailer to the boat hitch at the rear bumper. It was a common thing to see on any car in this region, and no one took any special notice.

They stopped about twenty miles outside of the main part of town, and ate a light meal. Colter and Sam seemed just right together, and Litvak openly envied them. His wife had died several years before, before they had had any children. He talked freely of his sadness, with that special brand of intensity that can only be Russian. In anyone else, it would be taken for self-pity, but from Litvak, it was philosophy.

Night had fallen as they finished their meal, and they stepped out into the darkness outside the roadside cafe with the intense awareness that the operation was about to begin.

"Good night for it," whispered Litvak.

"Let's hope so," agreed Samantha.

Colter just nodded, and opened the door of the car.

*   *   *

Krasnevin put down the phone and went back to the sideboard to pour himself another measure of vodka. They refused to let him be. He used to think he would never need to be away from the center of action, of power, but now he liked the relative quiet of the seashore. He could just hear the waves, lapping at the shore below.

When the phone wasn't ringing.

They called him all day, they called him all night. It was one thing to be informed, but another to be pestered. Still, he knew that it was a hollow complaint. He had fought hard to be the one they called. He enjoyed his time here, but he enjoyed his power, too.

He would return to Moscow in the morning.

It was past eleven; he would just have this one last glass of vodka and then retire for the night. He had sent the servants off to bed almost an hour ago. He had been trying to read, but his concentration was faulty when it came to fiction. The reality of things was so much more exciting.

The reality of things was that the CIA was in disarray. The reality of things was, the Doctor was performing his secret tasks perfectly. It was the perfect covert operation. Known to no one, penetrable by no one. It could not be stopped, it could not even be altered. It was flawless.

And the Voices had stopped.

Krasnevin had reached that perfect place, that state of being that the Hindus referred to as Nirvana. He was in balance with his world as he perceived it. His very being, his very purpose for living on this planet at this time and in this place, was satisfied.

The Voices were quiet.

Krasnevin took another sip of the excellent vodka that was kept stocked at the dacha, and closed his eyes. He sent his thoughts flickering over his own merits.

*   *   *

Mitch Colter was eleven feet away from him.

When a fortress is built, its central idea is that an enemy penetration will come with some notice. For instance, an aerial bombardment. With Litvak's help, Colter had had no need for such a formal announcement.

Colter was outside the window, watching as the head of the KGB took another sip of vodka. Litvak was right beside him, back to the wall, eyes sweeping the landscape for any trace of movement, any surveillance at all.

There was none. Unbelievably, once they had managed to get over the fence and past the rather elementary field-motion detectors, there had been little security of any kind. It was as if the Russians expected the terrain and the circumstances to do their work for them. Which is exactly what had happened. Colter and Litvak had been waiting for more than two hours, perfectly silent, waiting, watching, ready to strike when Colter gave the signal.

Colter didn't seem to be human. He seemed to Litvak to be a perfect waiting machine. Never tired, never impatient, never trying to stretch or condense the time. He was just waiting.

But now Krasnevin had drained the last of the vodka in the glass, and he stood up and took it back over to the sideboard. He looked at the bottle for a long moment, deciding whether or not to have a headache in the morning, and then apparently remembered he was planning to return to Moscow. He put the glass away, and turned for the main stairs.

Colter was moving before Litvak was even aware of it. They had spent almost twenty minutes unlocking the side door when they had arrived, and Litvak had all but forgotten that the way was open and clear.

Colter ran in a half crouch, faster than Litvak would have thought possible for a man his size, and was on top of Krasnevin in an instant. He placed both of his hands on Krasnevin's back, and slammed him into the wall next to the staircase. Krasnevin grunted in pain.

"Silence." Colter was listening, watching for an additional bodyguard.

"Who - who are you?" Krasnevin rasped.

"You almost died right then. I said silence." He brought a small Russian-made pistol up into Krasnevin's line of sight. Litvak came up behind Colter, having secured the door. He was tense but operating coolly. He nodded to Colter.

"All right. No reason I shouldn't introduce myself.

You've heard my name, I think," Colter told his prisoner, fixing him with a curious gaze. Krasnevin had seen that look before; this American was a killer.

"My name is Colter," the American told him.

Krasnevin began to sweat.

* * *

Colter took Krasnevin out of the main room and into the small storage cellar common to the homes along the bluff - what was called a root cellar in the American Midwest - Colter had spotted it and unlocked it over two hours ago. The Russian's hands were wired together.

Litvak backed the move like a seasoned pro, never giving Colter a second's alarm. They were, in fact, both a little impressed with the fact that they were laying hands on the head of the KGB, but their training was in movement now. They might shake later, but they were steady now.

Krasnevin had begun to come unraveled almost at once. A man expecting to go peacefully to bed in his secure, guarded fortress is ill equipped to be led forcefully into a small, cold, enclosed space by enemies he never imagined could be within a hundred miles of him. He instinctively tried to plead with Colter.

"Listen to m . . ." he began, and Colter slapped him across the face with the back of his hand. Before Krasnevin could cry out in reaction, Colter's hand had closed around his Adam's apple, pinching the nerve, closing the airway, and putting pressure on the carotid artery all at the same time.

In the sudden, surprising wave of pain and fury, Krasnevin was dimly aware that Colter was leaning in close to him, to whisper in his ear. The American spoke so softly that he had to strain to catch the words.

"If you speak *one more time* without being told to, I'm going to rip out this piece of windpipe and toss it in the corner over there. Did you hear that?"

The Russian nodded, choking and near unconsciousness, and Colter eased the strength of his grip. He pulled the lids of the Russian's eyes open one at a time and examined the man's pupils. Satisfied, he let go of Krasnevin and resumed his listening watch.

Krasnevin had gone into a kind of shock. No one had ever struck him in the face before. It was such a common thing. It was no big deal to many people, and he had certainly slapped people himself, in the past. But no one had ever *dared* to do such a thing to *him*. He had been assaulted, raped. He was humiliated, and there wasn't a thing he could do about it.

And it had happened so *fast*! He had never seen it coming. Colter moved like lightning, and with deadly, calm assurance. Krasnevin did not doubt for one second that Colter would in fact cripple or kill him instantly if he did not follow the man's instructions. The Russian wallowed in an agony of self-pity and frustrated fear.

Then the KGB professional in him began to function again, reminding him that he was still alive. Therefore, this was not to be a simple assassination. If that were the plan, he would already be dead. So it seemed likely that they wanted something from him. Something he could use to make a deal with. *He wasn't dead yet.* A glint of flinty determination came back into his eyes.

Litvak came up to them from the darkness and nodded to Colter, signifying that all was well, no alarms had been sounded. Colter grunted, taking one more look around the gloomy darkness, and pointed to the corner of the cellar. Litvak nodded and began to pry loose the floorboards and set them aside.

When there was a space large enough to accommodate a man, Litvak took an entrenching tool from a pack by the door and began to dig out a shallow grave in the dirt under the floorboards. Litvak became warmed, and took off his shirt.

Krasnevin's eyes widened as he saw the muscled back of the sinister-looking Ukrainian work to dig out dirt that Krasnevin owned. They weren't even paying any attention to him! His new-found resolve faltered as he reconsidered the possibility that these men were carrying out an elaborate assassination after all. He knew that Colter was an assassin, the top man in the West. The night seemed to close in on him. He wanted desperately to talk to Colter, to agree to give him anything he wanted. But he couldn't open his mouth without remembering Colter's admonition to silence. The image of a wet, glistening section of his own trachea lying on the dirty ground swam before his eyes.

Litvak had fashioned a hole, of sorts, in the bare earth. Despite his effort to remain perfectly silent, Krasnevin involuntarily whimpered.

Colter glanced at him, reacting to the small, wet sound. His eyes narrowed, and he appeared to be considering options. He moved over close to where Krasnevin was, and sat down next to him. He stared into the frightened Russian's face for a long time, thinking. The rhythmic *ssshic*! sound of Litvak's spade in the earth seemed loud enough to wake the dead.

"Who's been killing CIA agents, Krasnevin?" Colter finally asked.

"We don't know!" came the automatic reply. Krasnevin lied fluently and well; he had practiced all his life.

"Wait. I should have told you. If you lie to me," Colter said reasonably, "I'm going to hurt you. Okay?

Now tell me the true answer; who's been doing the killing?"

"I swear to you, it's the truth! Good God, is that what this is all about? Our people are as baffled as yours! We have no idea!" the man cried, really warming up to the lie now.

So Colter broke his finger.

He reached out quite calmly grasped the little finger of Krasnevin's right hand, and bent it back until it snapped. Quickly and surely.

Krasnevin's mind couldn't accept that much pain, racing from his finger up his arm to his brain, where it exploded in a white-hot fireball. But as he opened his mouth to scream, Colter's viselike grip was once again at his throat, stifling the release. The pain took his breath away, and sweat broke out all over him, running freely down his sides, his back, his face. He shuddered with the need for air, and Colter released him. He collapsed against the side of the wall, the air whistling out and in past clenched teeth.

"On your feet," Colter commanded. He lifted the injured Russian with ease and propped him against the wall of the cellar. "It's a warm evening," Colter declared conversationally, "You won't need your clothing."

With that, Colter reached up and grabbed Krasnevin by the scruff of the neck, then turned and gestured to Litvak. Litvak came directly over to him.

Colter unbuttoned the shirt Krasnevin wore and removed the terrified man's tie. He ripped the shirt open as Litvak went to work on the sleeves, using a folding razor knife made in the Philippines. The shirt fell away, and it was when they began to remove the trousers that they encountered the first sign of real collapse.

"Please. . . please, no . . ." Krasnevin was ashen.

But they continued, just as if they had not heard the

blessed sound of the successful interrogation. The trousers fell away under the ministrations of Litvak's razor, and then they bent and removed the Russian's shoes and pulled off his socks. Colter straightened up in front of the nearly naked man, eyeing the Russian-made underwear. He nodded to Litvak.

The knife flashed in the faint light from the moon outside. In seconds, Krasnevin was completely naked with his hands tied behind his back, nursing a freshly broken finger and facing two armed professionals. Pain and terror were his whole world, and earlier confidence was merely a memory.

Strip the men, make the women disrobe in front of you, so the rule went. You stripped men to show them how powerless they were, and forced women to disrobe in front of you to advance their feelings of vulnerability and even complicity. Once a woman has revealed her body to you, by her own hand, she was halfway there. Never, never let a subject of interrogation retain any article of clothing during the questioning, no matter how brief. Even underpants would provide the subject with a troublesome sense of security.

"Please. . . please . . ." Krasnevin intoned dully, twisting his body and raising his right knee slightly in a pathetic and futile effort to hide himself.

He had been living a safe, protected life for too long. Apart from the injury to his finger, which was extremely painful but not life-threatening, Krasnevin had not been damaged. Fear was his main enemy, but this thought did not occur to him. He was simply overwhelmed. He had been out of the field for too long, and was hopelessly unequipped to deal with an interrogation of this caliber.

"You ordered the CIA killings, didn't you?" Colter asked.

Krasnevin nodded.

"I didn't hear your answer. You can speak."

"Yes. . . yes."

"Who's doing the actual killings?" Colter's tone was perfectly conversational now, almost offhand, as if the answer really wasn't that important. To reinforce this feeling, Colter nodded for Litvak to continue digging in the shallow, grave-sized pit.

"His name is Turpenov. Code name Doctor."

"Only the one man?"

"Yes. He is. . . my own man. A special. KGB has no file on him."

"Who is next on the list?"

"No, he. . . He's in London. He will execute Lawrence Archer there. . . Please, you do not need to kill me."

"Why?"

"Please?" The Russian blinked, not having understood.

"I asked why. Why did you suddenly decide to declare war on the CIA?"

"I. . . I . . ." Krasnevin searched Colter's cold eyes, seeking for a way to explain the forces which drove him, and the power of the need behind his crusade. "My father was murdered by Agents of the West . . ."

"No, your father got drunk and fell asleep in the snow. I read the autopsy."

Something happened inside Krasnevin's mind when Colter said that. It had to do with the fact that Krasnevin had always suspected, really known that his father was not a hero, but he had built up the power to change that reality. Now that power was gone. Krasnevin's mind came a little farther off the hinges.

"You. . . lie," he snarled, spittle dripping from the downward curve of his lip. He was breaking, in front of their eyes. He appeared feral, subhuman. "I will kill you."

Colter ignored the pathetic threat and glanced at the grave, his mind already on the next set of questions to ask, regarding contact procedures to be used with the Doctor. That was when he saw movement.

Unbelievably, the broken madman had gathered himself for an attack. He had gone into a semi-crouch, ignoring his own pain and nakedness, and taken the instinctive opportunity presented when Colter turned his head away to glance at the pit. He launched himself at the big American head first, with a wild scream of fury, intending to sink his teeth into the man's unsuspecting throat and rip the life out of him. It was unreasoning, it was suicidal, and it almost worked.

Krasnevin was totally in the grip of instinct now. He had been reduced by the brutality and humiliation of the interrogation, but something came loose in him when Colter painted such a casual picture of his heroic father passing out in the snow, *as he secretly knew it had happened*, and he just went berserk.

Any other man would have been crippled or even killed by the sudden, lighting-fast attack. Colter, however, reacted before he could even think about it. In fact, it was much like punching a printed circuit; the decision-making process was completely bypassed. Colter's chin went automatically to his chest as he stepped *forward* to meet Krasnevin's lunge.

The Russian's move was fully committed, and he had no choice but to take the full impact right in the teeth. Colter felt the wet, crunching jolt of impact as he took the force of it on the forward part of his skull, just above the hairline. The night darkened for a moment, and his ears rang, but he remained standing. He stepped back quickly, now in his automatic fighting stance, to see if it was over.

It was. The naked man on the ground was spitting out blood and pieces of his teeth, making wet little noises. His eyes were unfocused, and his jaw hung at an odd angle, leaking warm, coppery blood into a puddle in front of him. All the fight seemed to have left him.

But he had screamed.

Colter felt the painful spot on his scalp where he had smashed into the man's face, finding some swelling but only a drop or two of blood. Litvak came over to him and examined the head for injury.

"Nothing."

Colter nodded, getting ready to finish the assignment quickly and get out, when both Litvak and Colter heard a sharp, metallic *click* from outside the cellar, as the door opened and revealed the silhouette of an armed KGB guard.

They reacted instantly, but differently.

Litvak was an operative. A mole. A Ukrainian patriot, schooled and practiced in the arts of selfdefense and the tradecraft of the intelligence game. His instinct was to clamp his hand over Krasnevin's mouth so that no further sound could come out and to pull him back into the shadow, out of sight, hoping to avoid detection.

Colter's reaction was to kill the guard.

The guard was simply running to see what the matter was. He had been sent by his team leader in the direction of the small root cellar, and he simply could not absorb the information his eyes sent to his brain in time to save his own life. He saw the naked Krasnevin being held in restraint by a shadowy figure, and he saw another figure, a man holding a small handgun. His flashlight showed him just enough of the weapon that he was about to be able to identify it as a Czech-made 3.6mm military pistol, when all the light in the world exploded in his head.

Colter shot him twice in the center of the forehead. The weapon was not silenced, and the resulting *Crack!* *Crack!* sound of its firing was enough to disturb the night. Litvak and Colter glanced at each other, very well aware that the only part of the plan remaining was escape and evasion.

But first, there was the matter of Krasnevin. The pit that Litvak had been digging beneath the floorboards had never really been intended as a burial place for the KGB chief. There would be no need to hide the body. Still, it had been left to Colter whether to leave him alive or not. For Colter, it was simple.

Krasnevin would die.

For one thing, Krasnevin had seen Litvak, and would never rest until the agent was found and thrown into the darkest hellhole that Number Two Dzerzhinsky Square could provide. Colter had extracted enough information to know that the killings would stop with the death of Krasnevin. Krasnevin's death was part of the job.

He motioned for Litvak to turn Krasnevin over to him and take the point position at the door, making ready for their escape.

Litvak went to the door, and Colter faced Krasnevin. Krasnevin had never imagined that anyone could be so frightened of anything. The look in Colter's eyes seemed to literally freeze his blood. He knew deep inside that no one had ever seen this look before and lived. He knew he was about to die.

At that precise second, a 9mm bullet from an AK--47 combat assault rifle hit Litvak in the right eye, killing him instantly. Although he dropped to the ground and was quite obviously dead, bullets kept striking the framing of the doorway where he had been leaning.

One gun, Colter automatically counted. He noticed only peripherally that Krasnevin had managed to flip himself over backwards at the first sound of gunfire, hiding himself behind and partially shielding himself with two crates of canned sturgeon.

Colter ignored Krasnevin in favor of the assault rifle. If there was occasion, he would finish Krasnevin, but if he didn't get himself out of the box he was going to be in when that rifle outside was joined by another weapon or two, it just wouldn't matter to him at all.

He scrambled to the door jamb, finding the angle from which the bullets had come, and took a quick, precautionary peek out the doorway. There was nothing to be seen, but he could hear the sounds of running boots now and men yelling in the distance.

Krasnevin shrieked in Russian, screaming something in utter panic from his hiding place in the shadows. Colter snapped off a shot in his general direction to discourage this behavior. He was already making his move.

Next to the door was a crate of Stolichnaya vodka, the silver-label variety that doesn't get exported to the West. It's about a hundred and twenty proof, and the case was opened. Colter took out one of the bottles and cracked the neck of it against the stone wall, shattering it. He splashed the sharp-smelling contents over the floor of the cellar, and threw the bottle away.

He looked out the doorway, and ran like hell.

He made it to a pile of stacked firewood without being seen. Then shots began to come from the direction of the main house, so Colter ducked down and fired three shots back into the cellar, trying to strike a spark with the steel-jacketed bullets off the stonework of the walls.

"STOY!! STOY!!" screeched the voice of Krasnevin, thinking that his own men were shooting into the firetrap. But strangely, it was this very plea that caused them to do just that. A man in combat is not likely to restrain himself from shooting at an enemy just because the enemy yells for him to stop. These men were soldiers. They didn't recognize Krasnevin's voice for the simple reason that it had never sounded that way before. They thought they were hearing the surrendering cries of the intruder-enemy.

Five or six weapons opened fire on the door of the cellar at once, and flames burst out inside almost instantly.

Colter was halfway to the cliff face by the time the KGB men had surrounded the cellar and organized a fire-control team. He didn't know that he would be pursued at all, but he assumed that he would be. If Krasnevin could make himself understood even slightly, there would be men following him. Maybe Krasnevin was already dead, but Colter never considered relying on the possibility.

Colter reached the cliff face, and quickly counted down the three radio-aerial towers which projected up from the wooded coastline. He raced to the third in line and found the doubled nylon sailor's line wrapped around the base. He slipped the Czech pistol into his belt at the small of his back and went over the side, rappelling down the bluff as fast as he could safely go.

At the bottom of the cliff was a beach. It was, more than anything else, a worn-out place in the rocky shore which had been filled in with white sand shipped from Yalta. Samantha was waiting there. She was dressed in a wet suit which was painted a color the Navy SEAL had developed: It was a kind of grey that almost disappeared in any light. She had a Zodiac inflatable boat pulled up onto the beach, waiting for Colter. In the Zodiac were two SCUBA setups. Litvak's getaway plan had involved returning by back roads to Odessa, so she wasn't expecting him to come down the rope with Colter.

Colter hit the beach and began pulling on the line. That was when the soldier stepped out of the shadows and went for Colter. He was a complete surprise, having waited in ambush since spotting Samantha and, totally on his own, surmised that she was waiting for an accomplice. He had not been issued a radio. After all, he had an AK-47.

Mitch Colter was called "Triphammer" for a reason. Normally, CIA code-names were assigned on a more or less random basis, and Colter had had his share of "bird-names" at the beginning. "Triphammer" had evolved as more of a nickname. It has started after Colter's development of a particular combat move, a killing blow which he had developed himself. No one else seemed to be able to master it, and indeed it was very hard to practice, so it had come to be regarded as Colter's personal signature, in a macabre way.

He used it now. The soldier was too close for any other choices, and there was no time. Moving with a grace and speed unusual for a man so large, Colter darted at the armed man in front of him and took a low stance directly in front of the man's right boot, keeping his own weight on his back leg. Colter's left foot shot out in a short, vicious arc, clipping the KGB soldier's ankles out from under him. At the same moment, he had hit the man sharply under the chin, using the heel of his right hand. The man's head snapped back as he began to fall, and Colter put every ounce of strength he had in his body into the follow-up strike, which was delivered with the right elbow. With feet planted and back braced, Colter delivered a terrible, crushing elbow-strike just below the man's chin, just as his head was recoiling from the impact of the first blow. It gained its additional force from the man's own falling body. The KGB man never had a chance. The killing blow broke his neck, severed his spinal cord, and ruptured his trachea. He died in seconds.

Samantha watched for the amazingly few seconds it

took, like a rabbit caught in a pair of headlights.

Colter checked the soldier to make sure he was dead, then resumed pulling on the line down which he had descended to the beach. Seconds later, it released from the top and fell all the way to the sand beside him. He gathered it in quickly and threw it behind the scrub-brush at the base of the cliff. He ran to the Zodiac, and helped Samantha push it into the water.

She clambered aboard, and he turned the bow physically outward and away from the land, and then climbed aboard, at last. He started the small outboard engine and set their course.

Once established at an acceptable speed and in the correct direction, he turned the throttle and rudder over to Samantha and looked back for signs of pursuit. There were none.

He stripped off his shirt and threw it into the stern of the Zodiac. He took the pistol out of his belt and tossed it over the side. He peeled his wet trousers off and threw them aside, reaching for a Body Glove suit which was waiting for him, also worn by the SEAL.

He went to his SCUBA gear, which was the military version of the U.S. Divers' triple-tank setup in a stream-lined plastiform shell. It contained the regular instrument panel running from the regulator, which contained a compass. He checked it and his watch, and nodded to himself.

* * *

Stanislaus Swarbrizk was the commander of the night patrol boat assigned to the sector of the Black Sea. He was a good commander and a natural military man. He understood the need for regulations, and he lived his life by them. He had risen to his present lofty position because of this. His men knew him to be fair, and a good man, but one who always went by the book.

The radio operator of the GHISTI-211 Kilo-class cruiser turned up the gain on his set. He turned to the commander and said, "Sir, it. . . There seems to be some sort of emergency at the KGB enclave."

"What sort of emergency?"

"I can't tell, sir, they're trying to set up roadblocks around the area and get a helicopter into the air, but their communications seem to be ineffective."

"Very well."

Stanislaus Swarbrizk had just noticed a speck-return on the radar panel of the boat. It could be just "noise," or it could be a small boat, or it could be dust on one of the circuit boards inside the machine. He looked for it on the next sweep, and it went away.

"Should we offer to render assistance, sir?"

"The KGB can take care of itself, Sparks," returned the commander. "If they need us, they'll let us know."

In point of fact, if it had occurred to anyone at the dacha that Colter might have been trying to escape by water, they would have sent out the proper request. And then Stanislaus Swarbrizk would become a relentless engine of search. The insignificant "noise" he had spotted on the radar screen would have been run down. The men would have been called to general quarters and the guns manned.

And it still would have been too late.

Colter and Samantha had donned their gear and gone over the side of the Zodiac, having reached the point predetermined back at the Maeva Beach Hotel. Colter's knife had surgically slain the inflatable boat, and it was on its way to the bottom. The radar return Swarbrizk had seen was its last gasp, as it folded in on itself.

Colter and Samantha followed it down, and Colter's Tekna underwater light showed him the direction he needed on the transceiver he took from the pocket of his stab jacket, the vest which allowed him to control his positive and negative buoyancy. He watched out for Samantha's depth as well, and at ninety feet he held her still and gave her the hand signal to stop. He pressed the button on the transceiver in his hand, and it lit up like a Christmas tree. They were right on top of the sub.

It was hard to see, but they were only fifty meters or so from the underwater rendezvous. The sub had been "sleeping" there for thirty-six hours and more, and would wait longer yet before making its way out. It was invisible to the coastal watch, and would stay that way until they were good and damn sure no one was looking for them.

Colter led Samantha to the dive hatch, and pressed the signal button three times, then once. The outer door opened, and she slipped inside. Colter followed her in, and the steel door fitted by the Electric Boat Company slid back into place.

Safe.

CHAPTER TWELVE

"So. The great Mitch Colter finally misses a target, eh?" Fairbanks tried to manage an effect of grim satisfaction. The decoded cable in his hands was Colter's notification from the sub that Krasnevin might still be alive. It also informed him that they had been correct in their suspicions of Krasnevin, and that the assassin, code-name Doctor, was still out there. Colter had had the temerity to suggest Fairbanks use the "Kremlin Zipper" to inform the Soviet Premier.

Fairbanks flipped the decoded cable onto the desktop in front of him and leaned back in the custom-made chair. "Left Krasnevin alive, by God!" he exclaimed to Harold Miles, who was sitting nearby, seeming to be carefully studying his own shoes.

"Still, I don't think you could exactly call the op a failure, sir," the mild voice returned. "We know now that it was, in fact, Krasnevin who was pulling the strings."

"Yes, of course you're right," said Fairbanks, reaching for the special telephone on the side table. "It just comes as a shock. Normally you cross the man's name off as soon as Colter gets the assignment. Shame about Litvak, too. Not like Colter to lose a man. Of course, it's unusual for him to take one along, too." A voice buzzed in Fairbank's ear. "Let me speak to the president, please."

"How soon can we get them here?"

"Well, that's what I'm going to . . ." The telephone came to life again. "Good morning, Mr. President. . . Fine, thank you, sir.

"They're fine, thank you.

"Yes, sir, I'll tell her.

"No sir, it's nothing like that. The fact is, Mr. President, we've just had some good news.

"No sir, not exactly. But we did find out who was behind it.

"Well sir, I'm sorry to have to tell you that it was Krasnevin. The head of the KGB himself. Apparently he had suffered some sort of psychological. . . difficulty, and had gone off on his own personal campaign against the Imperialist Yankee Spy Machine, or something like that.

"Exactly.

"No, no. Not himself. He was running a profes-sional assassin for the actual terminations. We had always suspected that, you'll recall."

Harold Miles looked out the window, fighting to keep a straight face.

"We don't know, sir. Just a code name.

"The Doctor.

"Not necessarily, sir. At least not immediately. He's just a hired gun. He won't be doing any more killing now, I think it's safe to say.

"Well, that's just it, Mr. President. He's still alive, although he's been badly burned. He was interrogated by one of our agents, and. . .

"Well, actually it was the man named Colter, that we. . .

"Yes, sir, the same one.

"Yes, sir.

"Anyway, the point is that Krasnevin is still alive. As long as he can communicate with the Doctor, he's dangerous. I'd like to stop him, and to do that I'd like your authorization to use the Intel-link with the Kremlin. The Soviet leadership should be alerted at once, I'm sure you'll agree, and this method. . .

"It's called the Zipper.

"Yes, sir. Rhymes with Gipper.

"Very good, Mr. President.

"Thank you, sir, I will. Good day."

Fairbanks hung up and massaged his brow with his fingertips, eyes tightly shut. He muttered to Miles, "The old moron actually thought the head of the KGB was running around the world shooting guys *himself*! Jesus!"

"He okayed the Zipper?"

"Yes. Go. Do it," said Fairbanks, suddenly very tired. "Let's get this thing over with."

* * *

Krasnevin opened his eyes and was aware that his physical agony was being dulled by painkillers of great strength. He had been badly burned across the backs of his arms and on his neck and scalp. His broken finger had been set and splinted, but he was still in an agony. An agony of failure.

The specially equipped hospital plane landed at Moscow's Sheremetyevo Airport and rolled out toward the VIP ramp at the far end of the field. The KGB ambulance would take him to the clinic. He couldn't afford the hazy thinking induced by the drugs. He had to think.

He could taste the dental plaster in his mouth, and he knew that his jaw had been wired as a result of his last-ditch rush at the agent Colter. He had partial memory of the KGB men rushing into the flames for him, and he could remember seeing the body of the traitorous Ukrainian who had helped the animal Colter. Colter had not been found.

That, he knew, was the key piece of information he had to think about. He remembered Colter's eyes. He remembered something Colter had suggested about his father. . . That wasn't important, it was only important that Colter be found and killed. That was it.

He tried to assess his position. What would he tell the Premier? He had to find out more information quickly, and he had to do it quickly.

The aircraft was met at the VIP ramp by a high-security team of guards and a team of doctors from Moscow's elite Trauma Center. Krasnevin pretended to be unconscious as he was carried by stretcher to the waiting ambulance, which instantly began the long drive to the Kremlin with the kind of hurried caution which could only be inspired by having the head of the KGB as a passenger and patient.

As the bleak scenery flashed by the windows, the Voices seemed to return to Krasnevin, whispering the name over and over. . .

Mitchell COLTER. . .   Mitchell COLTER. . .

* * *

The special CIA Intel-Link began to feed the information to the Zipper. The equipment itself was actually an adjunct of Einstein, programmed to operate only on concurrent signal with the White House. As the matching coded electronic pulse came in, the information was scrambled and transmitted in a single, very brief electronic burst.

Instants later, a strident buzzer sounded in the Kremlin, indicating that a message had been received from the president of the United States via CIA Langley, classified eyes-only for the Premier. It caused a sensation.

The special equipment had been used only once before, over two years ago, during a crisis precipitated by the idiotic self-styled *Imam* in Teheran.

The officer in charge now was a KGB major from Smolensk who had only recently been assigned to staff duty here in the Kremlin. He had to consult the Operations Orders Manual to find the correct procedure to follow in handling such a transmission. He raced through the pages of the thick book, finally finding a one-page memo concerning the unusual procedure.

Because of its classification of Eyes Only/ Premier/ No Copies, the message was in plain-language form, in English. The first thing he had to do was to get a witness in the room. Just as he was searching for instructions as to the proper witness, the door behind him opened and the Premier's personal aide came into the room.

"I am instructed to tell you, Comrade Major," the man said in a formal tone, "to extract the message from the machine and to then seal it in this." He produced a green State Document pouch. "I am to witness these actions. Neither one of us is to know the content of the message. We will remain together, the pouch in our mutual possession, until the Premier has seen it. Please proceed."

The KGB major was desperately relieved to be told what to do. He was suddenly and horribly curious as to the content of the message, but acted disinterested. He lifted the message off the printer, covered by a blackon--red cover sheet, and placed it in the pouch.

The aide locked the pouch and taped a small paper form in place over the flap. "Your signature, please?"

The Major signed it, and then the aide countersigned it. "Comrade Major," the aide continued formally, "You are relieved of duty here. You will accompany me, please."

The two men left the room, passing the off-duty KGB captain who had been summoned from the ready room to sit in at the major's duty-station. The major was on his way to hand-deliver a message to the Premier.

* * *

Mitch Colter had had a disagreement with the captain of the submarine. The sub commander had orders to take the pair of them to the U.S. sub-pen at the secret location everyone in the area knew of, about fifty nautical miles north of Athens in the Aegean Sea. There, he was to hand them over to the air force, which would provide military jet transportation for them back to Langley.

Colter wasn't going back to Langley.

He discussed it reasonably with the sub commander, who was a very decent guy and an able officer named Webber. He had his orders, and he was bound to follow them. Colter finally nodded, and made sure that Webber understood that the navy's responsibility ended when he was landed at the Greek sub base, and that if the air force screwed up, it was nothing to do with him and would not reflect badly on him. Webber knew damn well that Colter wasn't going to go back to Langley, but he couldn't see that it mattered much, and so he tacitly agreed to look the other way while Colter made fools out of the air force.

The small attack sub had slithered through the Bosporus in the shadow of a Turkish freighter, and Colter and Sam had been duly impressed with the job the men of the boat made of staying invisible. They were professionals.

Samantha had had some bad moments when Colter told her about Litvak. She had never been involved in combat, and although she hadn't seen or heard any of the action, she knew as Colter spoke that she had stepped past an innocence that could never be regained. She read Colter's After-Action Report.

"You're very resourceful," she said.

"Yeah."

"They pay you well? For this kind of work?"

"Yes."

"You enjoy it, then?" There was brittleness, tension in her voice.

Colter considered how to answer. Obviously she had been shaken by reading the AAR. Colter briefly regretted letting her read it, but quickly dismissed the feeling. It was done.

Suddenly, she was seeing him as a murderous, merciless fiend without feelings. Despite her training, she was inexperienced in the field. She was shocked, horrified by the death of Litvak, whom she had instinctively liked and admired. Colter did not feel like justifying himself to her, now or later. He decided to level with her. She'd either be able to take it, or not.

"Look," he said, sitting next to her on the tiny bunk in her "stateroom" on the boat. He fixed her with a serious intensity in his grey-green eyes and said, "I like you. You are an especially intelligent, vital young woman. I like the way you handle yourself. I like you in bed. We just did an important thing together . . ."

"Great. Here it comes," she cut in hotly, "But you

have to understand this and that, Samantha, you weren't there - when you're *really* saying you're just a woman, and this is a man's business!"

"Be still." Colter spoke quietly, but with such deadly weight that Samantha was, for the first time since she had met Colter, a little bit afraid of him. She kept still.

"Don't judge me, Samantha. You don't know me well enough to do it fairly.

"You asked me if I enjoy it. The answer is no. But I'm very, very good at it. I didn't enjoy what I did to Krasnevin, but it was the only thing I could come up with in the time we had. And don't forget-it worked. Krasnevin is through, as soon as Langley gets the information to the Kremlin.

"And don't lose any sleep over the Russian soldiers I killed. The one up in the cellar was willing to kill me. He just wasn't fast enough. The one on the beach . . .?"

"I'd never seen anything like that before. What was it you *did* to him? That's wasn't karate, that was - " She broke off, looking for a phrase that didn't exist.

"That's why my callsign is Triphammer. He got too close, and he ran out of luck. That's what it comes to.

"Litvak is dead because he wasn't lucky. And I take responsibility for that, because it was my op, but the plain fact is he wasn't lucky. That's the only way I have to deal with that loss right now. It'll be hurting me for a long time, and I'll probably replay that situation a million times, trying to make it come out differently. But it won't do any good. That's my personal hurt, though, and I don't have to show it to you or anyone else. Understand?"

"Mitch, I - " she began. There were tears starting up in her dark eyes.

"Wait," he cut her off, showing her his palms. "You don't understand yet. I've been doing this for a long time, maybe too long. But that doesn't mean it hurts me less. It's just that over the years I've had to learn how to live with it. When I was green, a guy explained it to me like this, and now I'm explaining it to you. If you stay in the field, you'll learn, too. You'll have to."

"Okay."

"There's only one unbreakable rule in the field. *Don't die.* At the moment, Litvak took the chance and got caught I didn't, and I'm here.

"Do they pay me well? You bet they do. Because I *don't* enjoy it. What I enjoy is living on Bora Bora, and being with my friends, and swimming and diving and sailing and making love and getting a little high once in a while and not having to watch my back all the time. That's what I enjoy. But I'm good at this, and sometimes people need things done for good reasons, that can't get done any other way. Not just the good old American government, either. That's why Langley's so nervous about me. I work when I think it's the right call.

"Anyway, I didn't mean to make a speech, and I'm not apologizing. But I wanted you to understand the way it is. Okay?"

A tear traced its way down her cheek, and she swiped at it. "I'm sorry, yes, it's just that I. . . okay, yes. Okay."

"Okay," Colter said softly. He didn't take her hand, or hold her in his arms, but he sat with her, quietly, until the silence had changed into quietness and the air had absorbed the heat and the hurt out of the exchange.

A yeoman came by and knocked, asking if they would care for coffee in the wardroom, and they nodded to each other and followed the young man down the narrow passageway.

Webber was there, and he grinned at Colter. "Just got word that transport is all set for you as soon as we dock. You're going to have a hell of a time getting loose from your air force escort."

"I had an idea about that" Colter nodded at the young commander "Remember the way we came aboard? Don't suppose I could talk you into letting us swim ashore . . ."

The smile disappeared from Webber's face. He was desperately hoping this man was just kidding. He didn't want to have to try to stop him.

*   *   *

"Ident 9," the Doctor said.

"Field phone five," replied the mechanical voice.

"This is the Doctor."

"Stand by, Doctor."

As Yuri Turpenov stood waiting in the telephone booth in Zurich, he had no way of knowing that Krasnevin had come upon such bad times. There was no mention of any incident in the Western press, although Yuri had noted that the general euphoria of "glasnost" was seeming a tiny bit strained. Instead, he was thinking of his money.

He was a rich man now, even by the impossible standards of the West. His money was safe here in Switzerland, in brand-new numbered accounts. He had taken the extra precaution of having all the account numbers changed, just in case. He was not about to risk the possibility of his money being traced to any Russian source; not now, when he was so close to pulling the pin. Soon, he would disappear.

He had decided last night that he would not be returning to the Soviet Union.

"Ident, Doctor."

"Nine-One."

195

"Doctor?" It was Krasnevin's voice; Yuri recognized that, but it sounded different. It was as if the man were holding a rock in his mouth while attempting to speak. Yuri answered in the affirmative.

"Report, please."

"London assignment completed without complications."

"I see. Excellent." Krasnevin's voice was full of tension. "There is a new assignment. This is most urgent, Comrade Doctor."

"There must be some misunderstanding." Yuri was wary of this new sound in his master's voice. "I have not received payment for the London assignment."

"What?" Krasnevin stumbled. "Oh, yes, of course. Do not worry, Comrade Doctor, it will be taken care of within the hour."

"Very good," the Doctor went on, normally. "What is the new assignment?"

"Colter," Krasnevin spat into the telephone, "Mitchell Colter." He went on to give him the details of Colter's island home and everything else the assassin needed to know. He did it with relish.

Almost too much relish. "Is everything all right, Comrade? You sound. . . different."

"Yes, Colter. . . There was an accident."

"What kind of accident?"

"Nothing for you to be concerned about," snapped Krasnevin out of habit, and then quickly, "but see here, this assignment, it must be done quickly, as soon as possible."

"I see."

"Right away. Right away, you understand?"

There it was. Naked fear in the voice of the head of the KGB. "What is going on, Comrade?" he demanded.

"Colter must be. . . Colter has learned . . ."

"Tell me what has happened, Krasnevin." The tone was not curt, but it was a demand.

A wave of nausea washed over Krasnevin. The pain came back to him in waves, from his mouth, from the burns, from the humiliation. . .   "Colter knows . . .everything. He knows about *you*."

In halting, stumbling sentences, Krasnevin related an edited account of the circumstances of the attack at the Black Sea. He tried to concentrate on giving the Doctor a sense that Colter was a danger to him, as well as to Krasnevin. He wanted the Doctor to feel as threatened as he did.

Yuri listened patiently to the fevered confession from his KGB paymaster, contributing soothing noises and outraged grunts from time to time, as appropriate. When Krasnevin finished, Yuri said, "I understand. Don't give the matter another thought, Comrade. The man Colter has just contracted a fatal disease. Terminal, my word on it."

"Excellent! That's. . . excellent."

"There may be. . . unusual circumstances, however. I require payment in advance for this one assignment. It may be included with the fee for the London assignment."

There was a pause. Krasnevin leaned against the wall in the small room in the clinic where they had set up the secure telephone. He knew exactly what he was being told. The worm had turned. He would not be hearing from the Doctor again, ever. But he would accept the assignment, and who cared about the money, anyway?

"Of course. There is no problem."

"Good."

"The money will be there within the hour."

"Excellent."

"Comrade Doctor. . . use caution. This Colter is a

very dangerous man."

"So are they all, given warning."

"Colter is the best of them, he - "

"He is as good as dead."

*   *   *

The Premier was tired, very tired.

He sat in the back of the Zil limousine and wished that he could fall asleep in the heated comfort of the car. He didn't want to continue to bear the weight right now. But he would. He knew himself.

The car was on its way to visit the clinic, to see how Krasnevin was coming along. Actually, his condition wasn't so much a matter of physical details, but more dependent on the outcome of his next conversation with the Premier.

The Premier had received word from Langley, Virginia, that he had a madman at the helm of the Committee for State Security. He didn't want to believe it, naturally, but it had been convincing data, and so he had had the line at the hospital tapped and recorded.

The Premier absently touched the distinctive birthmark he had schooled himself to ignore. In times of trouble, he still caught himself at it. He glanced across the seat of the limousine at the man who accompanied him now for the visit to the KGB chief. The man's name was Volkov, and his codename was FENCER. He was a "special" gleaned from the elite Spetnaz units. He was part of the Premier's Kremlin guard.

The two men were whisked up the steps of the clinic and left alone with Krasnevin. They took off their coats and came over to the bed, where Krasnevin was pretending to be much worse off than he actually was.

"Don't speak, Krasnevin," began the Premier, and the tone all by itself made the KGB chief's eyes widen. "I have had a communication from the American CIA informing me that you are the one responsible for the assassinations of the CIA men. You personally, and your hired killer, this so-called Doctor. No, don't speak yet." This as Krasnevin tried to raise himself up, realizing that he was going to have to fight for his life.

"Let. . . let me explain . . ."

"No. There are only a few possible choices now. A public trial and expiation of guilt. You could disappear. You could succumb to your wounds which resulted from the accident at your dacha.

"My question to you, Comrade, is why? Why would you undertake such madness by yourself? Didn't you see what we've been attempting to reach with the West? And didn't you know the danger you put the future of your country in?"

"It's. . . it's wrong, Comrade Premier. Wrong to trust them. You would have seen. It could still be. The man Colter must die, first. Then. . . you would see, their intelligence organization would be in complete disarray . . ."

The Premier saw it then. The light of madness, irrevocably in possession of the man's wits. He sighed, inwardly. There were so many decisions men shouldn't have to make. But this was clear, at least. Krasnevin succumbed to his injuries from the accident, and so on. He would have a statement out by noon. He nodded to the man known as fencer.

Krasnevin was still prattling on about the downfall of the West when he noticed fencer at his shoulder. The man used a silenced .22-caliber pistol made by Winchester, with a clip holding nine shots. As he took it out of his holster, Krasnevin blinked once, then twice.

"No. . . You couldn't. . . You can't do this . . ."

199

The gun coughed, twice. Krasnevin died as the familiar stench of cordite replaced the smells of the hospital. The bullets entered his brain and lodged there, mushrooming and causing vast but invisible damage.

The Premier eyed the remains and nodded to fencer. "Stay and clean up, won't you? Then you can report back to your unit." The man saluted as the Premier walked away.

In the hall, he remembered Krasnevin's last words with sardonic amusement. You can't do this. . . You can't do this. . .

Of course he could. He was the Premier.

* * *

At a small cafe in the heart of metropolitan Zurich, the Doctor was sitting, sipping the rich, creamy cafe au lait, and thinking. He was caught in a brief moment of indecision. It was a rare experience for him.

The money from Krasnevin had come in quickly, as he had been promised. It was an enormous sum, the largest Yuri had ever handled in one lump in his life. The Swiss banking laws were as close to inviolate as could be found in the world, and with the help of an agreeable if over-precise banker named Veltern, Yuri had done his very best to make sure that the money was safely hidden away in a variety of untraceable accounts, both in Zurich and Geneva. His funds in the bank in Nassau were already suitably protected.

That was that. Yuri was certain that there would be no further income from that particular source. And it was more than enough to retire on.

The question which then presented itself was, why

go on? Why should he travel all the way to some island in the South Pacific to kill this last person? Why didn't he just disappear now? He was certainly prepared. Why not simply take the money and run? Why take one more chance?

He didn't like the idea of operating on a small island, anyway. Not enough people. Too hard to get out, if he needed to do so in a hurry. Big cities were much better for this kind of work. And there was an additional concern; after the balls-up mess Krasnevin had made, Yuri couldn't be certain he wasn't completely blown, real identity and all. This Colter man might even be alerted. Why bother?

The Doctor was sorely tempted to retire right now. He could catch the next flight to London, change airlines at Heathrow, and be in America by morning. Through an agent, he had purchased a mountain retreat in Oregon, situated on over fifty acres of land near a main highway and a town. His new identity was already established there. It was a wonderful place. Yuri longed to go there and begin a new life.

However, he couldn't take any chances at all. He didn't want to be hunted down. Not by the KGB, and not by the CIA or the FBI or anyone. He didn't underestimate the power of these organizations, and he didn't want to be in a perpetual state of alertness once he had disappeared. He wanted to *live* in Oregon, not survive there.

He could never be sure how much of what Krasnevin had told him was reliable, but he was reasonably certain that the damned fool had told Colter enough to make him a threat to Yuri's future, if the man chose to be. It was this extra measure which ultimately swung the balance in the decision-making process. As well, an innate pride in his own professionalism came into play. He had performed virtually to perfection, all the way down the line. It seemed a bit cheap to cut and run at this point.

After all, he had already been paid for the job.

He took out his passport and travel documents, and examined his choice of identity. Dr. Miller, Canadian. Was it too risky to take the identity of an M.D.? Krasnevin might have revealed that Yuri was in fact a doctor, and he didn't want to run any risks with this last target.

He decided to stay with his chosen identity. The papers were excellent, and Colter would never have the opportunity of looking at them, anyway. If things went according to plan, the man would never know what hit him.

The Doctor put away the documents and took out an airline schedule. He looked down the listings, searching for the exotic-sounding name. UTA French Airlines could get him out quickly, as far as the main airport, on the main island out there. . . there it was, Faaa International. From there, he could use the local service of Air Polynesie. . . Here. The name of the destination burned on the page.

Bora Bora.

PART THREE

THE GOODNIGHT KISS

CHAPTER THIRTEEN

Colter brought in the jib until it stopped luffing, but didn't tighten it to the racing-style tension which Rene always demanded of the boat. He was taking it easy.

Up forward, Samantha was standing easily beside the mast, one hand on the halyard, staring dreamily off into the distance. She wore the bottom part of a bikini and a lazy smile.

Rene had loaned Colter his treasured boat, the *Presque-Vivante*, as a favor. He had not actually been reluctant, but he had been very careful to go over each little idiosyncracy of the Morgan forty-five foot sloop's handling with Colter. She was a wonderful sailboat, and Rene took a child-like concern in her safety.

"Okay, that's about it," he had finally decreed to Colter. "But if anything goes wrong, anything at all, don't be afraid to heave to and call for help on the radio. Just turn her into the wind."

"Okay, Rene."

"You remember where the signal flares are?"

"Yes, Rene."

"And if you see heavy weather coming, bring her right back home."

"Yes, Rene."

Rene had to fly that morning, or Colter was sure

he would have insisted on coming along, but he promised to be waiting for them at the Yacht Club dock
when they returned in the afternoon. The boat had
been in the Bora Bora lagoon for a week, Rene having
left it there when he had been called unexpectedly to
take over another captain's flight. He hadn't had a
chance to sail her back to Papeete yet.

Colter and Samantha had brought their day-sailing
provisions aboard and cast off, heading out through the
Te Avenui Pass to the open sea. The day was perfect
and the breeze was soft and steady. It was one of the
last days there would be like this before the annual
arrival of the *mauvais temps*, a stretch of sultry, stale
weather which was endurable for about the first two
hours. After that, people began to become irritable
quickly, and life in the islands slowed down to a grumpy
crawl.

But it was not here yet. The warm sun and the salt
air filled the world. Colter's mind drifted to the lines of
Coleridge's "Rime of the Ancient Mariner":

> *The fair breeze blew,*
> *The white foam flew,*
> *The furrow followed free.*

And Colter looked back at their own free-following
wake, and was deeply content. There were times like
this, for him, when he was certain in his heart that he
was in the right place, in harmony with the essences of
Life. Death and darkness seemed very far away.

They sailed aimlessly for a while, taking whichever
direction the wind offered as favorable. The *Presque-
Vivante* lived up to her name, seeming almost alive as
she danced across the deep blue water. Samantha
seemed to throb with excitement and good health as she
scurried around the boat. She produced a small camera

and took some pictures. She got out suntan oil and rubbed it all over her body. She brought Colter some wine in a plastic cup. She inched out onto the bow pulpit, beyond the very tip of the boat's prow, and looked down at the water rushing under her. She laughed for no good reason.

A pair of porpoises appeared beside the boat and began to swim alongside, keeping up with them and moving from side to side of the sloop. Their rolling, jumping motions caused Samantha to squeal with glee, and after she had taken several pictures of them, she ran below decks, saying she was going to get some food and toss it to them.

"Don't bother, Sam," Colter said, "they won't eat it. They just want to play."

"Really?"

"Really. They wouldn't even notice. They're having fun."

She thought about that for a moment, and then turned to Colter with sudden tears in her eyes. "Jesus. Isn't that *great*?" she asked with a hush in her voice.

She was so full of child-like awe and undiluted joy that Colter experienced a wrenching pain somewhere in his center.

He felt very close to this sparkling girl, intensely protective of her.

There was too much motion on the open sea to permit a decent, leisurely luncheon, so Colter came about and set a course back through Te Avenui Pass to the lagoon. Once they were back inside the encircling reef, the water would be flat calm and they could drop an anchor. Colter knew just the spot.

Samantha screamed in good-natured fury when she saw that they were headed back in, threatening to mutiny if he was calling it a day already. He calmed his one-girl crew with a solemn seafarers' oath to go back outside the reef after lunch.

Back inside the reef, Colter lowered the jib and ordered Sam to gather it in, wadding it into the bow pulpit until they needed it later. He guided the *Presque-Vivante* northwards past the Hotel Bora Bora and around to the extreme northern end of the blue-green lagoon, to a little *motu* he had visited before with permission. It was actually owned by one of the island families, but as far as Samantha was concerned, it was a desert isle straight out of fiction.

It was isolated, about three-fourths of the way from the island to the reef, complete with palm trees and a beach of pinkish white coral sand. Colter brought the shallow-draft sailboat in close and turned it into the wind. He dropped the rugged old Danforth anchor from the bow, and donning a dive-mask, dove in after it.

Underwater, he was startled yet again, and as always, by the beauty of the submarine world and its difference from our own. He never grew blasé about it, and he never failed to be mesmerized by it. It was part of the reason for the task at hand.

He dove down and hand-set the old anchor in a formation of stone in the sandy bottom, safely away from any living coral or delicate underwater life. It was a simple enough job.

In Cozumel, Mexico, there is a gloriously beautiful system of coral and underwater life which has become a mecca for scuba divers from all points of the globe. They are systematically killing it.

Divers with less than a dozen dives in their lives are being guided through caves of coral. The young man from Dallas accidentally loses control of his depth and breaks off a piece of staghorn coral. He has a slight cut to show for it, but it's a slow death for the million organisms that lived in the coral, three hundred years in the making. The macho, beer-drinking bottom timer with three thousand dollars' worth of diving equipment on his body pulls himself along a coral wall by handover-r-hand effort against a three-knot current. He wears gloves, and it is a measure of his manliness that they are torn to shreds by the end of the trip. He is personally responsible for killing millions of living creatures, and if he knows it, doesn't care. In twenty years, the tourism will begin to fall off in Cozumel. In fifty, there will be stories about how beautiful the reef used to be.

So Colter always hand-set the anchor.

He surveyed the bottom of the keel on the way up, making sure that it was clean and in no danger of coming into contact with any subsurface coral heads, even should the boat swing on its hook. Satisfied, he surfaced and swam to the boat's stern, where he had placed the aluminum boarding ladder over the transom.

"You didn't tell me you were going to abandon ship," Sam remarked as he climbed aboard.

"That's why I came back," Colter replied, deadpan "Old rule of the sea - Women and children first." He picked the nearly naked girl in his arms. "And that's you."

And he tossed her overboard.

She hit the water with a splash, and came up sputtering and calling him names, but he had already gone below and didn't hear them. He came back on deck, carrying a watertight cooler containing food and wine, and met her at the boarding ladder.

"All ashore that's going ashore" he grinned at her. For an answer, she tried to squirt water at him through her teeth. She missed, partly because she giggled halfway through the attempt and nearly choked. She started swimming to the motu in a lazy backstroke. Colter lowered the slowly luffing mainsail and secured it, then set out after her, with the cooler in tow.

They were both hungry from the sailing, and they

demolished the simple lunch of cheese, meat, fruit and wine in a matter of minutes. Colter quickly deposited their trash back in the cooler, and led Samantha into the shallow, warm water to wash off the sticky juices of fruit and meat, and the sand that had adhered to their bodies.

They washed each other in the bright, sandy-bottomed lagoon, splashing water over backs, faces, hair. Her short, dark hair was sleek against her head and her breasts were buoyant in the water. As she ran her hands over Colter's smoothly muscled body, a familiar heat welled up inside her that had nothing to do with the island sun.

Colter felt the subtle difference in her touch, and began to become erect. He drew her to his chest and kissed her open mouth, running his hands over her back, up her sides, cupping her breasts. He ran a fingernail gently across a nipple, and heard her breath quicken.

She tugged insistently at the material of his swimsuit, freeing his now fully erect penis, and began to stroke him, slowly. She looked vaguely around them for a moment. They were right out in the open, in broad daylight. It was scandalous. But she could not hear any cries but her own . . . the very openness of it became an aphrodisiac, ringing a latent bell of exhibitionism in her. She looked into his eyes, and whispered to him as she unfastened her bikini bottom.

"Now. . . do me now. . . do it to me right here. . . now."

He felt her hands guiding him, and he lifted her up by the buttocks, helping her mount him. She moaned as he filled her, and locked her legs over his hips. She clung to him with feverish effort, rocking herself even further onto him and feeling the tension build through their bodies. Suddenly, her orgasm was very close, and she clutched him with all her strength.

"*Mitch. . . ?*" she voiced his name, urgently, inquiringly.

He altered the angle of their embrace slightly, and forced himself into a long, smooth, steady rhythm as he moved in her.

"Ah, yes! Yes! Ah, God! Yes!" she shouted as the ecstasy swept over her in waves.

He could no longer restrain his own orgasm, and clasped her to himself tightly as he came, burst after burst. Driven by the feeling of his ejaculation, her orgasm lengthened and deepened, going on and on and on until she felt she would go insane.

Afterward, they held tightly to each other for a long time, quietly, silently, in the bright sunlit water.

* * *

"I wish I never had to leave this place," she said.

It was some forty-five minutes later, and Colter and Samantha were walking, hand in hand, along the empty sands of the tiny islet.

"So don't leave," he replied.

"Yeah," she nodded, smiling.

"I mean it," he went on "Why the hell should you go back to the CIA? Or the United States?"

"Well, I can't just walk away."

"Why not?"

She looked at him, seriously now. "You're not kidding, are you?" It was a statement.

"No. I'm not."

The first thing that scared her was, she had already thought about it. This was an incredible place, he was an incredible man, and she was happy in a way she would not have believed possible. But she forced herself to stand back from the immediacy of it. To be realistic.

"You're talking about doing what you did. It was right for you, but that doesn't mean it's right for me. Not now, anyway."

"Why not?"

"I don't know," she answered honestly "I love it here, but I also love some things back there. There are people I have ties with, but I don't rule anything out. I'll know when it's time to leave, I think. I'm pretty sure of that, and it just isn't right now, Mitch."

He walked along with her in silence for a few seconds. Then he asked, "When do you have to go back to Langley?"

"Yesterday," she laughed. There had been some very cranky cable traffic and telephone messages after Colter and Samantha had eluded the air force in Greece and made their way back to Tahiti via commercial airlines.

"No, really," he pressed.

"Soon, I guess. There will have to be a debriefing, and I'm certainly due for re-evaluation, after what we did together. There'll be a step up in my career."

"Oh, yes."

"Steve Bishop gets in this afternoon, and he'll probably send me back on the first available transport. And I'll have to go."

"Yeah. I know." Colter squinted at the horizon.

"Anyway, stop talking about it. I'm here now."

He looked at her, admiringly. "You certainly are."

She turned to face him, striking a hip-shot pose, arms akimbo. She had turned a beautiful all-over brown in the last several days, since their return from the Black Sea. She radiated good health from every pore of her lush, long-legged body. Colter felt the familiar fires rekindling between his legs.

She was going to say something, when she noticed the bulge in his swimsuit.

"Oh, no, you don't," she grinned. "What do you think you're going to do with *that* thing?"

"Nothing," he said innocently, taking a side-step in her direction.

"You'll have to catch me first!" She ran away from him, along the palm-shaded beach.   He caught her.

* * *

Rene was waiting with cheerful Polynesian impatience.

He ordered another Hinano beer for himself, and two more of Christian's obnoxious rum concoctions for the new arrivals, a charter-boat captain and his mate. They had already been in the bar at the Yacht Club of Bora Bora when Rene had arrived an hour before from the airport. The newcomers were apparently fresh from the trip out to Bora from Papeete. Rene had listened with polite disinterest to their talk of the voyage across, and to their grumbling about the charter business generally. Their lone passenger, who was some Canadian doctor, had gone on to explore the island on his own.

Christian put two of the "Planter's Punch" specials on the bar along with Rene's beer. Rene shrugged at Christian as if to say, "It's on my bill, what are you looking at?" and Christian returned the shrug as if to reply, "Your bill, since when do you pay your bill around here?" and carried them over to the table where the three men had been sitting.

The men murmured appropriate thanks to Rene, who was wandering out toward the dock again, hoping for the first familiar sight of the sails of the *Presque-Vivante*.

Noticing, the charter captain called, "Patience, my friend. The water is safe, and there is plenty of daylight left. They will be bringing her in by and by."

"Everyone is in a hurry," his mate added muzzily "No one takes time anymore. Even this doctor of ours, he doesn't want to go sailing, he just wants transportatión. Why take a sailing trip if you're in a hurry? Take a plane! Asshole. Did you see him? He checked the headings on the chart on board! Asshole! As if I don't know how to hold a course."

"You don't know how to hold a course," the captain replied.

"Maybe not, but he didn't know that. He should have taken a plane ride, instead."

"And then we'd still be in Papeete, looking for a charter. All I know is, he paid the whole advance in U.S. dollars. I'll sail him around the world or around the harbor. I don't care."

"Here she comes!" Rene shouted.

The captain and mate of the charter boat joined Rene and Christian out on the dock, past the dining area not yet set up for the evening meal service. The beautiful white sails of the *Presque-Vivante* had just appeared, rounding the point of land closer to the main village.

* * *

The Doctor saw the sails at exactly the same moment.

He had stayed with his hired charter captain and the incompetent first mate in the Yacht Club bar just

212

long enough to establish that it was in fact Mitchell Colter that they were talking about. It was an incredible stroke of luck, and the Doctor was prepared to take advantage of it.

At first, he hadn't been able to believe his ears. No sooner had the chartered inter-island sailboat docked at the picturesque harbor of the Yacht Club and the Frenchman Christian had motored them ashore in the skiff than the airline captain had arrived, making noises about waiting for his friend Colter to return with the borrowed sailboat. The irony of it was increased when he learned the name of the vessel - the *Presque-Vivante*. Almost Alive. Yuri's sense of poetry was satisfied. Almost alive was the same thing as dead.

He had learned by surreptitious eavesdropping (did Frenchmen think that *no one* understood conversational French but themselves?) that Colter was not alone on the boat - he was apparently accompanied by a female. Too bad. Bad luck for her, but the situation was too good. He couldn't afford *not* to take advantage of the situation.

He silently commended himself for his decision to hire a charter boat to take him to Bora Bora instead of merely flying in along with the tourists. It had been a last-minute change of plan, and it had proved fortuitous. Besides, it offered an additional back-door escape route from the island should anything go wrong.

When Yuri was sure he knew what to expect, he had quietly returned to the charter boat and gone below to his cabin. He got out the special suitcase he had brought out of Russia with him weeks ago, which was constructed so that no pain-in-the-neck airport security device could detect any threat from its contents. It was becoming almost a standard-issue KGB device, very useful for bringing weapons of one kind or another along with you. Much better than the damned plastic pistols, which blew up in your hand as often as they performed properly.

Ah well. That was *almost* all behind him, now.

The case opened easily under Yuri's hands, and he checked its contents carefully. He then closed it again and carried it with him along the pier, through the hotel, and across the road and the dirt parking lot before doubling back to a rise of ground he had spotted from the water. It looked just about perfect. It had excellent cover, no dwellings, and a good vantage point over the Yacht Club dock area.

He selected his spot with care, finally choosing a volcanic outcropping of rock which had been overgrown with thick vegetation. He reopened the suitcase and assembled the RPG-7 combat rocket-propelled grenade launcher, piece by piece, with loving care. It was not a subtle weapon, but it was horribly effective, and no one would know where the explosion had come from. It would certainly kill Colter and anyone else on the small sailboat. This was Yuri's farewell assignment, and he had decided not to take any chances.

At that moment, he spotted the white sails skimming around the far point and heard the Air Polynesie pilot's shout of excitement and greeting from the bar across the short stretch of water.

He sighted the short, squat tubular weapon at the docking area, unconsciously measuring angles and distances. He adjusted the range setting of the sighting gate, and then set the weapon on his lap, mentally preparing himself. His eyes traveled from the Yacht Club dock to the approaching sailboat and back again.

He nodded, waiting. He would have an excellent field of fire.

* * *

It had been a fabulous day.

Samantha had released Colter from his promise to take them back outside the reef because they had stayed so long on the tiny deserted motu. It was midafternoon, and time to return Rene's boat to the Yacht Club anchorage. Besides, Sam was getting too much sun, and there was a long night ahead. She wanted to bathe and take a nap before dinner.

Samantha was almost reluctant to return to dry land, and as they came within sight of people on the shore and the dock at the Yacht Club, she pulled a T-shirt out of her bag and pulled it on over her head. Colter smiled his rueful smile at her.

"Modesty returns."

"Pity."

"Humor me. What would Michelle think?" Colter had made no secret of his relationship with Michelle, and the two women had even met each other, the day before. After one look at the girl's eyes, Michelle had known she was sleeping with Colter, and accepted it with characteristic good-natured grumpiness. As for Samantha, she had found Michelle enviably spirited, sexy, and strong willed. They liked each other.

"No one knows what Michelle thinks, about anything. She's French."

"She's gorgeous."

"She calls you 'Wonder Woman,'" Colter teased.

"I'll bet that's what she calls me," Samantha replied from the corner of her mouth.

They were coming in closer to the Yacht Club's docking area and anchorage now, easing across the smooth water of the semicircular bay formed by the island's natural shoreline. Colter decided to take the boat right up to the dock, since it was clear, and show off a little. After the unloading and cleaning-and-battening chores Rene would insist on, he could get Christian to tow it out to an anchor buoy for the night.

Colter told Samantha to come aft and take the wheel, and ran forward to strike the jib, which was no longer needed. He brought the big sail down with quick, powerful motions and stowed it in the bow pulpit. With a quick glance at the docks, he returned aft to take the helm again. He picked the easiest spot to put the forty-foot boat, and set himself up to reach it just as he turned into the onshore wind. The drift would carry the *Presque-Vivante* gently and safely up next to the dock with a soft thump.

Colter could see Rene clearly now, coming down the pier anxiously, probably searching for damage to his beloved craft. Colter noticed the presence of the charter-sailer at the anchor buoys, and remembered that it had not been there when they had left, that morning. He couldn't see the boat's name from where he was, but he seemed to remember it from Charter Row in Papeete Harbor. He made a mental note to inquire as to the skipper and cargo. He was not suspicious, but his habit was to keep informed of the new faces on the island.

Sam had gone below deck to grab her things and stuff them into her carry-all. She yelped as Colter suddenly brought the bow of the boat sharply around into the wind, causing her to lose her balance.

The air spilled out of the mainsail, and the *Presque-Vivante* instantly lost headway, drifting silently and slowly the few remaining feet toward the pier. Colter reached back and grabbed a coil of line, tossed it to the waiting Rene on the pier, and brought the rudder amidships.

"Toss me the bowline, Mitch," called Rene, running to the deep-water end of the dock. The bow of the boat had stopped drifting in, and was still some five feet away from the dock.

As Colter began to run forward along the boat's deck, everything began to happen at once. The hair on the back of Colter's neck stood straight up. There had been a puff of smoke from the jungle *right over there*.

Sam's voice: "Mitch?"

Colter turned, lightning quick, and too late. As Samantha had emerged from the cockpit hatch, about to complain about his ship-handling skills, she had had the briefest glimpse of the rocket as it hurtled toward her. Her blood ran ice-cold as she gritted her teeth, which was the only response there was time for before the rocket exploded exactly in the center of the boat's cockpit, killing her instantly.

The blast of the exploding missile threw savage gouts of debris flying everywhere, dismasting the *Presque-Vivante* and sending the heavy boom, still trailing the flapping mainsail, across the pier. It swept Rene Iatape into the lagoon, knocking him unconscious and cutting a wide slash across his abdomen. The boat's hull cracked approximately one third of the way forward from the transom, splintering outward and down, and she began to sink rapidly.

Colter had been spared most of the impact of the blast. At the moment of the explosion, he had been partially shielded by the superstructure of the boat itself, but he was knocked flying through the air by the shock wave. A sudden, jolting pain in his shoulder rendered him nearly unconscious, and he dimly realized that he had flown right into one of the permanent pilings at the end of the dock. He hit the water so hard he bounced off the surface once before splashing into the salty lagoon. Water filled his nose and mouth, and he fought back the state of shock which beckoned him.

Samantha is dead, he thought.

He had seen the impact take her. She could never survive the injuries he had seen; his memory burned with its picture of her last moment. He must put it aside.

It was aimed at me, he thought.

Then his thought became more organized. Someone had tried to kill him, and missed. Whoever it was was still out there. The puff of smoke. The killer might be reloading, right now. He would surely have seen that Colter had run forward on the boat just at the critical second. He would know that Colter wasn't dead yet.

What about Rene? he thought.

Not now! Colter commanded himself. First of all, survive.

He checked himself for injury, finding that something had gone wrong with his left shoulder. It was still numb with the shock, but it was likely to be disabling. Probably dislocated. He coughed out the saltwater in a stinging, retching spasm and tried to find something to get behind. An injured man in the water was too damned easy a target to survive for long. Not against a guy who was willing to use *rockets*, for Christ's sake.

He forced his lungs to accept a deep breath, and held it as he dived for the bottom. He swam strongly but awkwardly underwater, making for a row of fishing *pirogues* which had been beached beside the limited number of bungalows the Yacht Club rented out in addition to anchorage.

That was when he felt the second explosion.

He was lifted almost clear of the boiling water, and was smashed against the hardwood outriggers of the nearest *pirogue*. The world was upsidedown, a sudden fury of churning water and splintered wood. As his shoulder ligaments tore apart, pain shrieked into his brain and the light grew very dim. He tasted warm,

218

coppery blood and realized that it was his own, and then he lost consciousness.

* * *

The Doctor was in a stunned fury. It was inconceivable to him that he could have missed. The first rocket had already been triggered when Colter had scampered rapidly forward on the damned boat, like a monkey! Outside the kill radius, obviously. Yuri had kept his eyes trained on the body of his target even as he reloaded the rocketlauncher. He saw Colter's impact against the piling and his splash as he plunged into the lagoon, obviously injured but not dead.

Aiming his second shot, he praised himself for taking the extra precaution of bringing along the extra rocket-propelled grenade as an emergency fail-safe measure. But, incredible as it seemed, Colter had *dived and begun to swim under the surface of the water* as he triggered the second shot. The wire-guided device just couldn't be made to find him in time, and the explosion had been above and behind him. Yuri had no experience with the effects of this weapon in water; it was designed to pierce the armor of a light tank, not the warm salt water of a coral lagoon.

Yuri stared intently at the area of destruction caused by the second rocket, totally ignoring the carnage inflicted by the first. He could see that Colter had been thrown into a line of wrecked outrigger canoes and that he was bleeding. He appeared to be unconscious, but his head and shoulders were clear of the water, suspended over the ruined hull of one of the fishing boats.

He was a perfect target, immobile and defenseless.

And the Doctor couldn't touch him.

He had brought only the two rockets with him, the second one only as a backup. He had never considered the possibility that it would not be enough. He had no other weapon with him, because he had considered it unthinkable that anything more could be necessary.

He sat rock-still, immobilized by the unforeseen failure. He had never missed before, and a part of his mind was absurdly examining the experience with detached, scientific interest. *So this is what it feels like to fail*, he thought. Then, his sense of self-preservation took hold of him, and his thoughts became organized again.

First of all, survive, he thought urgently. He had taken two shots from the same spot. He had to get moving. Instantly, he began to break down the RPG-7 into its component parts, as quickly as he could. As he did so, he was thinking fast.

His original plan had called for one mysterious explosion, cause unknown, which would kill Colter and anyone close to him. Witnessess would, as always, give conflicting reports as to what they had seen, but the obvious thing to look for would have been explosives on board the ruined boat itself. Not an assassin with a sophisticated rocket launcher.

But he had had to fire twice. So the original plan was thrown away, and it would be known that it had been an attempt on Colter's life. The moment Yuri had triggered the second shot, he had revealed the presence of an assassin on the island. The question was, what could he expect to be the response?

If only he hadn't missed!

The Russian forced the useless thought from his mind as he completed packing the weapon into the specially fitted suitcase. The suitcase had become a problem; he might have been seen leaving the Yacht

Club area with it, so he should be carrying it with him when he returned. But he could not now take a chance on its contents being revealed. With no more rockets, it was useless, but it was a considerable threat to him. He would have to lose it.

The Doctor had two choices. Leave the island as quickly and as safely as possible, or stay and make sure the job was done. It was possible that Colter was already done, that he would die of his injuries. He might be bleeding internally, might even be dead already. But if he ran now, he could not be sure. He decided to stay.

His cover was still good, excellent. He was a Canadian doctor who had gone walking, looking around the island. Explosions at the Yacht Club pier? Good heavens! Anyone hurt? Good God, no! Perhaps I might be of help? After all, I'm a doctor. . .

That was it.

If he could manage to be allowed to examine Colter's injuries, all he would need would be a few seconds alone with the man. A steely, determined look, not quite a smile, came to Yuri's face as the new plan fell into place in his mind. It was going to work out, after all.

He carefully concealed the lethal suitcase under a growth of particularly dense bougainvillea, which looked like it hadn't been disturbed in thirty years. Then he moved quietly and cautiously away, back toward the road.

CHAPTER FOURTEEN

BLOOD POUNDING IN HIS EARS.

"Mitch?"

Colter heard his name called from the other end of the tunnel and fought his way uphill toward the light. He was dimly aware that he was in pain, but he knew even in his semiconscious state that there was an emergency. His body produced enough adrenalin to shoot him toward the light, not back down into the sleepy safety. He opened his eyes.

"Mitch?" Bishop repeated.

"What time is it?" Colter managed.

"Michelle!" Bishop called in the direction of the next room, then turned back to the big man lying on the bed."

It's about six P.M. You've only been out for a couple of hours, but you're damn lucky to be alive at all. You're in Michelle's place, and you're going to be okay. Your shoulder was dislocated, but we popped it back into the socket right away. It's going to hurt like hell for a while, but there's nothing broken."

Michelle came into the room and bent over him, looking carefully into his eyes. She checked the size of his pupils, looking for signs of a concussion, and felt his brow for a fever. Her face was grim.

"Rene?" Colter whispered, fearing the worst.

"Rene will live," she answered him shortly. "He is being flown to Papeete, to *L'Hôpital Publique*. You should have gone with him." She darted a furious glance at Bishop, whose face was an expressionless mask.

Colter's memory flooded back to him, unwelcome and burning. "Samantha . . ."

"Samantha is dead." Michelle turned, and left the room.

Colter thought for a moment. Then he asked Bishop, "How soon were you on the scene?"

"I got there just as they were pulling you out of the water," he answered.

"Tell me what you know," Colter demanded, his voice taking on a somewhat sharper tone.

Bishop related the story, as far as he knew it. The proprietor of the Yacht Club, Christian, had actually been the first person to get to Colter as he lay in the splintered wreckage in the lagoon. He had kept Colter afloat and cleared out his airway, which had come dangerously close to choking him on his own blood. With the help of a couple of young boys who had been drawn to the scene by the sound of the explosions, he had managed to float Colter's unconscious body gently to shore.

Bishop had rented one of those silly-looking plastic Citroens that pass for automobiles at the launch ramp, having come in on the afternoon flight. He had been almost to Michelle's Inn when he heard the explosions. He had hesitated after hearing the first, mentally checking off possible sources of the unexpected, powerful sound. At the sound of the second explosion, however, he had floored the little car's gas pedal and raced in the direction of the blasts. He had recognized the weapon.

He found the scene by following the crowds. Every

islander in that part of the island had come to see what had shattered the placid quiet of the Yacht Club's lagoon. It was a scene of devastation, of chaos. Rene's precious *Presque-Vivante* had sunk by the stern, and the wreckage was strewn everywhere. The torn and shattered corpse that had been Samantha Sandri was already wrapped in a piece of sailcloth on the beach when Bishop arrived, but the water near the broken sailboat was still pink with her blood. A team of men was working feverishly to remove Rene Iatape from the tangle of lines, severed halyards, and streamers of ripped nylon sailcloth in the shallows.

Bishop had realized immediately that Colter had been the target, and he furiously searched the area for any sign of his friend. He quickly questioned several bystanders, and was pointed in the direction of the far shore. He remounted the Citroen and raced around the edge of the bay, arriving at Colter's side just as he was being placed on the beach. His face had blood all over it, but he seemed to be breathing all right. His left arm was canted at a horrible angle, and Bishop instantly recognized the injury as a dislocated shoulder, having had one himself during his college football years. As Bishop searched for fractures and prepared to yank the arm back into its socket, a man had run up to them, stating that he was a doctor and asking if he could help. The man had held Colter's shoulder steady as Bishop pulled sharply on the wrist and elbow, popping the sprung joint back into place. Colter groaned initially, but then seemed much less agitated. The doctor had then told Bishop to go get some men to bring a stretcher.

Bishop might have done so, except that at that moment, Rene was being extracted from the wreckage and placed on a litter a little way down the beach, and people were calling out to see if anyone was a doctor or nurse, anything. Bishop sent the physician to Rene's aid, in terms that overrode the man's perhaps overprofessional reluctance to leave Colter's side.

It was only later, as Colter was being placed on a litter himself, that Bishop realized that A) the would-be assassin was still on the island, and therefore B) Colter was still in grave and immediate danger. He swiftly decided that Colter would not be leaving his sight, not for an instant. He told the rescue parties that Colter would not be taken with Rene to Papeete, that instead he would be recuperating under Bishop's own care, at Michelle's.

There was well-intentioned resistance to this idea, but Bishop had been adamant, demanding and accepting total responsibility for Colter's well-being. Bishop took what precautions he could in conveying the still-unconscious Colter to Michelle's Inn, which precautions mainly consisted of not letting anyone get very close to him. When Michelle herself found out what had happened, she had screamed abuse at Bishop for preventing Colter from being taken to Papeete, where he could get the best medical treatment available anywhere in the islands. She went white with shock as Bishop told her that Samantha was dead, that the killer had been trying for Colter, and that he would almost certainly try again. He told her with a quiet authority that Colter's best and only chance of coming through this thing alive was to stay as isolated and as closely guarded as possible, at least until he regained consciousness and was able to decide for himself. He convinced her that Colter's injuries were not serious enough to kill him, and allowed her to examine him herself.

"She has taken it very hard, Mitch," Bishop added with an implicit plea for Colter's understanding. "She's mad at me, and at you, too. We've brought death and ugliness into her home, and she's damn mad."

"How many people left the island with Rene?"

"Five. All Air Poly people, I checked."

"We need to seal off the island."

"Difficult."

"The Doctor is on this island."

"The doctor?"

"Krasnevin's assassin, the Doctor. It has to be him."

"Krasnevin is dead, Mitch."

"I don't give a fuck. If that's true, then somehow he got word to his pet killer first. It's him."

Bishop thought it over. "Possible . . ."

"Goddammit, it's *him*, I can *smell* him. The miracle is that somehow, he missed."

There was a sudden, sinking, crawly feeling in the pit of Bishop's stomach. "Doctor . . .? I wonder. . . Oh, sweet Jesus."

"What is it," Colter demanded, raising himself up on his good elbow.

Bishop's face had lost some of its color as he croaked, "I think. . . It's just possible that this Doctor was the guy who helped me set your shoulder." He stumbled through the details of the incident on the beach, the timely appearance of the man claiming to be a physician and his seeming reluctance to leave Colter's side, in spite of the manifest need for a doctor for Rene. Now it definitely seemed to Bishop that the man had wanted him to leave him alone with Colter. He had almost insisted on it.

Colter listened carefully, nodding his head. "That would make sense. The guy's got balls, I'll say that for him. He wouldn't have needed much time alone with me, not then." He looked at Bishop. "Looks a little bit like you saved my ass."

"I wish it was like that." Bishop shook his head. "It was just luck that kept me from leaving him with you."

Colter ignored this, asking, "Describe him. What does he look like?"

"Mid-early forties, about six feet, dark hair with a little gray, light eyes, blue, maybe gray, slim build. Speaks English well. Little or no accent. At least, I didn't notice any. No scars that I could see."

Colter drew a mental sketch from Bishop's description, then appeared to be thinking aloud: "Okay. He's gone to an alternate plan. He missed his target, and he didn't run for it. If he stays with his physician identity, he should be pretty easy to find, if he doesn't know he's being looked for. He had no reason to suspect that we're looking for him in particular, even though the police are obviously going to be investigating what happened at the dock. He may even try to come here . . ." Colter's voice faded away.

"Here?" Bishop prodded.

"It would make a certain amount of sense," Colter frowned, "for him to pay a courtesy call, just to see if the patient is still doing well."

"That *would* be balls. If he tries that, we've got him."

"Oh?" Colter asked, with a curious smile.

"What do you mean, 'Oh'?" Bishop returned, taken aback.

"Are you armed?"

"I - you mean right now?"

"Yes, you moron, I mean right now," Colter rumbled good-naturedly as he brought himself up to a sitting position.

Bishop opened his mouth to speak, thought it through, and then closed it again.

"So. You're unarmed," said Colter, beginning to flex the traumatized muscles in his shoulder. "And this guy, if he is who we think he is, has managed to bring at least a rocket launcher onto the island. Probably

227

other arms as well. He knows a lot of ways to kill, and he doesn't care who or how many have to die alongside his target." Colter took a deep, ragged breath, betrayed emotion held rigidly under the surface. "He's already killed Sam, and he wouldn't hesitate one second to take you, or Michelle, or anyone else who tried to stop him out, like a light. And you stand there, unarmed with your face hanging out, and tell me that if he knocks at the door, *we've* got *him*."

Bishop struggled to save face, saying, "Well, the airport is being watched by the *constabulaire*. I'll get them his description immediately. At least he won't be able to get off the island."

Colter grunted. "Another way of putting that would be, 'We can't get away from him.' And don't be so sure he hasn't got a boat somewhere, Steve. Go ahead and give the description out to the *gendarmerie*, but I don't think we have to worry about that very much. He doesn't want to leave the island, not yet. He needs an escape route, yes. But if this guy is Krasnevin's special, the Doctor, he's already decided to finish the case before he goes." Colter paused, struck by sudden thought. "I wonder if he knows that Krasnevin is dead? Are you sure Krasnevin *is* dead, Steve?"

"Positive. Terminated by KGB Agent Dancer, inside the clinic. Our own man there saw the wounds."

"Okay. I just wonder if our puppet knows that his strings have been cut."

"What difference does it make?"

"Maybe none" Colter spoke quietly, rising smoothly to his feet. From his full height, he looked down at Bishop. "Here's what I want you to do. Go back to the Yacht Club and ask around for the doctor who helped out this afternoon. Find out anything you can about him. You can say I've taken a turn for the worse, or something. Then come back here. I'm going to my house. I've got an Uzi hidden there."

"Wait a minute, Mitch, damn it, you can't just be going off on your own. You're in no condition to - " Bishop stopped in the middle of his own sentence as he saw the lights flashing in Colter's eyes.

"I want to thank you for looking after me this afternoon, Steve. If you hadn't got to me as fast as you did, I think I'd be dead now.

"But I'm not dead. What I am, is angry. Don't get in my way. If you want to help, then just do as I say, or stay out of it. This guy is much, much better than you are. He'll kill you quick if you make a mistake or become a threat to him.

"Until this guy is dead, anyone standing close to me is taking a big risk. I won't have that. You go back to the Yacht Club and find out where this guy is staying, how he got here, anything you can. But avoid him at all costs. Come back here in an hour or so, and I'll meet you and find out what you learned. After that, it's my show. Got it?"

Colter spoke with such calm, deadly assurance that Bishop realized immediately that no argument was possible. He found that he was very glad to be on Colter's side; the prospect of this man coming after *him* was not to be dwelt upon.

"Michelle is going to kill me, and then break my back."

"You didn't let me go. I just went."

"Why don't you tell her that?"

"You think I'm crazy?" Colter grinned. It was good to see him smile, Bishop reflected as Colter eased into his torn, salt-stained shirt as he made for the rear door to Michelle's bungalow.

Bishop turned back to the chair in which he had been sitting, and retrieved his jacket. When he turned around again, Colter was gone.

*   *   *

The Doctor watched silently as the young American friend of Colter's left the inn and walked off briskly in the direction of the Yacht Club. He quickly re-examined his options.

He could follow the friend. Perhaps he would be able to manage find out if Colter had regained consciousness, and if so, to find out something about his state of alertness. The injured Colter would surely know that an attempt had been made on his life, but what inference had he drawn? As far as Yuri knew, his cover as a charter-boat tourist was still good as gold. And no one would find out anything more by asking the charter-boat captain or his mate. Yuri had taken care of that.

He could do nothing. Posing as a tourist, he could merely wait until Colter emerged from the damnably located bungalow at the back of the prehistoric inn. The place was very hard to approach unseen.

He *could* press his cover, right now, and be finished with it. Make a "house call."

He decided to press it.

The Doctor had retrieved his black leather medical bag from the boat, and carried it with him as he stepped across the road in the fading light. The lights of the inn were on now, and a number of locals and two or three tourists sat in the warm twilight of the patio cafe, drinking wine and buzzing with conversation.

The Doctor stepped up to the bar rail and inquired in good French for directions to the room of the man who had been hurt earlier, down at the Yacht Club dock. Big man, shoulder injury, hard to miss. . .

"Oh yes, Mitch Colter . . ." came several helpful locals.

The barman, Jean-Louis, took in the black bag and replied helpfully, "*Oui, M'sieur Le Medecin; Un moment, s'il vous plait.*" He ran to fetch Francoise, his lover and chef. She had been helping out earlier.

Francoise emerged, wiping her hands on a dish towel, and asked Yuri what she could do for him.

"I'm a doctor, Madame," replied Yuri in his Americanized English, "and I treated this man Colter, and I just wanted to look in on him, and make sure that he's comfortable."

"You want the owner, M'sieur Le Medecin," and she turned, gesturing as Michelle came out of the kitchen into the soft evening light. "Michelle D'Alene."

"Sorry" Yuri replied to the introduction in courtly embarrassment, bending minutely at the waist as he took her hand, preparing to kiss it but remembering at the last second who he was *supposed* to be and turning the movement into a hearty handshake. "Forgot my manners, there. Name's Miller. Dr. Bert Miller. Pleased ta meetcha."

Michelle was relieved. She was fairly sure that Mitch was not too seriously hurt, but wasn't sure whether she would recognize internal injuries. She had been very cross with Bishop because of his pigheaded refusal to let them take Colter to Papeete along with Rene, and now a doctor comes to them! *Formidable!*

"But this is wonderful!" she sang to Yuri. "The big ape thinks he is indestructible, but I'm delighted to have you argue the point with him instead of me, for once. Come right this way, M'sieur, he is resting in my own bungalow, out at the back."

She led the Doctor out the breezeway at the rear of the building and across the open ground to her house. She was in front of him, and did not see him extract a silenced .32-caliber Colt revolver from it, nor did she notice as the gun disappeared inside the medical man's jacket.

When they were in the front room of the house, she turned to him and said, "Please wait here just a moment. I'll explain who you are and why you're here. He's. . . well, just wait, please." She went on through to the bedroom.

Yuri planned to use a hypodermic needle to kill Colter. The gun in his belt was merely a safety measure, in case something unexpected developed, and to insure his escape. He was sure that his cover was still intact, and that Colter had no reason to fear, never mind not to *allow*, the nice Canadian doctor to examine him. Therefore, he was checking the contents of the bag when Michelle stormed back into the room, fuming and swearing in French.

His hand automatically went for his gun, but he managed to stop just short of drawing or revealing the weapon. The outburst was merely surprising, not dangerous, his highly developed nervous system told him.

Michelle hadn't even noticed. "That cretin! I must apologize, M'sieur Docteur," she managed as she regained control, "for Bora's *enfant terrible*! It seems that he has gone. The big *bebe* has decided that he is well enough to travel, eh bien! *Enfin*, let him travel! *Bon voyage*!"

"But I thought that his injuries . . .?"

" . . .are in his brains! Yes. I'm very sorry for the troubles you have taken - M'sieur?"

Yuri had swiftly moved to the entrance to the bedroom, indeed so swiftly that Michelle had not had time to stop him. He checked the room swiftly, just to make sure that she was telling him the truth.

"M'sieur Docteur. I have told you, he is gone."

There was the first trace of suspicion in her voice, and Yuri didn't want to kill her if he could avoid it. It would slow him down.

"Yup, he sure is. Had a patient hide under the bed on me, one time. Afraid of needles, he was. Well, I guess he must be doing okay, then" he grinned at her, and gave her a little chuckle.

"Yes. He is, yes." Any fledgling suspicion Michelle had been growing was now diverted back into her annoyance with Colter. "To hell with him," she snapped, stepping outside the bungalow and holding the door open for the Doctor.

Leaving, Yuri asked, as casually as he could manage, "Where do you suppose he might have gone? Home?"

"Hah! Who cares? Probably! I hope a coconut falls on his thick head and he forgets his name. Better - he forgets my name!" Even though her characteristic response placed her in a steaming snit, she knew that she was secretly glad that Colter was well enough to travel. She was actually more hurt that he had gone off without telling her.

"He has a house on the island? I thought you had to be French to own a house here . . ." the doctor was commenting.

She said yes, and absent mindedly described its location for him, along with the circumstances of its ownership. As they came together into the bar area, she asked him politely if he would like to have a drink, or perhaps a glass of wine, as a guest of the house.

"Thank you, but I can't," Yuri demurred. "I'm afraid I have to be getting back. Nice to meetcha. Glad your friend is better." Yuri walked off down the road, in the direction of the Yacht Club, until he was sure that he was out of view of Michelle's Inn.

Then he stepped down to the water's edge, only

meters away from the road but nearly invisible in the full darkness. He made his way back in the direction from which he had come, past Michelle's, and stepped back out onto the road some distance beyond, in the direction of Colter's house.

He had a fairly good idea where the house was, from her description and from his study of the tourist map. He took the revolver from his waistband and replaced it in his black bag. He wouldn't need it now. If Colter had left at about the same time as the younger American, Yuri wasn't too far behind him. And if Colter was alone at his house, Yuri would make sure to get him, this time. Things were working out, after all.

He quickened his pace, smiling in the warm darkness.

* * *

"Anybody on board?"

The charter-sailer *Kili-Iti* was dark, even though Bishop could see that it had been connected to the dockside power. From talking to the barmaid and one or two locals, he had established to his own satisfaction that the doctor who had helped out at the scene earlier had arrived at the island on this charter boat, early that day. However, he hadn't been able to confirm this by talking either to the charter captain or his mate. He was told that they had been drinking pretty heavily, and had probably returned to their bunk aboard ship to sleep it off.

Colter had told him pointedly not to make any direct contact with the doctor, whose current *nom de guerre* was apparently Dr. Bert Miller. But no one had seen Dr. Miller aboard or anywhere else recently, and

Bishop felt fairly certain that he was was not aboard the *Kili-Iti*. And he wanted to talk to the charter's crew, even if it meant waking them from an alcoholic slumber.

"Aboard the *Kili-Iti*! Anybody home?" he shouted.

There was no reply from the dark, silent motor-sailer. Bishop looked around, but there was no one paying any attention to him, so he cautiously walked up the short gangplank and stepped aboard. The boat rocked only slightly as it adjusted to the additional, new weight on its decks.

Bishop's senses came to piano-wire tension as he tried to discern signs of life: snoring, music, or any other sounds from belowdecks. The companionway hatch was open, and he made his way cautiously through it in the eerie silence. He didn't like it. He felt that any moment he would be jumped from the darkness by a drunken, half-asleep sea-hand with a filetting knife or a shark gaff in his hands.

"Permission to come aboard?"

No answer. Nothing, not even a sleepy grunt of protest. Just the electric silence. Bishop didn't want to be taken for a thief, so he located the electrical panel on the port bulkhead and flipped a switch marked INT CAB LTS.

That was better. The boat's interior was flooded with a soft yellow glow, and Bishop felt less like an intuder. He was just beginning to relax, figuring that the captain and his mate must be having dinner ashore, when he saw the blood.

His skin crawled. There were only a couple of smears, on and around the lid of one of the sea lockers which doubled as benches in the galley. It was labeled "Running Rigging Aux," but Bishop had a sudden, sickening premonition of what he would find inside it. He disengaged the latch and threw back the lid.

He was right. Both the captain and the mate had huge, deep gashes (*incisions*, Bishop thought involuntarily) across their throats, and now the burnt-copper smell of blood assailed Bishop's nostrils as he fought back the bile in his throat. They had been stuffed into the sea locker like so much meat. Discarded and hidden.

Bishop stood there for long seconds, trying to think in the face of death. Finally, he shook off his inertia and closed the lid again, relatching the locker precisely as he had found it. Quickly then, as his mind began to react to his own situation, he lunged for the electrical panel, switching off the interior cabin lights as quickly as he could, plunging himself once again into darkness. He had realized that if the murderous Dr. Miller was anywhere nearby, he might see the lights inside the boat, and Bishop would be marked indelibly for the same fate as the two sailors and Samantha.

And Colter. He had to get to Colter. This was absolute confirmation in spades that the man who had played the Good Samaritan earlier that day was, in fact, the Doctor. Colter had to be told. As Bishop made his way aft, toward the hatchway, he had to fight his professional's impulse to stay a while longer; to search "Dr. Miller's" gear; to sabotage the boat so that it could not afford the assassin an escape route. He wanted desperately to spike the enemy's guns.

But even as he had the thought, he knew the priority was to get to Colter. And then, simply by chance, Bishop's eyes came to rest on the boat's shark rifle.

It's a common piece of seagoing equipment, like a fire extinguisher or a rack of life vests. After a while, you don't notice it. Standard equipment in these waters, it was mounted on brackets just inside the starboard side of the hatch. Bishop snatched it off the brackets and examined it.

It was a Winchester 30-30, lever-action hunting rifle, old but obviously serviceable and well looked after. And it was fully loaded. Bishop hesitated, deciding.

He took it with him. Chances were good that the Doctor wouldn't even notice its absence, it not being part of his own arsenal. Furthermore, Bishop might need it to defend himself before this was over. He ran the weapon down his trouser leg as soon as he got out on deck, making sure that no one was watching. He put his hand in his pocket and gripped the butt end of the rifle firmly as he walked, only slightly stiff-legged, back down the pier.

Within minutes, he was safely on his way back to Michelle's to keep his rendezvous with Colter.

* * *

Colter had used caution that bordered on suspicion to approach his own house. He was all but certain that no one could have predicted his arrival, but he was also certain that he was up against a professional, so he made absolutely certain that A) the house was empty and B) no one had been there since he had left with Samantha that morning, to go sailing.

He felt a sharp tug at his heart as he remembered her impatience with him while he had closed up the house with his habitual, meticulous tradecraft.

"Jesus Christ, Mitch, it's not as if you've got the crown jewels in there. Let's go!" she had urged. He had just smiled at her, and finished setting his telltales.

Now, he was glad that he had.

He forced the image of Samantha's face and form from his mind. When he was satisfied that the house was safe to enter, he did so quickly. The first thing he did when he was inside was to check and make sure that both his emergency quick-exits were operational. Now that he was in, he simply double-checked that he could get out.

Everything was fine, so Colter moved into his large bedroom and removed a section of the headboard of his bed. Behind the panel, recessed into the wall, he had fashioned a tightly fitted compartment known only to him. He reached inside it and felt in the dark space. His night vision was just fine, and turning on the lights was contraindicated in any case.

He pulled out a cloth-wrapped bundle and tossed it on the bed, opening it to reveal the serviceable shape of the Israeli-made Uzi submachine gun. He quickly ran the action, verifying that it was clean and working, and snapped a clip into place. He took a roll of black ducttape from a nearby drawer, and began to tape the second clip upside down to the first. Thus, when the ammo in the first clip was expended, Colter could speed-reload by merely flipping the used clip upside down. It was a trick he had learned long ago, and it saved precious seconds at precisely the right time.

Another trick was his choice of ammunition. He had managed to get hold of several boxes of Glazer cartridges in the proper calibers, through the Chinaman. These were outlawed in many countries. Instead of a normal lead projectile the Glazers threw twelve-gauge shot, suspended in liquid Teflon and jacketed in lead. At impact, the bullet ruptured, sending its contents everywhere inside the victim's body. It was devastating. A man hit in the arm would lose that arm, and no one had ever survived a hit in the torso.

Colter stripped off his ruined shirt and tossed it into a corner. He reached again into his hiding place, and drew out his Kevlar "Second Chance" body armor. It had been specially fitted for him by the expert CIA armorers at the Farm, and he had taken it with him when he "retired." He slipped it on, and buckled it securely. His shoulder was hurting badly, but his pace never slowed. He had no way of knowing how much time he had.

His plan of action, if he could call it that, fell into three fairly simple steps: Identify, Search Out, and Destroy. He was sure that Bishop's suspicions of the man on the beach were well founded, but he had to be sure. He needed to hear what Bishop had been able to find out. Then, and only then, it would become a fairly straightforward manhunt. Colter wanted to get himself as far away from any innocent bystanders as he could; that would probably mean luring the killer up into the jungle-covered hills on or around Mount Pahia. Therefore, he was going to need to take a supply of water with him.

Colter went to the cedar cabinet and removed a web belt and canteen from the bottom drawer, then went to the kitchen to fill it. Just as he completed this task and turned off the water, he heard a soft, chiming sound from the bedroom. It was one of his telltales.

At the bottom of the pathway up to the house, someone had stepped on one of the two pressure plates which were concealed in the ground. Someone was coming to see him.

Calmly but quickly, Colter strapped on the canteen and returned to the bedroom. He picked up the Uzi, and replaced the headboard panel. Then he froze, listening.

His hands moved silently over the Uzi's smooth metal.

He flipped the safety lever to OFF.

*   *   *

Yuri hadn't expected the house to be dark.

He stood in the pathway just below the house, thinking fast. If he were actually who he was pretending to be, the proper, expected action would be simply to march right up to the house and knock on the door.

But the house was dark.

If Colter was inside, surely there would be at least one light on, somewhere. Unless the injured man had been so exhausted by his ordeal of this afternoon that he had merely collapsed on the bed, heedless?

If Colter was not inside, however, things took on a different look entirely. Perhaps Colter had not come here at all, in spite of that hotel woman's guesswork. Perhaps he had gone somewhere else first, and hadn't arrived here yet. Perhaps the target would appear at any minute; that was also possible.

The Doctor couldn't be sure. He needed to know for certain. He stepped forward, through the gate. As he unknowingly tripped the pressure-plate chime in Colter's bedroom, the night-sounds of the island combined with a faint, familiar, city-type sound. It was barely audible, but Yuri Turpenov had had much experience separating one night-sound from another. Suddenly, it came to him with crystalline clarity.

It was the sound of a water faucet being turned off.

Colter was in the house, conscious and moving around, with the lights off.

Turpenov's interior alarms systems went off. He suddenly re-evaluated the possibility that he was blown. The image of the younger American leaving the inn with a purposeful stride came to him unbidden. He had been walking toward the dock area. . . the bodies on the boat. And Colter's house was dark.

Trap?

No. Not yet, it couldn't be.

Still, Turpenov was a professional and knew the first rule. He would just have to go on the assumption that his cover was blown, and proceed accordingly. He could no longer go to the door, passing himself off as a helpful tourist doc, but he *did* have the man Colter located, inside the house.

As the Russian glided into the shadows cast by the tall coconut palms, he thought, *This time I've got him.*

I'll just take out the whole house.

He had everything he needed, with him. Crouching now, behind a clump of bougainvillea, he opened his black bag and lifted out a soft brick of a putty-like substance favored by terrorists: Cyclonite-four, also known as plastic explosive. He attached a KGB-type detonator-timer to the entire lump, and looked at the house with an appraising eye.

Like so many island houses, it was essentially one large room under a roof, subdivided into separate rooms by mere panelling. Turpenov knew that if the plastique went off anywhere inside, this huge quantity of explosive would shatter anything and everything in the structure, blowing out the walls and collapsing the roof into a fiery inferno.

The Doctor moved closer now, picking a window through which to deliver the lethal surprise.

*   *   *

Colter had seen the Doctor disappear into the edges of the palm grove. Just for an instant.

It was enough. He had had his first glimpse of Samantha's killer. He was sure it was the Russian assassin now. The man even carried a black doctor's

241

bag!

He was certainly on no errand of mercy tonight, the way he was moving easily and swiftly from shadow to shadow in the moonlit night. He looked experienced, and calm. He moved like a professional.

Colter couldn't see where he had gone and wouldn't even try to guess what the man was up to. He was probably waiting for some sign of activity in the house, or even for Colter to emerge on the front porch in the morning. Anything was possible. Looking out the living room window toward the palm grove, Colter jacked a round into the chamber of the Uzi, and mentally prepared himself to wait for hours, or to move in an instant, whichever was needed.

With time to think, Colter found that he was a little alarmed at the ease with which the Doctor had located him. There were many people who might have told a helpful-seeming man of medicine where Colter lived, but only Bishop knew for sure that Colter had come here now. The Doctor must have been to the inn; Michelle would have been only too glad to have Colter seen by a doctor, and on finding that Colter had gone might have assumed that he had come here. That made more sense than finding anything out from Bishop. Colter hoped that Michelle was all right. He hoped that the Doctor had been plausible, and that Michelle had not suspected anything amiss, had not tried to interfere with the man in any way . . .

There.

There had been only a second's movement in the darkness, but Colter had been watching for it. He saw the object being thrown, and knew it instantly for what it was: a bomb.

Always, at the first moment of combat, there was that sense of being a spectator. There was a reluctance to move, to act, in spite of the intellectual cue. This form of inertia had killed many men in battle, frozen them like rabbits under a spotlight as the enemy tank hove into view for the first time. Many a trained soldier had found himself simply watching in open-mouthed amazement, realizing that the enemy was, indeed, willing to actually *kill* him. It is this form of shock which makes the difference between a trained recruit and a seasoned combat veteran. Veterans have learned to ignore this "spectator" effect, and as a result, usually live longer.

Colter was a veteran, and even though the balmy tropical night seemed inviolate, even though this could not be happening here, Colter reacted instantly and without another glance at the airborne explosive.

In three quick strides, he was at the specially designed window, which sprang open as he hit it in a flying dive. It opened outward, as a door, allowing the big man to fly clear of the house just as the deadly satchel of plastique crashed through the kitchen window, disturbing the night-quiet with the distinctive sound of breaking glass.

Colter hit the ground with the back of his right shoulder, already rolling to absorb the impact of the fall, and was on his feet and running for the cover of the grove of palm trees before the tinkling sound of broken glass faded away.

And then a volcano erupted behind him.

The ground shook violently, and there was a blinding flash of white-hot light which destroyed Colter's nightvision even at the distance he had managed from the house. The blast of the shock wave hit him with the impact of a giant fist and sent him flying headlong into the darkness.

The Russian had used much more explosive than was necessary. The house simply burst like a balloon, sending sections of wall, flying glass shards, pieces of furniture and clumps of roof thatching everywhere. The blast drove all the air away from the center of the house, creating a vacuum. When the initial force of the explosion was spent, the air rushed back like an express train to fill it. This created a second shock wave, but in the other direction, which flattened the few remaining sections of the structure. The return of the air also brought oxygen, to feed the freshly kindled fire.

The house was simply gone. Fire spread quickly through the splintered remains, obliterating anything recognizable and casting horrible, unnatural shadows in the smoky light.

Colter's body armor had repelled what might have been a killing blow from a shard of razor-sharp metal, and he found that he was uninjured, except for his newly painful shoulder. He looked meditatively into the flames of the ruin of his house, his eyes pale and hard.

But he did not linger. The Doctor now thought that he was dead, and his guard would lower. And looking across the clearing, Colter could make a very good guess as to the Russian killer's exact location.

Colter began to move.

CHAPTER FIFTEEN

The Doctor's ears were still ringing from the explosion, so he could not be sure what he was hearing. There seemed to be excited voices shouting nearby, coming from the direction of the road. That was to be expected, of course, but Turpenov knew that he didn't want to be nearby when the crowd gathered, if there was going to be one.

Yet he didn't want to leave, either. His impulse was to go closer to the ruins, to see if he could find some positive trace of Colter's corpse. He knew that no one could survive such an incredible conflagration, but his training made him desire absolute proof. He had not *seen* Colter die.

Usually, he arranged a killing so that he was present: if not face to face with his victim, then at least observing from nearby. This man Colter had proved harder to kill than most, but that hadn't been Turpenov's fault. Anyway, the man was certainly dead now.

Yuri looked at the silenced revolver in his hand. He had taken it from the black bag as soon as he had thrown the bomb, as a precaution. Had Colter somehow survived the blast and dragged himself clear of the wreckage, Turpenov would have merely walked up to him and put two shots into his brain. He considered putting it away, but decided to keep it at hand, for the present. He was finished now, on his way home, and didn't want anyone getting in his way. If that young friend of Colter's had found the bodies on the *Kili-Iti*, he could take care of that on the way. But Colter was finally dead.

He fought back the recurring desire to approach the ruins of Colter's house to find the actual proof of his success and began to back cautiously away from the firelit clearing, into the deeper darkness of the palm jungle.

* * *

Colter knew that he was in the right spot to detect any movement from the Doctor. The man wouldn't have moved too far away from where he must have been to throw the bomb. Colter kept his face oriented away from the flames, allowing his night vision to return.

Just one glimpse of him, Colter thought grimly.

Colter himself would have been hard to spot. He had taken a charred piece of planking which had been thrown clear of the destruction and used its charcoallike surface as guerrillas use lampblack or shoe polish, to blacken his face in smeared stripes, and the same with his throat and arms. The Kevlar body armor was dark gray itself, and Colter's jeans were dirty and non reflective. He had rubbed enough soot and charcoal into his hair to take the shine away, and only his eyes were pale enough to see. He presented an altogether frightening aspect.

He heard a sound.

The ringing in his ears had faded, and he was just

bringing the Uzi to bear on the area from which the small noise had come when the unexpected occurred.

Nestled in the palm fronds some forty feet above his head, a fully mature coconut, loosened by the shock wave from the explosion, quietly disengaged itself from the tree and began to fall to the earth, gathering speed at the rate of sixteen feet per second every second, toward a spot some five meters in front of Colter and slightly to his left. At impact it was traveling at exactly forty-four miles per hour, and it made a hell of a noise.

Colter's instinctive reaction was to shoot it, and he did. Even as he loosed the five-shot burst from the Uzi, completely destroying the coconut, he realized his mistake.

By then, however, it was too late. The noise of the rapid-firing combat weapon had destroyed any hope of surprising the Doctor, and it had also given his position away. Colter took cover, just as two supersonic bees flew past his head and tore twin trails through the jungle behind him.

Silencer, he thought automatically.

Colter moved quickly but quietly to his left, keeping close to the ground and deep in shadow, trying to get into a position which would prevent the Russian from moving any farther away from the road than he was now. He didn't know what the other man's reaction would be, but the Doctor had to be surprised, and thinking fast.

Maybe Colter could get him to make a mistake.

* * *

Memories were flooding into Yuri Turpenov's consciousness, unbidden and unwanted. Night. Jungle.

Gunfire. Heat. Listening with straining, desperate concentration to any sound, every sound, coming from the darkness. Lightheaded and breathless, Yuri tried to think, to *concentrate*.

He couldn't believe it. Colter was alive. Not only alive, but armed and moving around in the jungle close by. How in the world . . .?

The Russian was sweating now, straining in the effort to keep his mind on the situation at hand. If he lived, he could figure it all out later; but if he didn't get his mental energies under control, and right now, Colter was going to kill him.

Choices. Make a choice. What are the choices? the killer screamed silently.

The memories persisted. The haunting similarity between the situation he was in now and the countless nights in the Mekong Delta which had formed him into what he was rushed in on him. For a moment he was confused; he couldn't remember who the unseen enemy was. Green Berets? ARVN troops? No. This was not Vietnam. That was another lifetime ago, in his youth.

This was Bora Bora. An island in the South Pacific . . . and Mitchell Colter was the enemy.

Choices. He could not hear Colter moving, but he reasoned that the man must be changing his position. Which way?

Logically, Colter would try to prevent him from getting out. Therefore, he would try to block him from regaining the road. Or would he? He might take the high ground, to block him from going deeper into the island's protective, concealing jungle. The deep jungle on the hills and mountainsides of the island seemed suddenly very attractive to the Russian. It was his area of expertise, his personal background, his style.

But Colter might be expecting him to move in that direction. That left. . .

248

Of course.

Back to the house. There would be other people there by now, curious islanders drawn by the blast and the flames. The American would not be expecting him to move in that direction, and he would be able to simply walk right through the clearing, past the ruins of the house, and into the night on the other side of Colter's property. Into the jungle, and the hills.

Turpenov's earlier zeal, his killing lust, was a dim memory at this point. Colter was alive, and dangerous. He would set another kind of trap for Colter, later. Meanwhile, he had to survive.

The Russian slipped the silenced handgun under his jacket, into his belt, and picked up his bag, already moving silently toward the flickering light and sounds of the excited Tahitian voices.

*   *   *

Colter was uneasy. It wasn't right, somehow, but he couldn't figure out what was wrong.

The Russian wouldn't, *couldn't* simply wait him out. This was Colter's territory, his *turf*, and the Doctor would know it. Furthermore, there wasn't enough cover here in the grove to play a waiting game. No; the Doctor is going to have to move.

But he wasn't moving.

Colter had been in a perfect position for minutes now, and he felt sure that the Russian could not have gotten by him undetected.

So where was he?

Colter went over it again, mentally putting himself in the Doctor's situation. Back to the road? Not likely he'd be willing to expose himself that openly, not after the kind of shock he'd had. He'll want to get hidden, get away, get away from Colter, away from the fire and the crowd of. . .

Shit.

Not *away* from the crowd, *toward* the crowd. It was the classic unexpected direction, providing both surprise and the cover of milling bodies to get clear. From there. . .

Colter was already moving. His quarry wasn't going to come this way or he would have done so by now. The bastard was running, and that was his first mistake. Colter knew the island as well as a native, and he knew how to track an enemy, even at night.

As Colter trotted around the high ground behind the remains of his house, he could see the shapes of perhaps a dozen of his neighbors, come to help out in the emergency.

Then, at the other side of the clearing, Colter saw him. At first he wasn't sure, in the failing light and the smoke, if his eyesight was tricking him or not. He stopped and took a better look just as the figure, still carrying the unmistakable black doctor's bag, melted off into the darkness at the far edge of the clearing.

Colter took a drink of water from his canteen. He knew the terrain in front of the Russian, and knew that the man would be forced to move fairly slowly. There would be fewer chances to pause and refresh himself from now on, he knew, and he didn't make the mistake of ignoring the fact that he had been recently injured. As a result of the adrenaline pumping through his system, he didn't feel tired, but he knew the kind of exhaustion a night-track through the jungle could inflict. He took another drink of blessed, cool water, and replaced the canteen.

He moved out, arriving quickly and with little effort made to remain unseen. In fact, he had considered taking the time to give someone at the fire a message for Bishop, but decided that he couldn't spare the seconds.

Facing the darkness, Colter considered the moves that his target was likely to take in view of the terrain. He would probably want to get his back against the cliffs of Mount Pahia for safety, and he would be looking for a good natural layout to trap and ambush anyone following. Colter knew of several possibilities. He would just have to follow, stay invisible, and see what happened.

Colter disappeared into the darkness.

*   *   *

Michelle had seen Bishop return to the inn, walking with a curious, stiff-legged gait, but she had been too busy with her customers at the time to confront him. He had disappeared out the back breezeway, headed in the direction of her bungalow. She had been about to follow him when Levalier, drunk as usual, had set up a fuss and distracted her.

When the sound of the explosion reached her ears, some minutes later, she felt her skin crawl. It had come from the exact direction of Mitch's house. Suddenly dizzy, she sat down to await bad news.

It wasn't long in coming. First some boys from Viatape came running along the road, yelling about a huge explosion at the big American's house. Right behind them, three men from the Club Med staff came running in to use the telephone at the inn. While one of them summoned the Fire Department, a pitiful service but the only one on the island, Michelle managed to extract a fairly coherent account of the incident from the other two.

They hadn't witnessed the actual blast, but they were sufficiently graphic in their descriptions of the result to make Michelle feel faint with nausea. She drank a little water and was mentally preparing herself to go to the site of the fire when she remembered Bishop.

She found him in her bungalow, sitting calmly at the back door with a rifle across his knees. He was looking out into the darkness of the jungle, but gave a start as she opened the door, stopping himself from bringing the rifle up to firing position as he recognized her.

"Oh. It's you," he said uselessly.

"Just what the hell is going on here?" she demanded.

"Was that an explosion, a while back?" he countered.

"Yes. Mitch's whole house is blown up. No one knows if he was in it, oh, God, Steve . . ." She choked as her frustration and anger gave way to fear and despair. "He's dead, they. . . they're saying he's dead, and I - " she stopped, unable to continue.

"Michelle?" Bishop's voice was different from its usual casual tone, somehow. "Don't worry, now. He's not dead, he's fine. Get a hold of yourself," he comforted, moving toward her.

"How the hell do you know that? Bastard! You stand in my house with a gun in your hands, in my house!" she screamed at him.

"Calm down! Tell me what you've heard!"

"Don't tell me to calm down! Get out of my house!"

"Michelle," Bishop began with icy quietness, "it's important that you tell me what you've heard. Sit down, please." She sat, reluctantly. "Now listen to me. A man has come to Bora to kill Mitch. He tried this afternoon, but he missed. Mitch knows who he is, and he's watching out for him to try again. I don't think that anyone alive could kill Mitch Colter when he's been alerted this way. There's been a big noise, but no one has seen a body, have they?"

"I - I don't know. No, I didn't hear that."

"No. That's good. That means that we assume that Mitch is still alive."

"I'm going up there," she said determinedly, rising.

"Not right now. Sit down, please." She sat. "Just listen. You can go later if you want, I can't stop you. But Mitch and I talked about this man. Mitch sent me to check up on him, and I did. Now, I'm supposed to wait right here for Mitch to come and find out what I learned, understand?"

Michelle was somewhat comforted by the fact that Bishop persisted in using the present tense with regard to Colter. She had involuntarily been thinking of him as dead already, and she found the CIA man's strong, quiet denial of this to be soothing. She nodded, trying to focus on his words.

"So Mitch knows where I am. I'm right where he wants me to be. I don't know what that explosion was all about, but we should both stay right here, until Mitch comes. *He will come, Michelle.*"

"When?"

"I don't know. But it doesn't matter, and I'm going to tell you why. "When Mitch realized that this man was after him, his first reaction was to get away from anyone else, so that no one would be hurt, understand? He wants to protect you, and me, and everybody else from getting hurt by accident. See?

"But now listen; even if things go wrong, Mitch would be wanting you to stay here with me. I'm sure he's all right, but even if he isn't, our job is to stay right here until this thing is over. There's nothing you can do to help him other than stay out of the way. If he needs us to help him, he'll know exactly where to find us, and he won't have to go looking all over the island. Understand?"

"Yes. I - when was he supposed to come back? To find out what you learned?"

It was already past the hour that Colter had mentioned, but Bishop saw no point in adding further alarm to Michelle's emotional balance. "He didn't say," Bishop lied levelly "He just said to wait here."

"Who is this man? This man who tries to kill Mitch?"

"He's a . . ." How to put it? "He's a Russian, a very. . . dangerous man, but Mitch will take care of him, don't worry."

"A Russian? What Russian? There are no Russians on the island."

"He's pretending to be a Canadian doctor named Miller, but he's. . . what's the matter? Michelle?"

Her color had suddenly gone bad, even under the tropical tan. Bishop was afraid she was going to collapse.

"Oh, *Le Bon Dieu, non*, I. . . "

"Michelle!"

"I. . . I have done a terrible thing, I. . . I did not know . . ."

Michelle gave Bishop a halting account of the Doctor's visit, telling him that she had shown him right into the house here and given him directions to find Colter's house. He had seemed genuine, just a friendly tourist trying to help out.

Slowly and carefully, Bishop led her through the entire encounter, assessing the damage. Under his gentle prodding, Michelle remembered one tiny moment of unease.

"When he finally introduced himself, it seemed to me for a moment that he was about to kiss my hand. Americans or Canadians never do that, and I forgot about it then, but I remember being curious. Enfin, he shook my hand like an American."

Bishop nodded, and continued his questions until he was sure that he had an accurate, complete picture of the incident. He told Michelle that it was all right, the Doctor could have gotten the same directions by asking almost anyone, Michelle had not done anything wrong. In fact, had she seemed suspicious of the man, he might have. . . hurt her.

With Bishop's permission, Michelle went back to the inn to tell her staff that she didn't feel well and was going to lie down. On her way back, she selected a bottle of good French cognac from the bar.

While Michelle busied herself with opening and pouring the cognac, Bishop went back to his post, listening carefully but deep in thought.

What he had told Michelle was true, as far as it went. Mitch would indeed expect Bishop to remain where he was, and to make sure that Michelle came to no harm. Bishop had no idea what had happened, what had caused the explosion or where Colter was at the moment, but he knew to stay put. If the Doctor had died in the explosion, Colter would be here in minutes, if he was able to move. If they had both died in the blast, staying here on guard couldn't hurt anything. But if Colter had died alone in the explosion, what then? Would the Russian leave the island? He could sail the *Kili-Iti* alone, Bishop was sure; hell, he could use just the engine as far as Papeete. But what if he noticed the missing shark rifle? Would he suspect that Bishop had discovered the bodies?

Also, and Bishop would not mention this to Michelle, the Doctor was now aware of the special

255

relationship between Colter and Michelle, and he had actually been inside this bungalow. He knew the exact layout. It was not a comforting thought.

Bishop again considered changing their location. He could easily keep watch from one of the hotel's rooms. He could take Michelle with him. But he decided against this action, for the reason that things might start happening very fast, and he wanted to be exactly where Colter would look, if the going got sticky.

He worked the lever-style action of the old rifle, chambering a round. Michelle started, surprised by the ominous sound, and looked at Bishop. He returned her gaze evenly.

"So. We wait?" she asked.

"We wait," Bishop replied.

* * *

It was past midnight when the Doctor set his second ambush.

He knew he was being followed. He had known for over an hour, or suspected, anyway. As inconceivable as it was, the man Colter had managed to second-guess his route of escape from the devastated house, and *follow*. Turpenov didn't know of anyone who he had ever heard of doing such a thing, even the wildly reckless Rangers in Vietnam. The Doctor doubted whether he himself could have done it. This Colter was turning out to be more than he had bargained for.

When he had set the first ambush, he had still been hoping that he was wrong, that he was not being tracked, at night, through jungle. He was hoping that he was merely responding to perfectly normal, understandable paranoia. Still, he had set up the trap as though Colter was right on his heels. He used a natural formation of the terrain, a section of sloping hillside which funneled between two massive shoulders of volcanic rock. He had passed between them normally, making a definite but not an obvious track. Then he had doubled back, and climbed up onto the higher of the two shoulders, gaining a vantage point over the narrow passage. From his position, he had been sure that anyone following him would have naturally proceeded through the narrow space and into his field of fire. He had set himself, and waited.

Colter had not come.

Just at the point when Yuri had begun to sell himself on the idea that it was merely his imagination, he had spotted movement from a clump of brush *across* from his own position, on the other shoulder of rock! Colter had avoided the ambush and had almost overtaken him! He had known the terrain so well that he was cautiously avoiding all possible dangerous features of it, even going to the length of climbing steep rock out of his way to do so.

The Doctor had moved on, swiftly.

Now he was trying again. The chase had taken both the hunter and the hunted a good way up the slopes of Mount Pahia, and Turpenov was encountering steadily steeper terrain. He had found a cleft in the rocky hillside, at the top of a lava scree, a small field of loose, gravel-like rock. No one would be able to move across it undetected, and from the Russian's place of concealment he would have acceptable angles of fire. Colter would have to cross it, if he meant to continue the chase.

The wind, stronger at this elevation than at sea level, had blown the clouds away. The moon cast a bright white wash over the killing ground, almost a glare. Yuri felt more confident, this time. Colter had been cautious and strong, and skilled, and lucky, but his luck was about to run out.

The Doctor had never missed, at this range.

*   *   *

Colter stopped to rest. He removed the canteen from his belt and took three big swallows. His shoulder was on fire, and his legs were shaky with the strain he had put them under. The improved light up here was in his favor, he decided, and that was just as well, because he was close. He could feel it.

Colter wasn't sure that the Doctor had set an ambush back at the narrow defile between the rocky shoulders, but he thought so. His quarry was still being careful to leave the minimum trail, so Colter figured that he was well aware of the fact that he was being followed. That was all right. They were on an island; there was nowhere the Russian could go.

He replaced the canteen in its cloth jacket on his belt, mentally reviewing the lie of the ground just ahead. There was a lava scree which would require him to come out into the open in order to cross it. Beyond, the rocky base of the cliffs of Mount Pahia. Another excellent spot for an ambush.

Colter wasn't wearing a wristwatch, but he could tell from the position of the moon that it was well past midnight. He wondered, briefly, what Bishop was doing; whether or not he had had the sense to stay at the inn, regardless of the inevitable reports of fiery death and destruction at Colter's house. He could only hope that the younger man had not been rattled too much, and that he had Michelle safely under his wing. At least Colter had been able to chase the killer out to a removed location.

Without moving from his shadowy-dark location, Colter exercised the muscles in his legs, back, and arms, to prevent them from becoming stiff. When he was satisfied that everything was in working order, he moved out, keeping close to the ground as he approached the edge of the jungle which formed the lower border of the scree.

Looking out over the field of volcanic gravel, he easily spotted the route by which the Doctor had ascended. It would have been impossible for the man to have passed without leaving a clear trail. From the look of it, Colter guessed that the man would be hiding now, somewhere along the top edge near the base of the cliffs, waiting for Colter to follow the trail out into the open. Therefore, Colter would not do so.

The big American considered his options. If the Doctor was indeed hiding where Colter thought he was, then the Russian had unwittingly put himself in a box. He would be hard pressed to get out of his present location without Colter seeing him, even from here. Colter wondered if he was aware of that fact. The only way for the Russian to move from there would be straight up the cliff face, or back the way he had come. In a pinch, he might also try to edge his way sideways, along the rocks, trying to reach the tangle of jungle thirty or forty meters to his left. But for that, he had simply picked the wrong night. There was no way that Colter could miss him, if he did that. Not in such strong moonlight.

So Colter could simply wait. Wait him out. The man was edgy, he had no water, and he couldn't get out. Or Colter could circle, using the jungle for cover, and try to come at him either from the side or from above.

As Colter lay on his stomach, thinking, he noticed that the moonlight's shadow had crept minutely away from him and that the muzzle of the Uzi was now exposed to the glowing light. He drew it back into darkness.

Suddenly, Colter's eyes narrowed, and he looked up at the silvery orb in the sky with renewed concern. He had forgotten just how fast the moon moved; and how fast the shadows changed. It was true that the whole area was brightly lit at the moment, but it was equally true that it wouldn't stay that way. Colter figured that he had less than an hour before the shadows would darken the Doctor's hiding place and begin to creep swiftly across the open lava field, as the moon began to sink behind the bulky tower of Mount Pahia.

He reluctantly decided that he could not just wait. If the Russian realized that he was trapped, he would have a very good chance of escape in the first few moments of the cliff's moonshadow. Colter would have to go after him.

Colter silently backed away from the open field and began to circle to his right, moving swiftly.

* * *

The ambush had gone sour, the Doctor realized, and that was not the worst of it.

He had been so intent on the kill, so sure that Colter would present him with a target this time, that he had not taken the basic, standard precaution of providing himself with a back door. And when he had begun to suspect that the American had smelled the trap, he had been horrified to realize that he could not get out safely.

It was a stupid, amateurish mistake in a field where you didn't get to make any mistakes. Turpenov was stunned to realize that he, the Doctor, had made it. He fought back the panic of the caged animal, and tried to think.

Maybe he's not even out there, he tried wildly.

Nonsense. Believe that, and you'll certainly die, he answered himself mentally. Although it was true that Turpenov had not actually seen Colter following him, and even allowing for the possibility that the movement in the brush which he had seen at the site of the first ambush was merely the rustle of some innocent night creature, Yuri knew that Colter was out there. He just knew. He could sense him.

He was unbearably thirsty. Parched. He had not had a drink of water since. . . God, how long ago? He had been sweating, and using terrible amounts of energy, and he was now seriously dehydrated, he knew. His doctor's bag contained many useful things, but plain, ordinary water was not one of them. He had some Dexedrine with him, but taking it would merely exacerbate his condition. He needed a drink of water. It began to absorb his thought, taking on the proportions of obsession.

He gave up hoping for the success of the ambush. Colter was not going to be stepping unsuspectingly out into the clear, he realized now. His full attention turned to the problem of getting out, getting away. The sides of the cleft in the rock seemed to press in upon him. He searched the area for any possible escape route.

It was then that he noticed the movement of the shadows and quickly came to the same conclusions that Colter had only moments before. Salvation!

In a matter of minutes now, the entire base of the cliffs would be plunged into total darkness! That would be the time to move. The only question remaining was, in which direction? He didn't want to move at all without some indication of Colter's whereabouts, for fear of running right into the man as he ran for the safety of the jungle.

Maybe Colter hadn't realized what was about to happen to the shadows. If the American. . . no. No, it didn't really matter, because he was out there *somewhere*. He might be in place at the bottom of the scree, or he might even be moving up the hill through the jungle, in a flanking move. It didn't matter, as long as the Russian could find out exactly where. He had to think of a way to get Colter to reveal his location. And it would have to be done at precisely the right moment, just before the moon went behind the mountain.

Hope returned to the Russian assassin in a flood as the beginnings of a concrete plan formed in his mind.

*   *   *

Damn, the moon was moving fast.

Colter had managed to reach a position which was just about on a level with the area of rock the Russian was hiding in, but only after some difficult travel. The vegetation at this altitude was somewhat more sparse than at sea level, which necessitated a more circuitous route from place to place. By the time Colter arrived where he was, the moon had traveled an alarming distance toward the mountain. The area would be darkened in shadow in a matter of minutes.

Colter took another drink of water and was replacing the canteen when he heard the Doctor's voice.

"Colter!" came the disembodied sound. "Mitchell Colter!"

Colter waited, listening in silence.

"I know you are out there! Please!" the Russian

262

continued "It's over! I'm hurt! I thought I could go on but. . . all I want is to escape from here! If you will agree to let me leave the island, I'll quit. I'll throw out my weapon."

Colter moved swiftly and smoothly, in a combat crouch, in the direction of the voice. If he could get him to disarm himself, under whatever conditions, it was desirable to do so. Colter figured that the Russian was about twenty meters or so in front of him, still hidden in the rocks. And still dangerous, in spite of his claimed injury.

"Colter?"

The Russian sounded bad. The man had to be tired and, unless he had water in that bag, dehydrated. The assassin had had a series of nasty surprises all in a row, and he might be desperate enough to actually believe that Colter would let him live. It happened, in extreme situations like this. The quarry without hope can talk itself into anything.

Colter looked at the moon. There would be darkness over the whole area in seconds. It was worth a try.

"Throw out your gun."

"Yes! Yes, here it is!" the Doctor croaked weakly. But no gun came out.

Suddenly the shadows raced across them, and their arena was plunged into darkness.

* * *

The Doctor was moving to his right at the instant the shadow fell over them. He had formed a mental picture of the ground immediately in front of him, and ran for all he was worth, even though he was temporarily blind. Exposure to the harsh white moonlight had taken away his night vision, but he knew that Colter would have the same problem. Even so, he kept low as he ran, expecting gunfire from behind him.

He was not disappointed. Just as he jogged sharply behind a large boulder, there were two short bursts of automatic fire from behind and above him, horribly close. The bullets struck amazingly close to him, but he was spared from harm by the rocks. As the Russian heard their impact on the surrounding boulders, he noticed the absence of the characteristic ricochet sounds. That meant that Colter was using special ammunition. Glazers, he guessed automatically and correctly, and felt a chill streak up his spine. He had seen the effects of such cartridges. He raced on.

The Doctor raced into the jungle, recklessly, heedless of his back-trail, going as fast as he could. He no longer cared if he was easy to follow.

That Colter *would* follow, he was sure; that the American would continue to take precautions against traps and ambushes, he could surmise with confidence. The man was not superhuman, after all. He would *have* to exercise reasonable caution. And that was what Turpenov was counting on.

He had no intention of fooling around any more, trying to best *this* adversary, not one-on-one on the man's home ground. It had been a mistake to try.

It was time for a change of tactics.

*   *   *

Back to square one, thought Colter disgustedly.

The Russian had only wanted to pinpoint Colter's location, he realized belatedly. He wasn't hurt, and he hadn't disarmed himself. The Doctor was still loose, but he was still on the island, and Colter comforted himself with the thought that the elusive killer was at least no better off than he had been before.

Colter had heard the man running, and had fired in the hope of bringing him down with a lucky shot; as he expected, he had missed. But he had been able to get a good fix on the Doctor's direction of travel, and he mentally prepared himself to go back to tracking the man through the jungle. He would follow him all night. All night and all the next day, if he had to.

Colter moved silently down the hill from the base of the cliffs and back into the jungle, moving cautiously but steadily in pursuit.

CHAPTER SIXTEEN

Michelle had been asleep for almost two hours when Bishop heard the noise.

She had tried to stay awake with Bishop, but the strain of the day plus the tots of good French cognac combined in a one-two punch which Bishop encouraged her not to resist. She waved him a sleepy goodnight and went to her room. That had been at about half past one in the morning, and it was now well past three. Two more hours until the island dawn.

Bishop had taken to the habit of walking around the outside of the bungalow, on patrol, at irregular intervals. He took the shark rifle with him, but what he was looking for was any sign of Colter.

He was just completing his circuit of the house when he heard it. At first he thought it was just a falling coconut, but it happened again. It was no coconut; someone was moving around out there.

Bishop peered anxiously in the direction of the sound. It was too dark to see anything moving, and the sound had stopped.

The CIA man ran lightly across the yard, to a spot about halfway between the house and the jungle, and called out.

"Mitch?"

A low moan came from somewhere nearby.

"Mitch!"

"Over here!" hissed the reply. "I've been shot!"

It didn't really sound like Colter's normal voice, but it was largely *un*-voiced. Who knew what Colter had been through, and how he had been wounded. Only Colter would know to come here for help, reasoned Bishop, almost unconsciously willing it to be Colter, alive. He moved toward the voice.

"Where are you?"

"H-here," answered the voice, and the rustle of bushes came from the same spot.

"Don't move, I'm coming," cautioned Bishop as he covered the twenty meters or so between himself and his injured friend. He dashed through the darkness to the line of shrubs at the back of the property. The shark rifle in his left hand was forgotten, a useless weight to carry as he went to the aid of his wounded friend.

"Mitch?" he called again, arriving at the approximate spot.

From behind the line of bushes, a man stood up, his right hand extended fully in front of him, a silenced pistol in his hand pointing directly at Bishop's face.

In an instant, Bishop realized that he was about to die. Freezing-cold electric chills sprang from the base of his spine and sped up his back, numbing his brain. His stomach contracted, and he had to consciously fight back the impulse to urinate. The rifle in his hand might just as well have been hanging above the mantelpiece in his den in Fairfax, Virginia, for all the good it would do him now. He had made a horrible, ghastly mistake, and there was no way he could take it back. The nerve endings in his face tingled, expecting to feel the final sensations of his life at any instant.

"Drop that rifle." It was a quiet command.

267

Bishop dropped the Winchester immediately. A faint glimmer of hope came into him with the realization that the man behind the silenced pistol hadn't killed him already. Apparently the man didn't intend to kill him; at least, not right now.

"Turn around." The same quiet tone, but under it there was. . . what? An edge of shakiness, of. . . *fatigue*, Bishop decided. The man was exhausted. Bishop turned around, slowly.

The Doctor came up silently behind him and placed the muzzle of the silencer at the base of Bishop's skull. With his free hand, he carefully searched the young American for a second weapon. He took his time, not speaking, using professional care. He emptied each of Bishop's pockets in turn, examining and discarding their contents in the dense undergrowth. He carefully ran his hands all over Bishop's body: back, front, legs, arms, crotch, hair, ankles, and shoes. Not once did the pressure of the silenced barrel of the gun vary at the nape of Bishop's neck. It was a constant reminder, and Bishop did not even consider trying to jump the man.

"Take three steps forward," the Doctor ordered.

Bishop fought back the hysterical response of, "Mother, may I"?, wondering how it could even have occurred to him, as he took three steps forward, and stopped.

In truth, Bishop was experiencing a perfectly normal shock-type reaction to the stress of the situation. He was alive, and he hadn't expected to be. He would do anything the Doctor instructed him to do in order to stay alive, and do it cheerfully. He subconsciously wished to communicate this fact to the Russian, but he did not speak.

Behind him, he could hear that the Doctor was picking up the Winchester, probably examining it. Bishop couldn't know whether the man would recognize it as being the shark rifle from the *Kili-Iti*, but he fervently hoped not. Bishop's chances of surviving until dawn were not good, but they would be even worse if the Doctor were to realize that Bishop had been aboard the chartered boat.

"We're going inside the house," the Doctor spoke softly behind Bishop, "through the kitchen door. Walk slowly, with your eyes to the front. If you move suddenly or unexpectedly, I'll kill you. Nod your head if you understand."

Bishop nodded his head, and felt himself prodded gently from behind with a fingertip. He started to walk slowly, and with his eyes to the front.

When they arrived at the kitchen door, Bishop stepped slowly up to the unlatched door and opened it, proceeding on into the kitchen. When he was well inside, the Doctor spoke again.

"Stop."

Bishop stopped. From behind him, he heard the man fumbling one-handed in the dish drainer, then turning on the tap at the kitchen sink. For several minutes, all Bishop heard was the sound of the Doctor's glass being filled, then drunk, then refilled.

When the man's thirst had been quenched, there was silence for a few seconds, and then the sound of drawers opening and shutting. This continued for about a minute, until the man gave a small grunt of satisfaction, apparently finding whatever it was that he had been searching for.

"Is the woman in the bedroom?" came the whispered voice of the killer from just behind Bishop's ear. Bishop had a bad moment then, of acute anxiety. He remembered that the Doctor had been in the house earlier, and that he knew its layout. But although Bishop had resigned himself to play along with the man for as long as possible, he had not mentally abdicated his responsibility for Michelle yet. He didn't want the Russian to go anywhere near her, and he considered lying to the man; telling him that there was no one else in the house, or even that the police were coming. He considered jumping the Doctor right then and there, before things could go any further.

He felt the barrel of the silencer being placed at the base of his skull and heard the Doctor whisper, "It's up to you. It has to be the truth, the very first time."

"Yes," Bishop nodded, obeying the First Rule.

"Is she the only other person here? No children?"

"No."

"Pets?"

"No."

"Very well. We are going into the bedroom now. Move."

They proceeded into the bedroom of the bungalow, Bishop still in the lead. When they entered, the sleeping woman stirred, and then blinked awake. She had been sleeping on top of the covers, clad only in a light cotton shirt which was many sizes too big for her. *Probably one of Colter's*, Bishop thought idly. She sat bolt upright when she saw the look on Bishop's face, and when she recognized the man behind Bishop, she automatically clutched the unbuttoned shirt front.

She opened her mouth to speak, but the Doctor cut off any sound with a preemptive command.

"Silence!"

Michelle stared first at the Doctor, then anxiously at Bishop, who tried to communicate some feeling of calm to the frightened woman.

The Doctor tossed the object he had found in the kitchen drawer onto the bed. It was a roll of Johnson & Johnson adhesive tape, almost new.

"I want you to bind her wrists behind her back," the Doctor instructed Bishop, "and then her ankles. Move."

Bishop went to the bed and picked up the tape, moving slowly, careful to keep his hands in the Russian's line of sight. He gently took Michelle's wrists and guided them together behind her, then wrapped the tape around them several times. The taperoller itself was equipped with a sharp metal edge to be used for cutting off the end. He then repeated the process with her ankles.

"Now your own ankles. And knees. Take off your shoes."

Bishop complied, and when he had finished, the Doctor inspected the bindings for tension.

"Both of you. Lie flat on your stomachs."

When Bishop's wrists were pulled up behind his back, he realized that the Doctor had put down the gun; the Russian was using both hands to tape Bishop's wrists together. But by then it was much too late to take advantage of the fact.

For that matter, Bishop thought with a sinking feeling, it was now too late to take advantage of anything. Both he and Michelle had been immobilized. They were alive, but they had been rendered harmless.

But the Doctor was not stopping at merely binding wrists and ankles; he was a professional, and half measures were an amateur's mistake. He taped Bishop's elbows tightly together, then his thumbs. Finally he jammed a piece of wadded-up cloth into Bishop's mouth and taped it in place. Then the man turned to Michelle and methodically repeated the process, taping her knees, elbows and thumbs together. Then he turned her over onto her back, and began to look for something with which to gag her.

Her sleeping shirt had fallen open, exposing her breasts and torso, and she spoke.

"Could you at least close my shirt? I - I don't like it like this."

The Doctor's eyes flickered over her momentarily,

and she felt her skin crawl. They were feral, animal's eyes. There was no warmth at all in them, only cold, metallic speculation.

"Be quiet," was the only response he voiced. He grabbed a rustcolored Hermes scarf from the dresser and jammed it into her mouth. As he taped it into place, he seemed to smile in the darkness. "You needn't be embarrassed. I'm a doctor." He stood back, having completed his work, and let his eyes rove over her once again.

"Not that you have anything to be embarrassed about, Mademoiselle. Your body is very. . . attractive."

Michelle's eyes flashed with hatred, and she drew her knees up protectively in front of her as the Russian continued to speak.

"This man Colter, he is coming. He is . . ." The Russian had to take a moment to shake off the amazement he felt at the pursuit Colter had mounted. "He is not like other men. I have never before encountered such a man. I just hope that he values your continued good health. For all our sakes. Otherwise, you will not be alive to see the sun rise this morning."

He said this with such casual, offhand authority that both Michelle and Bishop felt their stomachs tighten.

The Doctor moved to Michelle's dresser and picked up a spraybottle of perfume, which he then balanced carefully between the shoulder blades of the bound Bishop, still on his stomach on the floor. "I'm placing this bottle here," he explained, "so that you won't try to loosen the tape. I'm going out of the room for a moment, but if you move, even slightly, it will fall onto the floor, and I will hear it. If that happens, I'm going to come back in here and shoot you in the leg. You understand?"

Bishop nodded, and the Doctor left the bottle in its delicate balance. He turned to Michelle and removed the tape from her ankles and knees, using the cuticle scissors which he had found on the dresser top. He then helped her to her feet, and led her out of the bedroom.

He searched the house quickly but carefully, making sure that the front door was locked and latched and that the windows were secure. He held the gun in his right hand, having left the shark rifle inside the kitchen door, and guided the woman firmly with his left. There was no one else in the house. As the man had claimed. Good.

He propelled her into the kitchen, and paused to listen. The perfume bottle had not fallen, and all was quiet. So far, so good. He raised the revolver and pressed its muzzle against Michelle's temple. "We're going to go out the kitchen door, you and I, and walk to the bushes at the back. I left something there, and we're going to retrieve it. If you try to get away, I'm going to hurt you. Understand? All right, move."

The Doctor propelled Michelle quickly and smoothly across the back yard to the spot from which he had trapped Bishop. He didn't know how close Colter might be behind him, so he kept the revolver at her head the entire time. If Colter were, by some miracle, already close by, he could not take the chance of trying to kill the Doctor at this precise moment. Not when Michelle would be almost certain to die from the reflexresponse of the Doctor's finger on the trigger.

When they came to the black bag, hidden in the underbrush, the Doctor forced Michelle to her knees, gun still at her head, and quickly picked up the bag with his left hand. He then put his whole left arm around her at the neck, and set out for the return to the house.

Once inside again, the Russian allowed himself a deep sigh of relief. The trickiest part was over. He moved Michelle to one of the two kitchen chairs and sat her down in it, awkward though she was with her hands and elbows bound behind her. He quickly retaped her knees and ankles, and went to check on Bishop.

The bottle of perfume hadn't moved from its balance point, and so he returned to the kitchen before the woman could begin to try to loosen her bonds.

He took the Winchester rifle and put it on the draining board, next to the black bag. He opened the black bag and stared inside it, taking inventory both of its contents and of the state of the overall situation.

Two hostages. One too many? Perhaps he should kill the man now, just to avoid having to keep track of both of them. No, he decided, he had better keep them both alive for now. He might have to kill one of them when Colter arrived, as a demonstration of his seriousness and to throw Colter off his emotional balance. He would keep the woman alive until his eventual escape was guaranteed.

He did not doubt for a moment that Colter would arrive soon, probably before dawn. It didn't matter. It was too late now.

Two guns. The rifle and the handgun. That was good. Very good. It might even prove to be decisive. Did Colter know about the rifle? Probably, he decided, but he would have to find out.

"Where did the rifle come from? Is it yours?" he asked Michelle.

She turned her eyes away from him, defiant.

He continued to stare at her for a long minute, thinking, deciding. Then he reached into the black bag and withdrew a papersealed disposable syringe. He tore the paper covering off and took a small vial of clear fluid from one of the pockets inside the bag. He then filled the syringe with an amount of the tiny bottle's contents, and turned again to Michelle.

She had watched him prepare the injection, and was

wide-eyed with fear. Her lips trembled involuntarily.

"This is morphine," he told her "It won't hurt you, but it will make you sleepy. Just hold still." And with that, he bent over her and pulled the shirt off her shoulders. He gave her the injection in the triceps of her left arm, without the benefit of an alcohol swab.

As he waited for the drug to take hold in her, he resumed his analysis of the situation. While he was thinking, he mechanically threw away the syringe and returned to the doctor's bag.

Stupid to even ask her about the rifle, he mentally chided himself. The man was carrying it, he's the one to ask. Anyway, the man seems to know how to handle himself in this kind of spot. That perfumebottle trick is difficult for most people to handle without training. Was the man a professional? CIA, perhaps? Have to find out. Colter will be here soon.

The nearly naked Michelle was trying to focus her eyes. She seemed to be having some trouble with her eyelids, and the Doctor went over to examine her. When he was satisfied that she wouldn't be causing him any trouble, he spoke to her.

"Just stay right in this chair. If you try to get up, you'll fall and hurt yourself. Don't go to sleep. Just concentrate on staying upright in the chair."

With the revolver in his belt, he picked up the black bag and the rifle and went into the bedroom. He found Bishop exactly as he had left him, and went over to him and removed the bottle from the man's back. Instantly Bishop tried to exercise the tense muscles of his neck and back. Turpenov took the cuticle scissors from his shirt pocket and sat down on the bed, leaning forward and cutting the tape of the gag. He pulled the cloth from Bishop's mouth and sat back.

"Just stay on your stomach," he began softly. "I have one or two questions to ask you, and I want you to answer me quickly and truthfully." The Russian took the revolver from his belt and showed it to the bound man. Turpenov didn't want to take the time to strip the man's clothing off him if he didn't have to. It would be standard procedure, but maybe this young man was enough of a pro to have given up the idea of resistance.

"Why should I tell you anything? You're going to kill me anyway," Bishop asked.

"Don't do that," said Turpenov almost lazily, swinging the barrel of the silencer sharply into the bridge of
Bishop's nose. The cartilage broke under the impact, making a grisly snapping sound and causing blood to spurt from the nose, over the lips and into a puddle below Bishop's face. Bishop was stunned, both by the injury and by the casual manner with which it was inflicted.

"My first question is," the Doctor was saying, "Who do you work for?"

"Jesus! Bastard . . ." Bishop was spitting blood.

"Who do you work for?" came the repeated question.

"Work for?" replied Bishop angrily, using the pain in his face to clear his mind. "What do you mean. I don't work for anybody, for Christ's sake!"

"I don't have time for lies. Tell me quickly, or I'll hurt you again."

"Jesus Christ! I'm telling you! I'm unemployed! I was a Los Angeles police officer for nine years, but I got fired so I came to Tahiti, that was ten months ago, and I just . . . don't work. I sure wish I knew what the hell is going on. What the hell do you *want*, anyway?"

It was a good try, as good as Bishop had in him at the moment, but it wasn't nearly good enough. The Russian had been around, and he knew a backup story when he heard one. Bishop hadn't been in the islands

276

for any ten months, not with his skin still as fair as it was. And the Doctor had observed the American patrolling around the house, rifle in hand. No. Bishop was lying, and Turpenov knew it.

The Russian calmly reached down from the bed and felt Bishop's right leg, above the knee. He located the spot he wanted, and placed the muzzle of the silenced pistol against it.

And pulled the trigger.

Bishop screamed in pain as the slug tore its way through muscle and skin, leaving a clean but bleeding hole behind it as it thudded into the floorboards. The stench of cordite was thick in the air, and Bishop struggled with wave after wave of nausea, pain and fear. He was drenched in sweat.

"You lied."

"God! I-Jesus God!"

"It didn't hit the bone, or any major blood vessel. It will be painful, but it's really not much, as gunshot wounds go. I will inflict an injury like this on your body each time you tell me a lie. I know how, and I've got time."

So saying, Turpenov picked up a stocking lying nearby, and applied it as a tourniquet to the leg above the wound. The pain receded in Bishop's leg, mostly due to the effects of the mild state of shock into which he had entered.

"So," Turpenov continued as if nothing had happened, "Who do you work for? The CIA?"

"Y-yes."

"Very good. Now listen carefully. Are you the only CIA agent, aside from Colter, on this island? Be careful - I may know this answer already."

"N-no," Bishop lied deliriously, unsure now why he was continuing to lie except that his captor might be tripped into a wrong decision if he had wrong information. "There are - two more of us."

"Where?"

"Hotel Bora Bora."

"Names?"

"Lewis and. . . Decker," improvised Bishop.

"Where did this rifle come from?"

"Behind. . . the bar. The bartender loaned it to me. . ."

"Which bartender? Here at the inn?"

"Y-yes."

The Doctor was inclined to believe this because he was convinced Bishop couldn't be holding back any more, and he didn't want to spend any more time making sure. He decided that the situation was acceptable. As long as he knew who the other CIA men were, he could take appropriate precautions. And the origin of the rifle was no longer a mystery.

"Does Colter know that you got the rifle from the barman?"

"Y-yes," Bishop lied instinctively, "he told me to."

The Doctor's eyes narrowed.

He had been hoping that the second gun would be a surprise to Colter. If Colter hadn't known about the Winchester, then the Doctor might have been able to convince Colter that he was disarming himself by throwing out the revolver. Then, maybe, Colter might have shown himself, in which event Turpenov could have taken him down easily with the rifle. That was a solution much to be preferred over some others, but the crippled CIA man was undoubtedly beyond lying at this point. Too bad.

He attended to Bishop's leg wound, easing the tension on the tourniquet slightly, and then he opened the black bag again and prepared a second injection of morphine, slightly heavier than the one he had given Michelle. When the dope was on its way through

Bishop's system, he rose and went back into the kitchen, finding Michelle as he had left her. She would unknowingly begin to lean to the left or right, then jerk herself back upright, trying to focus both her vision and her attention and not quite able to manage it.

The Doctor settled down to his preparations. He moved Michelle's chair, with her in it, near the back door. He took the other chair and placed it for himself, out of the line of sight from the back yard but close to the woman. He brought the black bag, the rifle, and the silenced handgun to his spot. He sat down, and tried to relax. After a while, the first hints of gray came into the light at the eastern horizon.

He waited.

* * *

Colter had been almost halfway down Mount Pahia when he had realized the Doctor's probable destination.

He had been following the other man with professional calm and care, content to take all night and all the next day if he had to. But as he made his way through the jungle, he had mentally placed himself in the Russian's predicament and reviewed the man's choices. This exercise, given all the givens, led him in only one plausible direction: hostages.

Colter had then realized that the man's chosen direction of travel was almost directly toward Michelle's Inn. He could have chosen any of a dozen other, more promising headings by now, had he intended to stay under the protective cover of the island's dense vegetation, but he hadn't. Two plus two still makes four, even in the South Pacific. He was planning on taking Michelle hostage.

Colter didn't doubt for a minute that he would be able to manage it. Bishop might, just might get lucky and prevent him or even - too much to hope for - kill him, but the probability was that this Russian would bring off a safe capture. He would want to talk, but he would want to be holding a gun to Michelle's head while he did so.

Even so, Colter could not allow himself to abandon the caution he was using in the tracking of the Russian killer; although his stomach tied itself in knots with worry for the woman and his friend, he forced himself to maintain combat discipline.

And so, as he followed Turpenov's trail, he tried to think ahead to his verbal confrontation with the Soviet assassin. Even as Colter fled from shadow to shadow, instinctively avoiding open places and natural ambush sites, he was going over the Russian's probable demands, offers, and proposals.

Escape, obviously. The man certainly had realized that he would not be able to kill Colter, not this trip. Would he try to trade? Michelle's life for Colter's? Or would he have given up altogether on his primary mission here, seeking only to get away safely? And what about Bishop?

What would I do, in his place? Colter forced himself to concentrate. He decided that in order to make sure of the success of the escape, he would have to keep the hostages, or at least one of the hostages, alive. He would need to keep Michelle with him until he was well away from Bora Bora. That probably meant that air travel was out. This guy had arrived by boat, and he would now have to leave the same way. He could scarcely board the regularly scheduled Air Polynesie flight to Papeete with a gun at Michelle's head. Unless he hijacked the whole flight. . . no. That was out. He would want to take the woman on the boat with him.

Once away from Bora, his chances would improve in a rather dramatic hurry. It was damned difficult to keep track of a small vessel in a big ocean. He would kill Michelle, of course. One less distraction to concern himself with.

He would pick an island from the many choices available: Maupiti, Raiatea, Huahine, Tetiaroa-perhaps he would even try to reach as far as the Tuamotus, or the Austral Islands, before returning to land. It would depend to an extent on the provisioning of the boat. He would sail in close, under cover of darkness if possible, then sink the boat, using a life raft to get to shore. He could then disguise himself in order to throw off any lingering police pursuit or passportcontrol people who might have been alerted to watch for him. He could establish himself nicely as a tourist. It would be difficult, but it wouldn't be impossible for him to get away cleanly.

Colter would have to get the man thinking about his escape. Perhaps he could distract him long enough to get him to make a mistake. Perhaps. . .

Colter arrived at the line of bushes at the back of the inn's property, at almost the same spot where the Doctor had tricked Bishop, just about an hour after the Russian had gone back into the house with Michelle, having retrieved his black bag.

The dawn's early light. The phrase resonated in Colter's minmd. The first traces of the new day were appearing in the form of a light, misty ground fog which hung low, close to the ground, in the palest gray light. It was not true dawn, but the morning sun's reflection off the atmosphere itself.

The dawn's early light. The phrase had connotations of battle attendant with it. There would be a combat here, this morning. Colter tried to center his faculties, bringing everything inside himself to bear on what lay ahead.

Colter was tired, and his shoulder was a dull red ache which ate at his mental focus. He stopped, hidden in the foliage, and drank the last of the water from his canteen, watching the house. The kitchen light was on, and there seemed to be other lights on in the house. Colter could not see inside from where he was, and he had to rest before he could reconnoiter further.

Of course, Colter realized, the Russian would prefer not to have to leave the way Colter had envisioned. He would much rather kill all three of them right here and now and slip away quietly using his cover identity, normally. That would always be his first choice.

But he would have to get Colter first.

Colter began to move, circling closer to the house for a better look. He kept well away from the bungalow itself, mainly concerned with primary reconnaissance; how many people were around, where were they, was the house secured, that kind of question needed to be answered. As the light began to improve, he found that he could see into the house fairly well. From behind the inn's generator shack, he could see obliquely into the front living room, and he could just see that the safety chain was in place on the door. He moved on to the inn itself, finding no one up yet, no sign of any awareness of trouble. He moved on.

At length, Colter completed the entire circuit of the bungalow, arriving back where he had started. He unclipped the canteen from his belt and prepared to go in closer. He hadn't learned enough. He needed to know exactly where Michelle and Bishop were, and if they were still alive.

It made sense for the Doctor to be in the kitchen, probably with Michelle. But Colter needed to get closer in to be sure. He returned to the cover of the generator shack, way off to the side, and checked the load of the Uzi. Then, keeping low to the ground, he ran lightly across the side yard, a silent specter in the approaching dawn.

He got to the side of the house, and froze. He waited, both for his heartbeat to slow and for any sign of alarm within the house. Hearing nothing, he raised his head to the level of the front-room window and turned his head to the glass. Before the visual impression had even formed in his mind, he had returned to his crouch beside the house. Now, he gathered up what he had seen, and evaluated it.

Empty. No one in the living room.

Very well. He didn't need to look again, so he moved up to the next window along the side, which looked in on the bedroom. Repeating the process, he took a peek and went back to a crouch.

Bishop, his mind identified the eyes' quick impression. *Bound with tape, face down on the floor. No one else*. Colter raised himself up and took another, longer look.

Bishop's face was a bloody mess, and he had a tourniquet around his right thigh above a leg wound, but he was alive. He had apparently been gagged, but the gag had been taken out. He looked dull and sleepy. Shock, probably. He wasn't being supervised at the moment, yet he wasn't working, trying to get free from his bonds. Interesting.

Colter moved on. He circled the empty front of the house and came up slowly, quietly, using terrible caution, under the kitchen window. He listened intently for a full two minutes, and then took his quick peek.

As he dropped back into the crouch, he had already begun to run. His brain had flashed the signal: *Get out!* to him, even before a concrete visual impression of what he had seen had had a chance to form. He ran back the way he had come, around the front and away to the side. Only when he was well clear and under cover did he try to assess his visual input.

The Doctor had seen him.

Or at least Colter thought he had. Colter had had a clear view of the well-lit room, which showed him the taped-up Michelle in the kitchen chair, alive but groggy, and the Doctor. The man was situated perfectly, tucked neatly into the corner by the back door, out of sight. The silencer-equipped pistol was in his hand, pointing at Michelle. As Colter had taken the quick look, the man's eyes had seemed to stare directly into his own.

Yet he had not reacted.

Why?

* * *

The Doctor thought he might be going mad.

He had been daydreaming. The onset of the tranquil island dawn had lulled him into a false sense of peace, of harmony with the world. He had drifted back in time, to a holiday he had taken eleven years ago by the Black Sea, in summer. There had been a woman from the Crimea. . .

And then he had seen Colter's face at the window.

It was gone before he could even be sure that he had seen it, before the image had had time to register. Now, he became unsure whether or not it had been there at all.

Was the strain of the night taking its toll? Was he seeing things? Had his subconscious summoned up the image of Colter, playing a trick on him?

Or was Colter really here?

Panic welled up in him as he realized that he couldn't be sure. How long had he been drifting like that? It couldn't be more than a few seconds. Could it?

He fought back the almost overwhelming impulse to get up, to run, to look out all the windows, to do something, and forced himself to listen. Listen and think.

As he strained to detect the slightest sound from outside, imagining that he heard the lightest of footsteps running away, he thought over the possibilities, ultimately deciding that there was no immediate cause for alarm. If he had just imagined Colter's face in the window, then there was no harm done. Nerves, that's all.

But if it really had been Colter, then the man would realize the state of the situation. In that event, the Doctor would most likely be hearing from him soon.

Either way, no harm done, he soothed himself. Just hold tight; you have all the cards.

*   *   *

Colter had moved as close in to the back of the bungalow as he could without exposing himself. He was still about twenty meters away from the kitchen door, but he had cover here, at the base of the closest palm tree, and the young bougainvillea bushes would make him difficult to pinpoint.

It was full dawn now, and time to get on with it. The later it got, the more people would be up and moving about, and the worst thing for a situation like this was complications. Colter had all the information he was going to get by his own reconnaissance, and whether the Doctor had seen him at the kitchen window or not, it was no longer to Colter's advantage to make the killer wait. He cleared his throat.

"Vrachya!" he called out. The Russian word for doctor.

There was a brief, surprised silence in the house, and then the reply: "Come out into the clear, Colter. Hands above your head. *Now*."

"Oh, I don't think so" Colter smiled. The man was putting his best foot forward. If *that* had worked, it would all have been over in seconds. "Let's just talk things over from where we are."

"All right, then, we talk. I have two of your friends in here, and I will not hesitate to kill them."

"Krasnevin is dead."

Silence from the house. This was a surprise to the Russian, as Colter had hoped it would be, and Turpenov was desperately trying to think what it meant. Colter gave him a few seconds with it, and then lent him a helping hand.

"Don't you see? There is no need for any of this! You have no contract to complete! There is no assignment! Do you understand?" Colter tried to sound as if he were frustrated by the Doctor's slowness to comprehend.

"It makes no difference," the killer replied uncertainly.

"What?" Colter sounded amazed. "Don't you realize what I'm telling you? The hit is cancelled, you stupid bastard! It's been called off!"

Silence. The man was actually thinking it over. Colter had to keep talking, trying to throw him, keep him off balance.

"Krasnevin is dead, for Christ's sake! He was put to sleep like a mad dog, right in the Clinic! *Days* ago! There's a new head of the KGB by now. No one cares about this business now, not any more. It's history. You don't have to kill me, and I don't have to kill you. There wouldn't be any point to it, now. It's all over!"

Inside the house, Turpenov had been thrown into a quandary by this unexpected information. If it were true, then the big American was making perfect sense. There was no assignment, and besides, he had already been paid. What was he doing here? The whole damn trip had been a mistake. He should have just taken the money and retired to Oregon.

It was unnerving that Colter knew about Krasnevin, and that he had called him "Vrachya," though. The Russian was suddenly feeling very tired. He wanted to go home.

"How do I know you are telling me the truth?" he called out the back door.

"Oh, come on," Colter replied, "figure it out. I'm the one who forced Krasnevin to talk. I was at his dacha east of Odessa. I told my people. You think Langley didn't let Moscow Center know? That the head of the KGB was the one who was killing CIA agents all over the world? What do you think the Kremlin would do? Let Krasnevin *live*?"

The logic was incontrovertible. The Doctor accepted the fact that Krasnevin was dead.

"All right. So?"

"So," Colter answered, knowing that he had reached the crucial stage, "you have no reason to kill me, and I have no reason to kill you."

"So then. . . what? You expect me to just walk away?"

"Why not?"

Turpenov felt as if there were bees buzzing around inside his head. He couldn't think why not, but his every instinct was tuned for the situation he *thought* had existed. He looked at the helpless, drugged Frenchwoman, and thought again of the wounded American in the bedroom. He thought of his escape plan.

"How do you guarantee my safe passage?" he called.

"First things first. I want to see the hostages alive."

"They are both alive."

"Yes, but you know I won't believe you until I see for myself. I tell you quite frankly, their good health is your ticket out. You know this. I can assure your safe passage to *your own* satisfaction, but first I have to see both of them alive."

After a brief pause, the Doctor asked, "Do you know any songs?"

"What?"

"Songs. Sing a song. Any song. Loudly. I want to be sure you don't change your position."

"I don't want to kill you! I'm not going to rush the house, not with hostages inside, are you - "

"Sing!" yelled the Doctor, strain evident in his voice.

Better not push him too fast, Colter thought. He began to sing the first song which came into his head, which was, absurdly, "Happy Birthday to You." He sang it slowly and strongly enough to carry into the house, but not so loudly that it would wake the sleeping inn. It was incongruous, in the shining dawn of Bora Bora, in this tropical paradise and in this deadly moment, but it missed being funny by a mile.

Colter had sung through the song twice when the kitchen door opened wide. He stopped singing immediately, as he saw Bishop, bleary-eyed and in obvious pain, standing awkwardly in the doorway. The Doctor was propping him up from behind. Bishop, whose gag had never been replaced after his interrogation, tried to focus his eyes, saying, "Mitch? You there, Mitch?" The Russian gave him a push and he tumbled out of the doorway, unable to catch his balance, and fell hard, down the steps and onto the ground below the door. He hit with a thud, and groaned softly.

Colter had had the Uzi trained on the doorway, but the Doctor had been too fast. He had disappeared again, somewhere inside. Colter waited.

Now Michelle was at the door. Colter's temper flared as he saw her state of undress, and he had to check himself sharply to keep from letting his outrage get the upper hand.

She, too, was definitely alive, but was having trouble focusing her eyes. The Doctor stood behind her, holding her by the bindings on her arms. He had pulled her shirt up onto her shoulders, at least partially covering her. The Russian held the pistol to her head.

"You see? Both alive," he called to Colter.

"What did you do to them?" Colter asked, as calmly as he could.

"They are under sedation. The man has a broken nose and a small hole in his thigh, but nothing serious."

"Looks like he lost some blood."

"Not much. He was quite reluctant to tell me about the rifle, let alone Lewis and Decker. He'll be all right. They will both be all right. They are alive, as you see."

Colter didn't know who the hell Lewis and Decker were, but the mention of a rifle was interesting. So there was a rifle in the house. . . Bishop had told the Russian about "Lewis and Decker" under force of interrogation, and "about the rifle . . ."

"Colter?"

"I'm here. I concur, and agree that the hostages are both alive."

"All right. Next step. Don't try anything, or I'll kill the girl," he threatened, coming up closer behind Michelle and repositioning the silenced barrel in front of her, pointing into her body just below her breasts.

"Mitch," she moaned, with soft fear.

"Next step," repeated the assassin.

"We're almost there," Colter told him. He would just have to take the chance on the rifle. From just the single mention of it, he was only guessing. "Now toss out the rifle, and we're there."

"No."

Bingo! thought Colter. "It'll be okay," he said aloud "You can keep the handgun, but let me see you lose the rifle."

"Why?"

"Because I'm about to let you go. I know the effective range of a silenced pistol, and I'm not planning to be anywhere close to it, but a rifle around makes me nervous. You don't need it any more."

"I won't use it."

"You'll still be armed. Come on. You've tried to kill me enough times. I'm being overcareful, all right. But after all, why not?" Colter held his breath.

Inside, Turpenov had begun to sweat. He had lost the initiative early on, and he didn't know how to get it back. It occurred to him that all he had been doing was giving up things, even though he still had Michelle and Bishop under his gun. The rifle made no difference.

He drew Michelle back from the doorway and picked up the rifle by its lever action handle with his left hand. His right arm was still around Michelle's front. He jerked on the rifle, causing the action to open the breech and eject the round. He tossed it down the steps, where it clattered uselessly on the ground.

"All right. I've done as you asked. Now what?" he demanded.

"Now you walk away," Colter answered.

"Just like that?" Turpenov scoffed. "What kind of an idiot do you take me for?"

"Not just like that. You close the kitchen door, leaving the woman on the outside, and you on the inside. After that, I never want to see you again. Leave by the front door, leave by a window, I don't care. Get off the island. I won't stop you. From the moment you release her, I have no further interest in you."

"What's to stop you from coming after me?"

"Good judgment. Just think for a minute, will you?" Colter called conversationally. "We're both pros. We're pretty good at this kind of thing. Why should I endanger myself further by chasing after an armed, trained man whom I have no reason to kill? Once my friends are safe, why would I risk everything to kill you?"

"You. . . you are saying you have no reason . . .?"

"Have you forgotten? We have no cause to kill each other. Under other circumstances, we might even have worked together, have been comrades in arms. When I take an assignment, I accept some minimal risk because I am paid for it, and paid well. No one is paying me for this. There is no reason for me to exert myself further.

"You, too, are a professional. Why play this dangerous game any longer if you don't have to? I'm not asking you to trust me; I'm just asking you to think the matter through and decide for yourself."

Turpenov was tempted. There was no reason for it any more. He had already been paid. He was still alive, and the American was indeed a professional. No one was paying him to continue the hunt. Up to this point, he had merely been reacting to the attempts on his own life. Still. . .

"Colter!" His voice was sharper now, carrying the energy of a decision made. "I will agree on one condition!"

"Yes?"

"Throw out your weapon."

"Sorry. I can't do that."

"Why not?"

"Because as soon as you leave the house, I will have lost track of you. I don't want to be unarmed until you're off the island. Simple caution."

"Come on. It's my only condition."

"It's unnecessary."

"Then I'm going to have to take the woman with me."

"No."

"One or the other, Colter."

"Look. We both know that if you take the woman, you'll end up by killing her. You'd have to, at some point. You don't want to do that, because then you'd be giving me a reason to come after you and kill you. And I would." The promise in Colter's tone of voice was a new element, and even the hardened man holding the gun on Michelle was chilled by it. The prospect of having this particular man on his trail was to be avoided at all cost.

"Colter. I agree with you. I just need to be sure of your inability to cut me down in the first few seconds, that's all. All I need is for you to throw your - what is it, an Uzi?"

"That's right."

" . . .to throw the Uzi out into the clearing to your far right, and the clip of ammunition out to the far left. What about that?"

Colter paused before giving any reply, his fingers already at work on the taped connection between clips. He seemed to be thinking it over, but he'd already made up his mind how he would play it. When he felt that he had given the Russian the impression that he had considered it carefully, he called out.

"All right. It doesn't matter. We'll do it your way."

The Doctor smiled. At last his head had cleared, and he had come to his senses. Colter had very nearly tricked him, with all that talk of Krasnevin's death and the lack of reasons to kill each other. He must have been more exhausted than he had realized, to listen to such nonsense. Colter had merely been trying to get the hostages clear. Very well, he would give him what he wanted. "Very good," he yelled "As soon as I see your weapon clearly, in two sections, thrown into the clearing, I'll let her go, and then I shall disappear. Go ahead."

Colter had figured that the Doctor wouldn't be able to get out the front door of the bungalow in much under five seconds; the latch was on the door, and it would slow him down maybe a few seconds more. Five seconds would be enough to retrieve the Uzi; screw the clip in the clearing. He already had the two buttobutt clips separated.

He tossed the clip which had been in place all night far across the clearing, in plain view of the Doctor. He jammed the other clip into his canteen belt, behind him at the small of his back. Then he threw the Uzi out in the other direction, but also in plain view. It landed about halfway between the house and the old generator shed. Colter figured that he could get to it, snap the fresh magazine in place, and be at the front of the house in time to see the Doctor make his run for it.

The Doctor, however, had changed his mind. He had decided against trying to escape. He felt almost lightheaded, giddy with the knowledge that he was going to be all right. He was certain that Colter had been sincere about Krasnevin. What the Doctor had momentarily forgotten was that Colter was a threat to Yuri Turpenov. That was the whole reason he had come to this ridiculously picture postcard place at all. And he had accidentally killed the girl on that sailboat. Colter would not forgive him for that. Colter had to die, that was all.

He figured that Colter would break from cover only seconds after the woman was free and the door closed behind her. His first move would probably be toward the house; he would want to see if the woman was all right after the fall Yuri would make sure she suffered.

He would also be drawn to the rifle now, the only use-able weapon around. Such a move would bring him close to the door.

The Doctor's plan was quite simple. He would stay at the door. Colter would expect him to be on his way out the front. It would be a simple shot. Impossible to miss.

"All right, I'm unarmed," Colter was saying. "Let her go."

With his right ankle, the Doctor reached around in front of Michelle's shins. He gave her a sharp push with his left hand and sent her flying out the door. The door closed instantly behind her, and the Doctor, crouched down behind it.

Michelle was helpless to stop herself, and might have been seriously hurt by the fall but for Bishop. He had kept quiet throughout the exchange between Colter and the Doctor, but he was growing steadily more alert, thanks to the pain in his face and leg. He rolled his body quickly as Michelle started to fall and got himself under her just in time to absorb most of the shock himself. They lay together on the ground, winded.

Colter observed this only peripherally, concentrating his attention on the kitchen door. As it closed, he began to move, counting seconds off mentally. He broke cover and headed for the Uzi. As he reached its resting place, his extrasensory alarms went off, and he knew with a sickening sensation that something had gone desperately wrong.

Thirty meters away, across the clearing, the Doctor couldn't believe his eyes. Colter had gone for the Uzi! He opened the door and vaulted down to the ground, pistol aimed at Colter's back. He ran as fast as he could, trying to close the distance between them before he shot; with this weapon and this ammunition, he couldn't be sure of a kill at this range.

Bishop saw what was happening and kicked his legs frantically, trying to get close to the rifle lying on the ground nearby. He yelled, "Mitch! Look out!" just as he managed to get his hands on the action of the Winchester. He closed the breech, scrabbling for the trigger, not even thinking about aiming.

It all seemed to happen at once.

There was a small *phut!* sound, followed closely by a deafening rifle report, a loud *CRACK!* which shattered the morning air, causing nearby chickens in a pen to start up a din of frightened chatter. The Doctor had taken his shot at Colter just before Bishop had found the trigger of the rifle.

Colter's interior alarm system saved him, sending him into a flying somersault. He had grasped the Uzi as he rolled and, using his own momentum, had managed to regain his feet. Even as the rifle shot sounded, he was snapping the clip into the breechslot of the submachine gun. The Doctor's pistol shot had missed him by feet.

At the sound of the Winchester going off, the Doctor had instinctively wheeled about, drawing a level bead on Bishop. He realized his mistake only when he heard the sound of the Uzi's breechbolt snapping a round into the firing chamber.

It was behind him.

He knew what was going to happen, and he knew that it was much too late to stop it from happening. The certainty of it drained him of energy. He never fired the shot he had aimed at the CIA man on the ground. He turned to look at Colter. . .

Colter fired three fourshot bursts into the Doctor. The Glazer slugs tore apart on entering the Russian's body and threw high velocity lead shot everywhere inside. Not one of the twelve slugs missed. His last thought was of the wild beauty of the Pacific coastline, and then something crawled up his spine and tore his brain in half. He was literally dead before he hit the ground.

Someone was yelling something in the courtyard of the inn, and now a couple of islanders came running back to cautiously see what the noise was all about. Colter stood where he was for a long moment, looking at what had once been an adult male Russian. Then he walked slowly and steadily over to Michelle and Bishop, his face unreadable.

The next day, there was a memorial service for Samantha.

CHAPTER SEVENTEEN

BLOOD POUNDING IN HIS EARS.

Colter was swimming at a steady, stronger pace now, as he neared the end of his swim. He felt fit, and the shoulder no longer bothered him at all.

He had been out to his secret cache in the old torpedo and had deposited what was left of the money Langley had paid him, via Bishop, for the Black Sea assignment. *Which wasn't a whole lot*, he thought ruefully.

As he neared the waters of the lagoon directly offshore from the Hotel Bora Bora, his temporary home while his own house was being rebuilt, he passed through the unimaginable beauty of that part of the living underwater world. He paused, unable to merely pass it by in transit, appreciating the colors and formations through the window of his facemask.

High expenses, too high, he thought, unable to keep his mind away from the events of ten days ago.

Samantha. Litvak. Minton, Archer, Forbes, Carlton, all the other CIA field men.

Samantha. Ah, God.

He couldn't stay with that thought. He had to start letting go of the pain now. It was done, she was gone, and he couldn't bring her back.

Expenses had been high in other areas, as well. The money Colter had earned on the assignment, including the bonus, would be all but consumed by the rebuilding of his house, plus the new boat for Rene. Colter smiled a little behind the mask. Rene had refused to let Colter do it, but Colter could be persistent.

He had gone to Papeete on the same plane with Bishop, right after the service for Sam. Bishop was hospitalized, and Colter looked Rene up at his home. He was fine, and didn't seem to have been hurt too badly at all. Colter took him around to see the boat brokers, dragging him all the way, telling him that he just wanted to look around. Rene had insisted that the insurance money would buy him a new boat. Colter knew that, but it would take months to work a deal, and it wouldn't be a good enough boat anyway. Not to replace the *Presque-Vivante*.

Finally, Colter saw Rene's eyes light up at the sight of an ugly old ketch tied up to one of the broker's piers. It was big and well made, but it had been neglected and it needed a lot of hard work.

Colter bought it for Rene, managing a huge discount on the price. That was because he paid for it outright, in cash. He told Rene to use the insurance money for the necessary repairs and that if he ever got the old tub to Bora Bora in one piece, Colter would help him paint it. Rene's eyes shone, and that was enough for Colter.

When Bishop was ready to travel, several days later, Colter cabled Langley that Bishop was to be granted two weeks' paid convalescent leave. Langley had agreed, and Colter had taken him back to Bora Bora.

Arthur White had been only too delighted to take in the two men. Colter had been something of a mystery man before the explosion and the gunfight, but now, for better or worse, he had become a legend

White was remodeling again, and let them have finished quarters in the unfinished section, with an open tab, compliments of the house.

Michelle had been sullen and withdrawn with Colter when he returned from Papeete, and he was troubled by her coldness, but he certainly understood. Colter had been responsible, in her eyes, for despoiling her island and her home. He had brought death to Samantha, and had nearly been the cause of Michelle's own end. The bloodstains in the back yard had disappeared, but her house was full of the memory of that terrible dawn.

She shunned his company, and he would not press, although he found that he was missing her more than he would have expected.

Colter shook off these thoughts, and kicked out strongly for the beach. He sprinted for about fifty yards, and then let his glide take him up to the steps which led up to the bungalow he was using. He took off his mask and snorkel, and then his fins. He tossed them up onto the porch.

"Hey! Watch it!" came a surprised shout. It was Bishop.

Colter climbed quickly up the steps from the water and shook himself like a puppy, spraying Bishop with salt water.

"You didn't see the sign? Trespassers buy the lunch."

"Quit it. This is a clean shirt."

"Shirts. You wear too many shirts. No wonder you till look like library paste."

"Dry off," Bishop said, tossing him a towel.

"Is that a drink in your hand?" Colter asked, rubbing a towel through his hair.

"I'll get yours in a minute. While I do that, read his," he said, tossing a cable onto the small patio table near Colter.

Bishop went inside to fix Colter a drink, and Colter

picked up the cable and glared at it.

It was a coded summons for Bishop. Return to Langley, next available transportation, urgent. Colter tossed it down in disgust. He went over to the porch rail and looked out at the lagoon and the dark blue ocean beyond.

Bishop returned to the porch and gave Colter a Chivas and ice. The big man turned to face him, and raised the glass in salute.

"Just came to say goodbye," Bishop said needlessly.

Colter gave a huge sigh, and took a sip of the drink. "I ever bother to thank you for what you did?"

"About fifty times."

"It was a terrible shot."

"I know, but what timing . . ."

"Thanks, Steve."

"Fifty-one."

"When are you leaving?"

Bishop up-ended his drink and set down the empty glass. "I just left. See you around, Mitch."

Obviously, Bishop didn't expect Colter to accompany him to the plane, or even to the launch. Colter was surprised, but not hurt. He wasn't big on goodbyes.

"Okay, see you around, Steve."

They shook hands, and Bishop went out, through the bungalow and down the walkway to the beach. He disappeared behind the trees and shrubs, but the Colter caught a glimpse of him at the top of the path, pausing to speak briefly with someone before he vanished.

Colter stared moodily out at the sea, quickly finishing his drink, not enjoying it, only seeking the mild anesthesia it would provide. He took it in large, icy sips, finishing it in minutes. He was thinking of having several more when he heard a soft knock at the door of the bungalow.

He opened the door, and was surprised to find Michelle standing there. She had been the one Bishop had stopped to chat with, Colter realized. She looked. . . sensational. She wore a white *pareu*, and her hair was softly shining. Her eyes were wet, and her lips were trembling, and she was beautiful. Colter stood there and gawked at her.

"You big stupid American," she began, "don't you invite a lady to come in?"

She came into the bungalow, and into his arms.